KRAVEN IMAGES

Alan Isler was born in London in 1934. In 1952, at the age of eighteen, he emigrated to the USA. He taught English Literature at New York's Queen's College from 1967 to 1995 and now lives in London. His first novel, *The Prince of West End Avenue*, was acclaimed on both sides of the Atlantic. In America it won the National Jewish Book Award and was one of the five fiction nominees for the 1994 National Book Critics Circle Award. In Britain it won the Jewish Quarterly Fiction Award. His new collection of novellas, *Op. Non. Cit.*, is published by Jonathan Cape.

BY ALAN ISLER

The Prince Of West End Avenue
Kraven Images
Op. Non. Cit.

Alan Isler

KRAVEN IMAGES

V

VINTAGE

Published by Vintage 1997

2 4 6 8 10 9 7 5 3 1

Copyright © Alan Isler 1996

First published in the U.S. by Bridge Works Publishing Co.,
Bridgehampton, New York

The right of Alan Isler to be identified as the author of this work
has been asserted by him in accordance with the Copyright,
Designs and Patents Act, 1988

First published in Great Britain by
Jonathan Cape Ltd, 1996

Vintage
Random House, 20 Vauxhall Bridge Road,
London SW1V 2SA

Random House Australia (Pty) Limited
20 Alfred Street, Milsons Point, Sydney
New South Wales 2061, Australia

Random House New Zealand Limited
18 Poland Road, Glenfield,
Auckland 10, New Zealand

Random House South Africa (Pty) Limited
Endulini, 5A Jubilee Road, Parktown 2193,
South Africa

Random House UK Limited Reg. No. 954009

A CIP catalogue record for this book
is available from the British Library

ISBN 0 09 970171 5

Papers used by Random House UK Ltd are natural,
recyclable products made from wood grown in sustain-
able forests. The manufacturing processes conform to the
environmental regulations of the country of origin

Printed and bound in Great Britain by
Cox & Wyman, Reading, Berkshire

For my sisters

Alas! Fond Fancy's but a cheat:
Food for thought is airy meat.
The artist of the mind grows thinner
For want of a substantial dinner.

Nicholas Kraven, *Tickety-Boo*

Prelude

**Leeds, England
April, 1941**

THE MEN STOOD AROUND THE OPEN GRAVE
looking down at the coffin. Nicko, almost seven, understood
that his father, Felix Kraven, lay within. Grandfather
Kraven, Nicko's 'Opa', stood a little behind the boy, supported by Onkel Koko and Onkel Gusti. The old man was
having difficulty breathing. Tears ran down his cheeks into
his beard, and sobs shook his body. Onkel Ferri, himself
shuddering and whimpering, stood beside Nicko, whose duty
it was to say *kaddish*. On the other side of the pit were his
cousin Marko, Rabbi Himmelglick, and Grandpa Blum. The
rabbi held one hand on Marko's shoulder. Nicko rather
resented that, even though he already hated Himmelglick.
The rabbi was a thin, humped old man, with a soft fleshy
nose badly peppered with blackheads. When he talked, scum
gathered in the corners of his mouth. Certainly Nicko would
not have wanted the hand on *his* shoulder. Behind Grandpa
Blum stood a few of his father's old friends, those who had
been able to make the trip north on short notice. All of *them*
surely knew how important Nicko was today, the mourner-
in-chief, the sayer of *kaddish*, much more important than
soppy old rotten old Marko.

The sound of a ball hitting a cricket bat (pok!) and muffled
polite applause reached the ears of the mourning party,
uncannily, as if from an immense distance. There must be a
school and playing fields somewhere beyond the cemetery. It
was warm in the sunshine, but when a cloud raced across the
heavens, darkening the land, the underlying chill in the air
made itself felt. The clouds were beginning to bank to the

north. Visible in the moist black sides of the pit were white, gleaming dots, roots sliced by the spade. Worms wriggled in the loose black earth at the head of the grave. Nicko tried to concentrate on them. Marko had once shown him what happens to a worm when salt was poured on it. Ugh!

Willie, the gardener, was to do Home Guard exercises on the Stray this afternoon. Only last week he had promised to take Nicko along to watch. But at this rate they would never be back in time, and besides, probably they wouldn't let him go. Daddy had spoiled all that. According to Marko, Nicko would have to sit and shiver for seven days. Onkel Ferri was already doing it. Perhaps it was time for Nicko to start. Nobody knew what Nicko had done, except for Mummy, and she'd never tell. Nicko stared hard at the worms.

It had seemed a long drive from Harrogate to the Jewish Cemetery on the outskirts of Leeds. Nicko had been assigned the limousine reserved for the ladies, a wretched, sissy thing. He and his cousin Tillie were allowed to sit in the fold-out seats at least, and Nicko could see where he had been rather than where he was going, an odd sensation in a car. Lucky Aunt Cicely had managed to seat herself next to the driver. The women were all dressed in black, and they had red eyes that wept buckets. Well, Aunt Cicely had stayed pretty calm. She turned back to tick Mummy off from time to time. 'Hush, hush, Victoria. Hysterics won't help.' Every now and then she would glance at the driver. It was easy to see she wanted him to know that *some* Jews could control their emotions, just like ordinary people. And Tillie had started off all right, too. She had tried to play round-and-round-the-garden with Nicko, just to cheer him up a bit. Nicko hadn't minded, even though it *was* a baby game and he preferred *not* to think of the garden. *Would* Mummy tell? Perhaps the police would make her. Nicko glanced through the rear window at the first of the limousines that trailed them. Marko was sitting with the driver.

Only if Nicko craned round to look at the road before them could he see the hearse. Poor Mummy had no choice. That was part of the trouble. It was right there on the road before her, right there between Aunt Cicely's head and the driver's. The coffin was as visible as it could be. Mummy kept her head down most of the time though, her eyes closed, steadily sobbing, occasionally howling. She kept her arms crossed, and she rocked back and forth. How unhappy she was!

In the cemetery's prayer hall Rabbi Himmelglick greeted the mourners. The prayer hall was a plain red-brick building; it might have been a warehouse or a large garage. The air inside was cold and damp. It seemed unaffected by the stove in the far corner, whose lid glowed redly in the gloom. There was a smell of wood rot and wet cement. Some folding chairs had been arranged with a centre aisle, as if in preparation for a lecture. The place of the lectern was occupied by the coffin, which rested on its bier. Two bulbs of low wattage hung naked on long wires from the ceiling. The windows had been painted black as an air-raid precaution.

'Which one is to say *kaddish?*' Himmelglick asked in Yiddish. Onkel Ferri brought Nicko forward. The rabbi removed a pair of scissors from a spectacle case, took Nicko's black velvet High Holy Days waistcoat between bloodless thumb and forefinger, and cut a small nick in the V of the garment just above the heart. Nicko was shocked: his velvet waistcoat! Himmelglick bared his teeth, not to smile but to speak, the scum collecting. 'Well, well,' he said impatiently, 'tear it, tear it.' His teeth were long and yellow, crooked and widely spaced. The stench of their decay was on his breath. Nicko looked up unbelievingly at Onkel Ferri, who nodded. The boy turned his back on the hateful Himmelglick and tried to tear his waistcoat, but it would not tear. The rabbi leaned over him, forcing his head back into the dingy beard, inches from the detestable mouth. He grasped the cut edges in his adult fingers and tore. The women screamed as the cloth ripped. The rabbi released Nicko, who ran from him, nauseated, terrified, sought out his mother and threw himself into her arms. Himmelglick calmly went about the room nicking the clothing of the Kraven men. Marko, lucky Marko, merely a nephew, was excused.

At the gravesite, from which he had banned the women, Rabbi Himmelglick bared his teeth. 'May he come to his resting place in peace,' he said in Hebrew.

There was a sudden barking and howling and growling and whimpering, and the low-pitched whine of a dog in misery. And then two dogs, common curs, rolled out from behind a large family gravestone, rolled and attempted to stand, stood at last, stuck rump to rump, pulling in opposite directions, squealing, barking, howling dementedly. The larger of the dogs was making headway, dragging the other after, inch by inch. The mutt's hind legs scarcely touched the ground, but the poor creature tried repeatedly to find purchase. The dogs zigzagged, paused, advanced, retreated, staggered, approached, sending up all the while their frenzied racket. And finally, as the mourners stood paralysed, the dogs tumbled with a terrifying shriek into the open grave itself. There they scratched around on top of the coffin, whimpering, squealing, trying to leap out in opposite directions into freedom.

At a discreet distance, beyond the earth piled high at the head of the grave, stood the gravediggers, an old toothless gaffer and his assistants, two brawny adolescents, nudging one another and winking. The gaffer cackled openly, lifting his spade to point out the dogs' progress.

What to do? How to get them out? Driven close to madness, they were not to be approached. Rabbi Himmelglick turned to the old gravedigger. *He* would be sure to know. Was he not a gentile? The rabbi pointed to the grave and shrugged meaningfully.

Lifting his head the better to throw his voice across the earth mound, the gravedigger released a short burst of thick Yorkshire dialect in which the only word intelligible as a word (but in any case meaningless to Himmelglick) was 'watter'. He made no attempt to disguise his merriment. Now he pointed with his spade to the grave, from which the pitiful howling and mad growling, the scratching and thumping, were still to be heard. He tried again, this time speaking slowly, but still producing incomprehensible sounds: 'Thee maun poot watter on they.'

Himmelglick turned back to the mourners and lifted his hands and shoulders just enough to indicate puzzlement. 'What's he saying, the imbecile?' he asked, baring his teeth. 'A disgrace,' he added.

Nicko alone of the entire mourning party could claim birth in the land of the gravediggers. He alone might be supposed to understand the old man's words. But of course one could not ask a child, a *kaddishl*. Onkel Ferri, close now to hysteria, began to laugh, but then, shocked by his own laughter, he misswallowed, started to cough, and came close to choking. Everyone pretended to notice nothing amiss with him. Opa was saying in a quavering voice, 'Enough, enough. I can't any more. Tell me, God, what have I done? I can't any more.' He wept without cease.

Grandpa Blum had crossed the Channel well before the turn of the century. Apart from the old gravedigger, he could claim to have lived in England longer than anyone present. His English, as a matter of fact, was almost free of a foreign accent. It was perhaps natural that he should presume to translate the words into Yiddish.

'I think he's telling us to pour cold water on them.'

'So?' said Himmelglick. 'Get water.'

Onkel Ferri, dangerously close now to convulsions, took this opportunity to withdraw. The dogs had by this time grown quiet, merely whimpering, as if they knew that help was on the way. Onkel Ferri returned after a few minutes with a bucket, its water spilling over on to his trousers and shoes. His coughing was mercifully over. He prepared to slosh the water into the grave. Everyone stirred and craned forward with interest.

'Stop!' shrieked Himmelglick. He had roused himself at the last moment. 'Wait!' He held aloft his prayer book, as if offering it for witness. 'Earth! The coffin must first be covered with earth!' His teeth remained bared, an indication of his alarm.

'We'll pretend, rabbi,' said Grandpa Blum grimly, 'that it's been raining all this time. The coffin simply got wet. Pour, Ferdinand.'

Himmelglick bowed his head. Onkel Ferri dumped the water on the dogs, who let out a scream in unison, parted as if by magic, shot out of the pit and took off at top speed for opposite sides of the cemetery, barking joyfully, leaping over graves, and finally disappearing.

Himmelglick bared his teeth and picked up where he had left off. 'May he come to his place in peace.'

Everyone in turn quickly shovelled a little earth into the grave. It sounded horrible when it hit the coffin, a sequence of hollow *crumps*. Then Nicko said the mourner's *kaddish*, repeating the words after Opa, whose voice trembled as he prompted.

Then it was over. Onkel Koko and Onkel Gusti, pale and dazed, supported Opa, one on either side of him, as the old man tottered from the graveside. Onkel Ferri held Nicko's hand and led him after. Poor Onkel Ferri's feet squished, and there was a thickening cake of mud around his shoes. Nicko glanced back at the grave. The gravediggers were already filling it from the earth mound.

'It's a hard thing,' Opa was saying, 'no, it's not an easy thing for a son to bury a father. But for a father to bury a son, it's a bitter pill, a bitter, bitter pill.'

8

Nevertheless, even though he certainly knew better, Nicko half-expected to find his father waiting for him when he got home.

Part One

New York
Early Spring, 1974

ONE

NICHOLAS MARCUS KRAVEN stood at his lectern in the well of the lecture hall. Of the two hundred banked seats before him only about thirty were occupied, and these at random intervals. A small knot of students here, another there, a couple toward the rear in passionate embrace, a knitter, a dozer, the odd revolutionary, a wilted flowerchild, a compulsive doodler, a mad grinner: in short, a perfectly ordinary class. It was 1974 and in recent years violent winds of change had blown through the groves of academe, uprooting the once sturdy tree of knowledge, scattering its fruit and leaving it to rot on inhospitable ground. So, at any rate, it seemed to Kraven.

He shifted his position, aware that the posture of graceful intensity he had sought – legs casually crossed, shoulders curved forward over his lecture notes, fingers gripping the lectern's high far edge – gave him not only the anticipated view up Miss Anstruther's hiked skirt but an unanticipated pain where the lower edge of the lectern cut into his diaphragm. Antonia Anstruther wore no panties. Three times a week between twelve and twelve-fifty she was to be found, impassive of face, arms crossed over bountiful breasts, seated always at eye level, a little to the left of centre, her legs parted, one heel raised and hooked on to the back of the chair beneath her. She neither moved nor spoke but gazed imperturbably at a point some six inches above his head. Once, early in the term, he had attempted to disturb her maddening composure by addressing a harmless question to her. She had merely closed her eyes and kept them closed until he, embarrassed by the lengthening silence, had redirected his question to the class at large.

Kraven stepped back from the lectern, absently massaging his diaphragm. 'We come now to a crucial matter.' He circled the lectern and leaned back against the table upon which it stood, a graceful posture, one of his best. 'I mean, of course, the state of Lear's understanding in the moments before his death. How we interpret this passage will determine ultimately how we interpret the play. We should expect to receive an answer to the question with which we began: What is the nature of the Lear universe?'

Kraven paused, allowing his gaze to travel earnestly over the faces of the students before him. What cared they for the state of Lear's understanding? It was enough, surely, if by the end of the term they all agreed on a common spelling of the mad king's name.

It would be incorrect to suppose Kraven unaware of his posturing. He stood, so to speak, outside of himself, not so much observing a genuinely scornful Kraven addressing the sons and daughters of anti-intellectualism in its revolutionary ascendancy as watching himself play the role of such a one. By now he had transformed his career into theatre, a private entertainment in which he starred, and thus he coped with his uncertain times.

The table shifted under his weight, producing an unseemly sound. Gabriel Princip grinned at him from his seat by the window. Princip, an organizer in the local chapter of Students for a Democratic Society, played his own role with an enthusiasm that matched Kraven's. His costume demonstrated his solidarity with the Movement, a T-shirt with jaundiced armpits, denim overalls on which were painted crude peace signs and the legend 'OFF THE PIGS!' and

14

scuffed sneakers. He was bearded and his tumbling torrent of unbarbered hair was circumscribed by a scarlet cloth of a kind that in Kraven's childhood was called a headache band. In this Princip had stuck a jaunty quill, thus making clear his sympathy for the plight of the American Indian. Kraven shifted his weight back to his feet and returned to his position behind the lectern.

'Let us turn to Lear's last words, his final utterance before he dies. "Look on her lips," he cries, "look there! look there!" ' Kraven allowed his eyes to glint. 'Undoubtedly you have asked yourselves, ladies and gentlemen, what it was that Lear saw.'

He smiled to show that his was a gentle, a friendly irony. He knew, his smile implied, that before this moment they had not even recognized the question. But that was all right, not to worry, absolutely no rancour on his part – so long as they addressed themselves to the question now. All this was in his smile. Thirty or so faces gazed blankly back at him, while the eyes of one still focused above his head. He wondered, not for the first time, whether Antonia Anstruther possessed tunnel vision.

Kraven expected no response at this stage. He glanced at the clock on the far wall. In ten minutes he would be on his way back to his office, the business of the day over. 'Think, ladies and gentlemen, think. "Pray you undo this button," says Lear. Whose button? His own? The dead Cordelia's? Have we here a clue to what it is the old king sees?' Kraven had adjusted his tone to indicate that this time he wanted an answer. The moment for amiable bantering was past.

Mr Feibelman, white-bearded and gnomelike, a retiree, raised his hand. Kraven ignored him. Feibelman was a man of quirky erudition, and hence a nuisance. Whatever the subject of class discussion, he would bring it around somehow to the Jewish Problem.

15

As Kraven looked elsewhere for a suitable volunteer, heads bowed over play-texts, hands began scribbling in notebooks. This predictable behaviour pleased Kraven even as it irritated him. Only Giulietta Corombona serenely met his gaze. Now she pursed her lips, moistened them with her tongue, and winked at him. Kraven was startled. She had transgressed the cardinal rule: *Female students must* never *reveal in public whatever 'special understandings' they had or hoped to have with their male professors.*

'Mr Princip, perhaps you would be good enough to share your thoughts with us. What is it that Lear sees?'

Princip's fellows, spared this time, looked up. Feibelman sadly lowered his hand. Meanwhile, the smile had left Princip's fleshy lips.

'The thing is, you told us that like when Lear says his fool was dead, he din mean the Fool, he like meant Cordelia.'

'Indeed I did. Although I'm sure I did not phrase it quite so felicitously.'

The class sniggered obediently. Someone else was in the hotseat.

'Well, I mean, how d'you know? The guy says his fool is dead, right? I mean, why not believe him?'

Why not indeed? Kraven had no idea. It was true that every editor of every modern edition of the play that Kraven had seen inevitably glossed *fool* as *Cordelia (a term of endearment)*. But why must the word carry that meaning here? It had never occurred to Kraven before to wonder. The fault of his own generation, he supposed, this unquestioning acceptance of authority. Still, he recognized Princip's ploy for what it was, a defensive counter-attack. In his mindless striking out, Princip had scored a palpable hit. Kraven summoned his forces.

'I take it, Mr Princip, you are prepared to demonstrate the relevance of your question to my own?'

Princip had lost the scent of victory now. He looked quite cast down. Well, the lad was obviously a prick, a prick of the first water. (Yes, Kraven was well pleased with his conceit.) A raucous buzzer sounded. Match and set.

'Saved by the bell, eh, Mr Princip? It seems you have the weekend to think of a reply.' Kraven's smile made clear his good humour. 'We'll pick up on Monday where we've left off. Meanwhile, ladies and gentlemen, I urge you to begin reading *Macbeth*.'

He gathered together his precious notes and strode triumphantly from the lecture hall. Princip, he knew, would absent himself from Monday's class.

Kraven began a private hum, the outward audible sound transformed magically within his cranium to voice and orchestra. In this way he edged into a group of young women who were streaming along the corridor. As the the crowd approached the stairwell it slowed down and constricted. Kraven cheerfully ignored the girls' jostling and, sinking deeper into hum and thought, was in this way agreeably titillated down the steps and out into the ardent April sunshine. He began the trek across campus towards his office, smiling a private smile and humming his private hum. '*Sapro, sapro* . . .'

* * *

MOSHOLU COLLEGE was located where an impudent finger of the Bronx reached for the private parts of Westchester. The campus had once been a 'correctional facility' for delinquent girls. Indeed, the searchlight turrets and conning towers that still surmounted the older buildings around the Great Quad bore witness to Mosholu's bleak beginnings. But in the early 1950s the former Asylum for the Reformation and Rehabilitation of Wayward Women (founded 1867) became Mosholu College, devoted to the preservation, the cultivation and the dissemination of the liberal arts. This task the college had faithfully executed until the eruptions on campuses across the nation in the late 1960s and early 1970s at last shattered its peace. In point of fact, the students of Mosholu had sauntered woefully late to the barricades. Now students tumbled and cavorted on the greensward, some intertwined in panting embraces; others threw frisbees, did handsprings, strummed guitars, scratched crotches, exchanged term papers, hooted, laughed, shouted. They turned on and made out. The bulls with their truncheons were long since gone. Only the odd member of the faculty sunk in thought – Kraven at this moment was such a one – picked his way absently around and between healthy young bodies, sound too in mind.

'Yoohoo, perfessor!'

It was Feibelman. Kraven picked up his stride.

'Perfessor Kraven,' panted Feibelman, drawing abreast, 'you got a minute?'

'Of course.' Kraven looked doubtfully at his watch.

'Your two o'clock office hour today, you could fit me in maybe?'

'Not a chance, I'm afraid. Too bad.' But Kraven recalled a recent decision of the Academic Senate, a body now infiltrated by student activist-nihilists and their faculty toadies: henceforth the college committees on promotion would take into account student evaluations of faculty performance. 'Still, if you can walk with me to my office, perhaps we can dispose of your little problem along the way.'

'It's like this. The Prizes Competition? I'm working on something, original research, could be I've got a winner.'

'Good, good.'

'Could also be a loser, you know what I mean?'

'The point, Mr Feibelman?'

'So, you should be so good, before I get in too deep...'

Kraven gestured impatiently.

18

'I been reading up on King Arthur. Now a person like you, an educated person, I put a premium on your opinion. What about Merlin? You think there maybe was a Merlin?'

'Pure fabrication. Merlin is the stuff of Celtic myth.'

Feibelman grinned happily. 'Boy, have I got news for you! Not only I can prove there was a Merlin but, a long story short, Merlin was a Jew.'

Kraven stopped in mid-stride. 'Good God, Feibelman, you must be mad!'

The sun glanced brightly off Feibelman's skull. 'In other words, what you're telling me, no work's been done on it yet?'

'Of course not!'

Students cavorted about them. Kraven began walking again, Feibelman trailing after, a little run and a hop. The old man was insane, that much was clear; harmless perhaps, but insane. Should he be referred to one of the college counsellors, one of the resident shrinks? Was there a rabbi on campus?

'Naturally, a feller like you, a scholar, needs a bit evidence, what you might call proof, am I right? Nowadays, who believes in wizards? Only loonies. So what difference to you I mention Geoffrey of Monmouth, I throw in Gildas or Nennius? A bunch superstitious, you should excuse the expression, farts from the olden days, you'll say. Nennius? He lived in the *ninth* century, dummy, you're gonna tell me. And if I should happen to mention Gildas was Merlin's contemporary? Big deal, right? Never mind they both talk about a wizard called Myrrdin, what did they know?' Feibelman paused, as if expecting a reply. Kraven merely hurried his pace. The old man began to wheeze, but his legs pumped along, he kept up. 'How do we get from Myrrdin to Merlin? Easy. Geoffrey changed the name. Why? If you ask me, what he wanted was to get rid of a possible pun.' He looked at Kraven knowingly. Kraven raised his eyebrows. 'In French,' said Feibelman. '*Merde*? Shit? Get it?' He plunged on. 'So now we come to the *Annales Cambriae*. What d'you know, here's Merlin again. Knuckle-brain, you'll tell me, the *Annales* is thirteenth century.'

Kraven coughed.

'But what do the *Annales* tell us? Get this: when the Battle of White Chapel was over, a feller called Merlinus, "a poet and a prophet", went berserk, *meshuggah*, what you British call bonkers. That's only background, that's nothing. So far, so good. Just the same, no cigar. But it brings me to my discovery.'

It also brought them to the building that housed the English Department, a quonset hut, really, which in former days had accommodated a string of solitary-confinement cells. Now Feibelman followed him to his door, waited while he unlocked it. Would he never be rid of the man?

'That I suppose is that, Mr Feibelman.'

Cunningly, Feibelman put a trembling hand over his heart. 'If I could just sit down for a minute.' He followed Kraven inside.

The office measured twelve feet by nine. It had once been the guard's communication room with the central prison complex; it was the only office in the Department, apart from the chairman's, that had a genuine window. Kraven had come into his good fortune shortly after receiving tenure when he had explained to a compassionate Mrs Trutitz, the Department's principal secretary, that he suffered severely from claustrophobia. Notwithstanding the window, the blind always remained discreetly closed.

Kraven had a desk, a comfortable chair (removed one carefree Summer Session from the Dean of Faculty's office over in the Administration Building: an open door, an empty corridor, and the chair, conveniently equipped with rollers, was his), a stuffed wastepaper basket, a filing cabinet in which were collected his precious notes, a bookcase, a grey metal folding chair for conferees, and a chaise longue, a gift from an Hermione Gumm of five years ago, whose mother was discarding it in favour of something more 'modren'. (Miss Gumm, to her credit – a definite A+ student – had immediately recognized its potential.)

The walls were variously decorated: a print of Sarah Bernhardt as Hamlet; a Shakespeare calendar, this month displaying a nineteenth-century German etching of an Othello who looked like Erich von Stroheim in blackface, his left hand gesturing heavenwards, his right apparently fumbling with his privates; last year's list of campus events; an enlarged photograph of Dame Edith Sitwell, gaunt in melancholic weeds; a rubbing from a pseudo–Gothic college fireplace that read 'and gladly wolde he lerne and gladly teche'.

The desk, the bookshelves, and much of the floor were piled with papers: departmental announcements, college notices, publishers' catalogues, paperbacks, invitations, examination booklets, student essays, sandwich wrappers, advertisements, requests for letters of recommendation. It was Kraven's policy to throw out all such detritus at the end of each semester. Thus he prepared for the new. Only his chaise longue and his comfortable chair were uncluttered.

Feibelman eyed the chaise longue eagerly. Kraven swept a pile of recent quizzes and other papers from the metal conferee's chair to the floor.

'Sit down, Feibelman. I can give you two more minutes.'

Feibelman sank wearily into the metal chair. He took a handkerchief from his pocket and began to dab his eyes and his temples, moving on at last to mop his bald crown. His beard hung in white glinting driblets. He held his sopping handkerchief by two corners, quickly twisted it into a tight tube, and draped it around his neck.

'A couple seconds, that's all.' The old man's wheeze moved by degrees through heavy into normal breathing. 'Oy.'

Kraven drummed his fingers on the desk top.

'So about my discovery. Naturally, you've heard of Gryllus's *Apologia pro vita sua*?'

'Discovered a few years ago – behind a chimney in Podsnap Parva, as I recall.' Kraven was on top of things all right. He kept up. 'Modelled on Augustine's *Confessions*. What of it?'

'You've read it, perfessor!' What a man! said Feibelman's expression. This is some perfessor I've got me here!

'Ah, as to that, it must wait its turn.' Kraven waved airily at his bookshelves. 'Not exactly in my field, you know. In fact, why don't you trot along to the History Department, talk to a medievalist. Dillinger's the chap for you. Have a word with him.'

'When I tell you what I got, you'll understand maybe why I don't go to the History Department. This is dynamite. You think I can trust just anybody?'

Kraven sighed.

'A long story short, Gryllus *knew* Merlin. How do I know? Simple. He says his monastery sheltered a *meshugana* called Myrrdin. This *meshugana* he also calls *poeta*, *vates*, *magus*. So it's not Merlin, you'll tell me please who it could be? Of course it's Merlin. Okay, so here it comes now. Lucky you're sitting down. Right there in the *Apologia* Gryllus records an actual incantation of this Myrrdin, a powerful spell he says the *meshugana* always muttered over the sacramental wine. Such a scaredy-cat is this Gryllus that he tells us he crosses himself while he's jotting the words into his memoir. Well, you have to understand, this was a *goy* from a long line of *goyim*. A monk, after all. And what was this spell? I'll give you one guess. Go ahead, be a sport.'

'Not a clue. And now, since you've got your breath back, I really must. . .' Kraven indicated the heaps of paper on his desk.

'A piece paper, you should be so good.' Feibelman held out his hand. Kraven plucked a sheet at random from his desk. The old man tore it in half and began to scribble. 'Here, this is how it begins.' He thrust the half-sheet at Kraven: BOREASQUE TAURUS ADONAIS. 'Nu, what you think of that?'

'Nothing at all.'

'You kidding me, perfessor? Okay, okay. Here.' He scribbled on the second half. 'It ends like this.' He tossed his writing triumphantly on the desk before Kraven's eyes: BOREAS PYRRHI HOC OPHINIUM. 'Well, *now* what d'you say?'

'You've lost me, Feibelman.'

Feibelman's face registered his amazement. 'But there it is, in front of your nose, the Hebrew blessing over wine! *Baruch atta adonai*, and so on. Of course, you've got to make allowances. By the time of the *Apologia* Gryllus wasn't a spring chicken any more. His memory, well, you can imagine. Besides, what did he know, the *goy*, of Hebrew?'

Kraven felt a moment of compassion. Poor, sad old bastard. He must talk to him, give him a few more minutes of his time. If need were, Kraven was ready to blow this spark of pity into a lively flame.

'You've come to me for advice, and you shall have it. Alas, Judaism has become your obsession. Lift a literary stone and there you find a Jew, or an antisemite. It just won't do.'

'You think my evidence is crap, is that it? Gildas, Geoffrey, Gryllus, they mean nothing?' Feibelman was on the point of tears.

'What evidence connects Geoffrey's Merlinus with

Gryllus's Myrrdin? Or, for that matter, Gryllus's lunatic with the one in the *Annales*? Wishful thinking, Feibelman.'

'And the spell?' He was slumped forward now, his horny fingers nervously combing his beard.

'It's no more than a coincidental combination of sounds. Look, has the Brooklynite's *shut the door* never sounded to you like the Parisian's *je t'adore*? You say we should make allowances for Gryllus, for his faulty memory, his superstitious terror, his lack of Hebrew. Should we not also make allowances for your obsession?'

Kraven paused. A tear ran down Feibelman's cheek. His jaw trembled, fluttering his beard. Kraven, compassionate, spoke more gently.

'Which of us, I wonder, has not at least once in his career pursued an *ignis fatuus* across the literary landscape? There is no shame in that. But the true scholar must measure his insights against the most rigorous of intellectual yardsticks, the probable truth. Only because I respect your scholarly integrity do I now advise you to abandon this harebrained notion of a Jewish Merlin.'

A sob escaped from Feibelman's throat. He shuddered.

'The path of the scholar,' Kraven went on, launched now on a set piece, 'is strewn with impedimenta. The truth may be found, it is there, atop a "huge hill, craggy and steep". But you must first climb it, muscles aching, over giant boulders strewn on a wild landscape, avoiding as best you can the gentle, chimeric path that plunges only downward to Bedlam or Bellevue.'

Feibelman slumped in the conferee's chair.

'As a member of the Prizes Panel, I must tell you candidly that while I personally would grant an unbiased reading to a paper written on this insane topic, it is extremely doubtful whether any other panellist would read past your opening paragraph.'

Kraven brought his wristwatch before his eyes and glanced significantly at the time.

A cowed and despondent Feibelman struggled to his feet. 'What it boils down to, I should forget the Arthurian topic?'

'Unquestionably. Stop the madness here and now.'

A woefully stooping Feibelman stumbled to the door. 'In any case, thank you for your time.'

'Not at all. We must chat again.'

Kraven got to his feet and locked the door. The conference had been exhausting. He needed what he thought of as quality time with himself. He lay down on his chaise longue and sank contentedly into his thoughts.

* * *

KRAVEN WAS NOT ONE who could trace his ancestry to the primordial ooze. Of the Kravens, he knew that they had migrated from somewhere in Poland to Vienna in the middle of the last century and from Vienna to London in this; of his mother's parents, he knew only that they had left Cracow for London as a young bride and groom, arriving in time for Queen Victoria's Diamond Jubilee. But it was the Viennese Kravens to whom he gave his allegiance. All the Viennese Kravens indulged a devil-may-care attitude towards money and expressed disdain for penny-pinchers. Thus they were distinguished in Nicko's mind from the Blums, whom the refugees from Vienna despised, and for whom the sum of earthly wisdom was to be found in such a popular gem as 'Take care of the pennies and the pounds will take care of themselves.'

It was from his father's family that he had assimilated a bittersweet sense of the Austrian capital – so much so, indeed, that he often felt he had lived there. The likenesses of his ancestors had been preserved in dozens of photographs, sepia toned, stiff, statuesque, self-consciously posed, all now in Kraven's possession. An anecdote of Opa's, of Onkel Ferri's, of his father's, and these long dead Kravens were released once more into life, almost as vivid to Nicko as those Kravens he knew, Kravens who had petted him, who had pinched his cheeks and fed him chocolates.

What he had as a child absorbed as unembroidered facts – the Kraven salon, for example, the pride of Vienna, where gathered painters and poets, musicians and journalists, bright eager young girls and their dashing escorts – were, after all, the reminiscences of exiles, refugees, lost and, but for one another, alone in an alien city. So they had clung together, deriving strength from shared memories of earlier happiness, memories from which anything less than the marvellous had been carefully filtered. In retrospect, the adult Kraven saw them, alas, as rather banal, mere sentimentalists, aspiring to what they were pleased to call *Kultur* rather than possessing it. (Cousin Marko, a natural Pavlovian, had once put on the turntable a record of Tauber singing '*Wien, Wien, nur du allein*' simply to prove how quickly the tears would form in his mother's eyes. 'Told you so, Nicko, under thirty seconds!') True, the Kravens had possessed a certain panache, a certain style, that distinguished them from the self-effacing English Jews among whom they found themselves. But as for the famous 'salon' of Viennese days, Kraven now rather doubted that it had achieved a level of intellectual attainment beyond that of the dreary cocktail parties he himself occasionally attended in New York.

The Kraven refugees had descended upon Felix's London home in 1938 and transformed it, not merely in tone, but in furnishings, for they had brought their best pieces with them. The language of social intercourse became German. The cuisine was altered to accommodate Opa's likes and dislikes. Felix was delighted, his wife less so. It was something to be a Kraven, a member of a moated enclave into which little Nicko had entrée by right of birth; poor Mummy, however, was, quite simply, not one of them. The Kravens stood against the world, a tight core of defence against hostile forces. And how could Nicko's mother contend with that? She became after their arrival in England an alien intruder in her own home.

* * *

KRAVEN MUST HAVE FALLEN asleep. A rap at the office door brought him to his feet so suddenly that he knocked over a column of books on the floor. Groggily, he kicked his way through them. But, the door now open, what he saw before him shook him fully awake. For there, a frown of engaging perplexity upon her angelic face, stood a young woman of supernal beauty. Lissom she was and lithe. Her blonde hair – her tresses rather – tumbled to her shoulders. Her flawless skin was lightly tanned, her dark eyes huge, her lips a delightful moue. She was clad in well-bleached jeans that lovingly clung to her. A bumble-bee danced merrily on her upper thigh towards a rose, a brilliant red, emerging from her crotch. She wore a sleeveless white blouse that moulded itself to her small bosom, from which, after the happy fashion of the day, her nipples asserted themselves. In her hand she clutched a sheaf of papers. Kraven was enchanted.

'You an English prof, and like that?'

'Indeed I am.'

'So I guess you know all about po-tree, right?'

'Try me, my dear, just try me. Ask me anything from Homer and Virgil to Eliot and Molesworth. Test me on pastoral, Petrarch, ploce, or prosody. If it's poetry you're after, Kraven's the name.'

'O wow!' she said. 'Gee, you really talk funny, like weird, y'know?'

27

Strange, thought Kraven. The linguistic stigmata of her generation, against which he so frequently fulminated, tripped with endearing sweetness from her lips, less blemishes than beauty marks.

'I guess you'll do. See, what I need is help. Like advice and that.'

Kraven ushered her into his office and closed the door. Swiftly he gathered a pile of papers from his desk and dumped them on the conferee's chair. 'Won't you sit down?' he said. She sat on the chaise longue and on the instant transformed it into a throne of state. Kraven turned his own chair towards her and sat down too. The rose, he saw, was short stemmed. It was a briar rose, ferociously thorned.

'Only speak,' he said. 'How may I help you?'

'I'm in Phys. Ed.' She blushed in her embarrassment. 'But like I write po-tree, I mean like my own.' She abased her eyes. 'So how do I know, y'know, if it's for real? Like, am I wasting my time?' She held the sheaf of papers towards him. 'I figured maybe you'd take a look, tell me what you think. Y'know, like that.'

Kraven had established a firm policy never to read student writing outside the requirements of his courses and his regrettable duties on the Prizes Panel. From this policy he had never wavered since that unfortunate occasion early in his career when he had condemned and derided the work of a student who, within two years of graduation, had won a National Book Award.

'I would be delighted, Miss . . . er, Miss?'

'Berkowitz. Nimuë Berkowitz.' She shook her head and scattered day. 'Gee, thanks!'

'Well, Nimuë, why don't you select what you consider to be the very best of them and give me that to read.'

She went carefully through the papers on her lap, biting her superb lower lip as she bent to the task, selecting,

28

rejecting, rejecting, selecting. Kraven watched her. As the poets of his own era of special competence might have said, he sat 'astonied'. At last, apprehensively, she handed him a sheet of paper. And there in firm round hand appeared the following:

'Relationships'
by
Nimuë Berkowitz

As you walk along life's highway
    You may often shed a tear,
    But remember while you're walking,
    I'm walking with you, dear.
As the road unfolds before you
    And your feet begin to ache,
    I'll be there to bathe them for you
    In the waters of a lake.
Up the hills and down the valleys,
    By the ocean's burning tide,
    Just give a glance to windward
    And you'll find me at your side
    Whither thou goest, there I will go,
    Hither and thither, yonder and fro.

'Nimuë,' said Kraven fervently, 'you are a poetess!'
'O wow!'
'Of course, there is work to be done, some polishing, some slight modifications here and there. Milton called even Shakespeare "a wild, untutored talent". But of your great gift there can be no doubt.'
'O wow!'
'Perhaps I should be rather more specific in my evaluation and criticism?'
'O yes!'

Kraven moved from his chair and sat beside her on the couch, his leg inadvertently making firm contact with her own as he held the poem between them.

'First, I would point to the splendid consistency of the central metaphor, life as a journey. Here you write in the grand European tradition, boldly elaborating an image that Dante himself, seven centuries before you, did not scorn to use.'

She squirmed with delight.

'Then, too, I was particularly struck by the sly introduction of the four elements, the old Ptolemaic cosmology being particularly apt here: the hills and the valleys, the wind, the burning tide – a particularly fine conflation of two elements in one, fire and water, poetic economy of an oxymoronic kind – and finally the ocean and the tears. Now, what does all this mean to the sensitive reader? Well, first, you succeed brilliantly in suggesting at once the timelessness and the universality of the experience; second, you draw together all Creation into a single harmonious whole, a unified poetic vision. But I scarcely need tell *you* this.'

'Wow!'

'The metre is cunningly chosen. It is spritely and optimistic, confident and amiable. More particularly, the rhythms are strong and insistent, quite regular through three stanzas, but pointedly altered in the concluding couplet, where the unexpected change focuses attention on the Biblical allusion.'

'Biblical illusion?'

'Whither thou goest, there I will go.'

'I got that off of a perfume bottle; it's called Moon of Galilee, and then it says "Whither thou goest," and that. Here, smell.'

The delightful creature thrust an exquisite wrist beneath Kraven's nostrils. He caught her hand in his and inhaled. All the perfumes of the fertile crescent mingled with a whiff of the gym. He retained her hand.

'New Testament or Old?'

'I beg your pardon?'

'The Biblical illusion.' She frowned. 'My dad, he's liberal and like that. I mean, he don't interfere much. Live and let live is what he says. But like he's kinda funny about some things. He don't know about Gabe, y'know, my guy. I mean, he'd like lock me in my room. So the Bible, well hey, I mean, he'd blow his stack.'

'The Old Testament, Nimuë. It's from Ruth.'

'Great!'

Kraven absentmindedly caressed her hand. 'Above all, I'm attracted to your poem's sentiment. It is at once sincere and emotionally charged, frankly passionate and unobtrusively calm.'

'No shit?'

'It is clear to me that you yourself have suffered, that you know what it is to be alone, to be misunderstood.'

'Right on.'

'And of course, as your poem reveals, you know the value to the naked human spirit of companionship, of the presence of one, just one, sympathetic soul vibrating to the needs of another. *Agape*, Nimuë, *agape* and *caritas*, transformed in an instant of unselfish giving, apotheosized, so to speak, into *eros*.'

'All right!'

'There is, as I've already hinted, some work still to be done with "Relationships". And no doubt your other efforts, however excellent, are in minor ways a trifle flawed. But if we were to work on them together. . .'

'Y'mean you would?'

'Not for the ordinary student, of course. I've other commitments, other obligations. But for a genuine poetess. . .'

'Gee, hey.'

'Alas, I cannot hold a poetry tutorial during my regular conference hours. But let's see . . . Are you free at eleven on Mondays, Tuesdays and Thursdays?'

'No, o jeez, that's when I gotta go to Indian Clubs, it's in my major.' She pouted. 'O fuck!'

'Never mind, we'll work something out. You have a telephone? Leave me your number, scribble it on the poem. Fine. Rest assured I'll be in touch.'

Kraven helped her to her feet and saw her to the door.

'*A bientôt.*'

'O wow!'

He watched her progress down the corridor. He noted the deliciously undulating buttocks. What was that? On the jeans' right cheek a curving dayglo arrow pointed outwards, above it the legend 'NO'; on the left another curving arrow, 'YES'.

Wow!

* * *

KRAVEN STOOD AT HIS OPEN OFFICE DOOR vainly sniffing the last traces of Moon of Galilee when the phone on the desk began to ring. He stepped back into his cell and shut the door.

'Kraven here.'

'Hello, lover.' The voice was seductive, throaty, entrancing.

'I was just about to leave.'

'Tonight?'

'Of course.'

'My place?'

'I'd prefer mine, if you don't mind.'

'About nine?'

'About nine. Er, Stella, there's not too much in the refrigerator, actually. Of course, I could get in some. . .'

'Sure, for a change. I'll make some lasagna and bring it down.'

'And a salad? I'll pick up the wine you like, the Cetonese.'

'Some Italian bread too. Oysters to start?' She laughed lewdly.

Kraven shuddered. How he hated those slimy horrors she so frequently fed him.

'What's with you, Nicko? Not up to it? You've been taking your vitamins, eating your eggs, and so forth?'

'For pity's sake, Stella.'

'Well then?'

'It's nothing, a run-in with a bastard student.'

'Because you'll need a bottleful of vitamins tonight. I picked up some perfectly smashing panties on East Sixtieth this morning, Knickers Unlimited, Ltd. Remember? I showed you, west of Second?'

She loved to model her panties for him. She would parade up and down before his astonished gaze, wearing nothing but the briefest briefs, undulating her hips, her full firm breasts moving to a dark inaudible music. Her body was splendid, and she was proud of it. Now in her mid-forties, winter's ragged hand had not defaced in Stella her loveliness. Time's trenches, tiny cross-hatchings on her face, scarcely visible at the slightest distance, merely augmented her beauty. Her dark hair, cut short, was shot through with grey, in Stella a visual pleasure, a sexual stimulant. Often, she no sooner entered his apartment than she lifted her skirt to show him her latest acquisition. He stirred at the memory.

'You don't sound any too keen.'

'It will cost you a groaning to take off my edge. Let's make it eight-thirty.'

'No, nine.' But clearly she was pleased. 'You know what you British say, Nicholas. Keep your pecker up.'

Kraven's affair with Stella was entering its second year. She lived with her husband, Robert, in a large elegantly appointed apartment two floors above him. Robert Poore-Moody, an American with an English-sounding name, was a

33

man whose occupation, so far as Kraven could tell, was chairing boards. Kraven had encountered him a few times in the lobby or in the elevator. They now exchanged nods, New York custom happily not requiring verbal greeting. Kraven in fact, and Poore-Moody no doubt too, regretted the first of these exchanges, for it had immediately enforced a pattern from which it now seemed impossible to depart.

Poore-Moody was a stocky pouter-pigeon of a man in his mid-sixties, a dead ringer for the late Mussolini. Who would have suspected that those thick short fingers, heavily matted with hair, were capable of the most exquisite petit-point? And yet such was the case. Kraven had seen examples of his work in the Poore-Moody apartment. And Stella had told him, on one of the rare occasions when she spoke to him of her husband, that Poore-Moody had for years engaged in warm correspondence with an English duke living in Paris, himself an accomplished amateur.

But on Thursday nights, with a regularity broken only by a necessary business trip, an occasional illness, and of course holidays, Poore-Moody drove his Bentley out to Brewster for a poker game with 'the boys'. Kraven could much more easily imagine him playing poker than plying a needle. His low brow fairly cried out for the extension a green eyeshade would grant. At any rate, from about eight on a Thursday evening until four or five on a Friday morning, Poore-Moody was gone. The vacuum his absence caused, abhorrent to nature, was filled by Kraven.

And this vulgar little man had been happily married to the marvellous Stella for more than twenty years. What could she possibly have seen (still see) in him? Not money, for Stella herself was moneyed, a daughter of the Boston Devereux. If not money. Then what? Sex? Of that possibility Kraven preferred not to think. Besides, it was clear to him that she also felt a warm affection for her husband – and a ferocious loyalty that forbade Kraven to talk to her of him and forbade her (except infrequently and then only appreciatively) to speak to Kraven of her husband.

Nor was this abiding love for her husband, especially in view of her passionate adultery, the most puzzling of Stella's oddities. Her breeding, education, and social ambience, after all, were quintessentially WASPian. She was a product of the best eastern schools, with a BA from Bryn Mawr and an MA from Harvard. Her Harvard thesis, in fact, had won a University Prize and was subsequently published as *The Perils of Parzifal: Proto-Cinematic Aspects of Wolfram von Eschenbach's Serial Romance*. Moreover, she engaged in Good Works, sought the Elevation of the Downtrodden, attended Charitable Evenings; in short, she expressed the Cultured Liberalism and Social Conscience of those who dieted from choice. Sometimes, when Kraven lay palpitating on the Poore-Moody couch, he heard Stella speak on the telephone to her social peers. There was no mistaking the cultured tones, the assurance of place, the sense of belonging, the familiar allusions to people with such absurd names as Muffin and Bunny, Lolly and Wills.

And yet with Kraven this American blue-blood, this offspring of the nation's historical élite, became a drab, a scullion, a daughter of the game. Sex became her *raison d'être*, food an important preliminary to fornication, vulgarity her mode. Proud of her cuisine, she refused to employ a cook. Kraven had seen on the weekly menu-charts pinned to her kitchen bulletin board the gustatory promise of *boeuf Wellington, truite amandine, pigeonneau à la crapaudine*. For him, however, she prepared liver and onions, corned beef and cabbage, or (as, for example, tonight) lasagna.

Why she should have elected to play this role with him he was unable to say. She had drawn him into a kind of Lawrentian triad, a grotesque parody, in which Lady Chatterley was actually married to the brutish Mellors and sought her sexual-spiritual salvation in an adulterous liaison with . . .

35

whom? Well, no, the role of sexual impotent was demonstrably not for a Kraven. The hypothesis would not hold. Once he had asked Stella outright why with him alone she opted for vulgarity. Did she not see that there was something psychosexually sick about it, something kinky? What drove her to transform the glory of their lovemaking into base coupling, the beast with the two backs, something squalid and lewd? But he had succeeded only in precipitating inexplicable laughter in her, wave upon wave, until at last, reaching for him, she had managed to blurt out, 'Come again?' More laughter, and then, coaxingly: 'Come again, why don't you?' He had, of course, dropped the matter. Still, he sometimes caught her looking at him oddly, as if *he* were the curiosity, not she. And once she had pinched him cruelly beneath the heart and slashed his ribs with her nails until she drew blood, merely to discover, she had explained, if he could feel with anything other than his prick. Perhaps she was mad.

Kraven poked about among the papers and books on his desk. Was there anything he needed to take home with him? Ah yes, here was the poem he had himself composed en route to the college that morning and jotted down immediately upon arrival, the newest item for *Tickety-Boo*, his bulging private file of light verse. *Tickety-Boo* had grown apace of late, had grown, in fact, in direct proportion as the number of his academic writings had declined. Now he wrote only poetry, or at any rate light verse, and in any case for his own eyes only. He glanced through this morning's effort.

To Stella

A sweet rotundance in the tum
Doth please as well as bouncing bum.
A bosom bursting from its bra

To tempt a bite mandibular;
And flesh so soft, so smooth, so white,
Which beauty lends to clothes too tight;
A *mons veneris*, from which source
Sweet gums and resins hotly course;
An eager mouth, deserving note,
That sucks me freely down the throat;
Fingers to which delighted balls
Oft sing their silent madrigals;
Do prove that in Poore-Moody's wife
I joy in paradisal life.

Not bad, not bad, he thought. The last couplet should be tidied up perhaps:

Do prove I in the Churl's sweet wife
Enjoy a paradisal life.

Possibly. Meanwhile it would take its place with a brief series inspired by Stella's recent fear, wholly unjustified, that she was putting on a little weight.

He dropped the poem into his venerable and otherwise empty briefcase. Anything else? Yes, of course: Nimuë's Passport to Parnassus. He must remember the bread and the Cetonese – and some antacid tablets: the spices in Stella's lasagna were subtle; one did not notice their viciousness until it was too late. '*Questa,*' he hummed gaily, '*o quella. . .*' As ever, his best hums were unpremeditated.

TWO

TOWARDS TEN O'CLOCK THE NEXT MORNING
Kraven rose slowly to consciousness, luxuriously, stratum by
stratum, stretching his muscles motionlessly, unwilling yet
to open his eyes. He enjoyed his limbs' refusal to obey the
brain's command to move, enjoyed even the panic their
refusal engendered. Experimentally he concentrated his will
on his toes, increased the insistence of the command, another
notch, another, and lo, his toes twitched, they shifted,
grudgingly, to be sure, but with ultimate obedience to
authority. He was not paralysed after all. Perhaps his rebirth
in America had confused the familial demons, had kept them
at bay. Kraven opened his eyes.

Squinting against the light that blazed in through the
windows, he was able to make out a shrouded form on
the far side of his bed. There was Stella, lying on her back,
the sheet pulled up to her shoulders. Stella, his beloved . . .
He smiled warmly at her. Last night she had been a
catwoman, an avatar of the non-sublimated libido. No wonder he ached in every limb.

Stella! He sat up in the bed. It was broad daylight, she
should have left hours ago. He looked at his watch: ten-
fifteen. Good grief!

'Stella!'

He thought to shout, but his vocal chords were not yet up
to the task. The shout was a croak, scarcely more than a

whisper. He started to lean towards her but stopped in horror. Her eyes were open wide, but the pupils had disappeared, had rolled up out of sight. Her jaw hung slackly. He leaped out of the bed and flung himself across the room, turning in a half crouch, horrified. She had not moved. The light from the windows glanced off the waxen pallor of her cheek, glinted on the ghastly white of her eyes, gleamed on the exposed teeth. His heart twisted painfully in his chest. She did not breathe, the sheet that covered her lay quite still. She was dead. *SHE WAS DEAD!*

What to do, oh Lord, what to do? Call the police, that was it. But perhaps Poore-Moody had already called them, perhaps even now they were in the Poore-Moody apartment. 'I am not one who panics easily, officers, but I know my wife. She'd never go out without leaving a note, a message of some sort. Something's happened to her, something dreadful, I *feel* it.' 'We'd better search the building, sir.' Kraven rushed to the window and looked down into the street. Nothing. Not a police car in sight. Clarence, the doorman, was picking his nose.

He should call a doctor. 'You say this woman is *not* your wife? But she *is* married? Have you notified her husband? I see. There'll have to be an autopsy, this is obviously a case for the coroner.'

It would all come out. The newspapers, TV. His career destroyed. No, he could not now indulge his private grief. There would be time enough for that. Stella, his Stella, was beyond help. His first duty was to the living. 'Hi there, this is Smedlow of the *Post*. Crime desk. We'd like to give our readers *your* side of the story.' BIZARRE DEATH OF PROMI-NENT SOCIALITE IN COLLEGE PROF'S SEX PAD. DA Vows to Press Vigorous Investigation. Interviews with Suspect's Neighbours. 'To look at the guy, you'd've said he was as normal as you or me.' 'You could tell he was a fruitcake, one of the quiet ones, kinda creepy.' 'He pinched me once in the elevator, don't ask where, but this *is* New York, y'know. Gee, it could've been me up there.' Special Feature on Page 27: Inside the Twisted Mind of a Sex Fiend!

Perhaps the thing to do was to put her clothes back on her, carry her into the living room, prop her up on the couch. Yes, yes! She had just dropped in for a spot of English breakfast tea. A neighbourly encounter merely, innocent of any significance. And then, all of a sudden, it happened, a heart attack, whatever . . . Ridiculous. If he couldn't bring himself to look at her, how would he be able to touch her? A shudder ran through him. He was naked himself. First dress, then think.

Keeping his back to the bed, he made his way crabwise around the room to where last night in lascivious eagerness he had thrown his clothes. He thrust one leg into his rumpled trousers, then the other, hopping, tripping, almost puncturing his head on a point of the bedside table. Calm down, calm down. Putting on his shoes he was facing the bed again. He forced himself to look at her. Oh God, she seemed to be grinning. He felt the madness rising within him, *hysterica passio*, down thou swelling mother! Kraven ran from the room.

It was intolerable, simply not fair. What had he done, what crime committed? Adultery? A twentieth-century common-place, as American as cherry pie. This was the Age of the Open Marriage, 1974, for pity's sake, when one selected, as in a supermarket, the brand of Lifestyle best suited to one's taste and pocketbook. From time to time one changed brands, moved to a different shelf, that was all. Given the kinkiness that was unashamedly going on out there, a simple case of adultery had become banal, almost charmingly old fashioned, a quaint relic of a simpler, bygone era. To be sure, in that 'simpler, bygone era' his own father had enjoyed the odd spot of adultery, as had all that generation of male Kravens. But that truth merely confirmed the point from another perspective: to commit adultery was to be human. Adultery was built into the human condition. One touch of nature makes the whole world kin. Yes, one had only to explain to Poore-Moody that Stella had loved both of them and he was bound to understand.

Kraven was pacing between the couch and the dining table in a room that still bore the visibilia of last night's entertainment. On the table lay the wreckage of the meal, the plates caked with tomato sauce, the crumbs of garlic bread, the left-over salad, the wine glasses, the empty bottles of Cetonese, the gutted candles. By the couch, the coffee table offered a scattering of crackers, the remains of a horseradish dip, and a small dish of those vile oysters swimming in their glutinous oil. It was astonishing how the mind under such pressure could record irrelevant detail. From the dozens of photographs on the surrounding walls, dead Kravens watched him. Opa was pointing his magic stick at the stuffed chair by the window. Kraven looked. There where Stella had left them prior to the Panty Parade lay her clothes, neatly piled. He scooped them up, shocked, and ran to the bedroom. Opening the door wide enough only to admit his arm, he threw them inside. His heart was beating madly again. He must get a grip on himself. Quietly he closed the door and resumed his pacing.

Simple adultery was not, after all, the problem. Poore-Moody was scarcely a child. He was in his mid-sixties. They were all adults. But it was a question of delicacy. Poore-Moody was the victim of a double sorrow. How did one break the news to the elderly cuckold that his wife lay dead on her lover's bed, that she bore in and on her body sure signs of her infidelity? Kraven, in terror of exposure, of condemnation or, worse yet, of ridicule, had managed to suppress his private grief. Stella was gone. He would mourn her when he could.

Into his inner turmoil the doorbell intruded, buzzing

41

loudly. Kraven jumped, then stood stock still. The police? So Poore-Moody had called them after all. He heard the sound of a key in the lock. The super must be letting them in. It was all over then? So be it.

'You decent, perfessor?'

Early Byrd, Kraven's cleaning lady, had let herself in.

His forehead was clammy with sweat. He heard her muttering along the short corridor leading to the living room, dragging her carrier bag of supplies after her. She appeared now in the doorway and let down her burden.

Early had once confessed that she would never see seventy again, but Kraven would have believed any age she claimed over forty. She wore her blue-black hair tied back in a tight bun. Her yellow face was wrinkle-free. She was short, solid, as if compacted for maximum efficiency. Kraven she thought of as one of her charges. Like Miss Hudson of his Harrogate schooldays, she had little patience with his nonsense. Now she stood surveying with undisguised distaste the disaster of the living room.

'Good morning, Early.' Kraven strove for hearty naturalness.

'You had yourself a party last night.' She shook her head and made tsk-tsking sounds. In his distracted state Kraven heard only snatches of her grumbling: '. . . man, a perfessor, live like a pig . . . thought I seen it all . . . don't matter if you black, white, or grizzly green, pig's a pig. . .'

'Sorry about the mess.'

'You wanna help, you can carry some of them dishes through to the kitchen. I scared to look in there.'

Kraven began to do as he was bid.

'Seeing as you up, I gonna begin in the bedchamber.'

'No!' Kraven shrieked. Oyster dish in hand, he leapt to bar her way. 'Stay the bloody hell out of there!'

Early's hand flew to her mouth; her eyes popped wide. She backed away from him.

'Didn't mean to startle you.' Kraven dropped his voice. 'All I meant was, no need to do the bedroom today. Took care of it myself, you see. Woke up with the lark, couldn't get back to sleep.'

'You putting me on. *You* took care of the bedchamber? That's something I gotta see for myself. Way you use it, that bedchamber make a hooker blush.' She grinned and shook her head. 'You one frisky fella, no two ways, frisky what you is.'

Early made for the bedroom, but Kraven stood his ground, blocking her path.

'You got someone in there.'

'No, no, of course not.'

'You crazy then. Lemmee see for myself. You change them sheets? They 'bout ready to crawl away.'

Kraven would not budge. 'Later. Look, why not make some coffee? I haven't had any yet. You'd feel better for a cup yourself.'

'I fine right now, don't need no coffee. Coffee, huh? Heh-heh-heh.' She shook her head. 'Sure I fix some coffee.' She turned and made her way to the kitchen. 'He frisky all right, heh-heh-heh. Clean the bedchamber hisself! Man think I stupid, heh-heh-heh.'

Kraven pressed his hand to his heart in a vain attempt to still its thumping. How could he keep Early out of the bedroom? Well, it was his apartment, wasn't it? He would just order her to stay out. Yes, but was the body to lie there all day? Early was slow and thorough, never leaving until late in the afternoon. He could pay her for the day and ask her to leave now, of course, tell her it was a Jewish holiday or something. No, that would only further excite her suspicions. Yet every minute that passed made it less likely that he would be able to rid himself of the body. If forced to wait until the evening, if forced finally to phone the police or the doctor or Poore-Moody himself, how then could he possibly explain his delay?

Early poked her head into the room. 'You want I fix you something to eat?' But the doorbell rang. 'I get the door. You suppose to help with them dishes.'

This time it must be the police.

In a minute Early shuffled back. 'Man say his name Widdershins, claim he a rabbi. You in?'

Widdershins? Widerschein! 'No, say I've left. Europe, you don't know when I'll be back.'

'Ah, Professor Kraven, *shalom*. What's a Jew doing?' Menachem Widerschein materialized from the dark hallway behind Early's back, gold teeth flashing, holding out his hand in greeting. Kraven shook hands glumly. But Widerschein, his eyes adjusting to the dimness, saw Kraven whole, saw him dishevelled and unclean. He jerked his hand free and wiped it on the side on his long silk coat. 'So, it's been a year already. Go know.'

Tears of frustration stung Kraven's eyes.

'The Talmud says, no need to tell you, "The road goes out, but the road comes back." ' Widerschein rocked gently back and forth. 'And Rabbi Akiba interprets this passage, "We complete the year and begin again." '

Menachem Widerschein turned up at Kraven's apartment once a year to collect money for the Children of the Spanish Inquisition, an orphanage located, he said, on the Hill of Evil Counsel in Jerusalem. At first Kraven had explained he was a secular Jew, scarcely a Jew at all by orthodox standards. Widerschein had shaken his head in mingled reproach and compassion. 'Yes, in Cordoba too there were some like you, in Cadiz, in Granada. And where are they now? Go ask Cardinal Ximenes, ask Leo X, ask Philip II, may their names rot in eternal shame, may the cholera eat their souls. The Children of the Spanish Inquisition makes it possible for you to be a secular Jew.'

From their very first encounter, Kraven had had his doubts about Widerschein. Why then had he always paid up?

Perhaps it was the sheer effrontery of the charlatan that had appealed to him, a kind of homage due *il miglior fabbro*, the better fabricator.

Now once again he dug into his pocket. Bloody hell, his wallet and cheque-book were in the bedroom. 'Unfortunately, at the moment. . .'

'Take your time. The first lesson the poor scholar learns is patience. "Charity is never late." '

Early's grin was stuffed with wickedness. 'I hears my coffee perking now. You wanna bet the rabbi he thirsty? I *knows* he feel better for a cup.'

Widerschein ran his fingers through his curly red beard.

'Rabbi Widerschein has many more calls to make. We mustn't delay him,' said Kraven.

'Naturally, I wouldn't want I should be a trouble.'

'You ain't no trouble, rabbi. Coffee up anyways.'

'Coffee, two years now, I don't drink.' He struck his chest with the back of his thumb and offered an illustrative belch. 'But perhaps a glass tea? Wouldn't hurt. A twist lemon, a lump sugar.'

Early returned bearing a tray on which sat two cups of coffee, a glass of tea, a saucer of lemon slices, a bowl of sugar cubes, milk, and suitable spoons. Putting the tray on the coffee table, she sat herself next to Widerschein. 'Help yourself.'

'*You rotten bastard! Why didn't you wake me? D'you know how late it is, for God's sake!*'

In the bedroom doorway stood Stella, stark naked, angrily scratching her hip. Kraven's jaw dropped, his scalp prickling. As for Widerschein, he clapped his hands to his eyes. Early grinned, delighted: 'What I tell you? He frisky, frisky what he is.'

Stella saw that she and Kraven were not alone. 'Excuse me.' She turned with solemn, stately dignity, re-entered the bedroom, and quietly closed the door.

'Near as I can tell, we needing another cup of coffee.' Early got up. 'Clean the bedchamber hisself, heh-heh-heh.'

To know Stella dead and yet to see her living! My God, did she always sleep like that? Kraven felt giddy. His lover still breathed, and he was released from Death Row, granted a full pardon, found innocent of all charges! The Kraven demons, who, in his late Onkel Ferri's sweetly demented imagination, stood ever on offensive alert, must indeed have been asleep.

Widerschein separated the fingers before his eyes and peeped about. He lowered his hands to his lap, his cheeks aflame. 'Your wife, Professor Kraven, you're married?'

'No.'

'So who says it's my business? Sometimes from immorality too we can learn a lesson. Meanwhile, what I have seen, maybe could be I didn't see. All I know is, like I say, go know. But it is clear that here there are private matters, delicate matters, no one should stick in his two cents. A stranger, I mean me, Menachem Widerschein, has no place. The tea, just the same, is delicious.' He took a large swallow and smacked his lips.

Early returned from the kitchen with another cup of coffee. She sat down close to Widerschein, who rolled his eyes heavenwards as if seeking deliverance, a man who had tumbled undeservedly into the Valley of the Shadow, where dwelled fornicators and gentiles. Early shook her head at Kraven. 'Heh-heh-heh.'

* * *

'NO, DON'T GET UP.'

Stella spoke totally without irony. It was inconceivable to her that Kraven and Widerschein would not seek instantly to rise to their feet. They watched her majestic approach, awed. She was clothed now, immaculate, cool, regal. She sat down on the ottoman at Kraven's feet, her unsupported back gracefully straight. Smiling, she radiated the room with light. Inclining her head towards Kraven, she took his hand in hers.

'What a horrid mess we sometimes make of our lives, don't you agree?' She sighed. Her smile was gentle, bittersweet; her eyes guileless, trusting, appealing. 'There's no point in pretending. Obviously Mr Kraven and I have a problem. It's not your problem, I know, but through our carelessness we have exposed you to it. I'm truly sorry. It's unforgivable. Dare we ask for your understanding, perhaps even for your help?'

'I with you, honey.'

'Rabbi?'

'The Talmud tells us that the olive tree, in its desire to praise the Creator of all things, twists itself, is bent and crooked,' said Widerschein mysteriously. Stella paused, expecting him to elucidate, but he merely closed his eyes.

'Upstairs in my apartment, at this very moment, my husband is frantic with worry.'

Early bit her lip; Widerschein bit his nails.

'My husband is the dearest, the kindest man that ever lived. I love him very much, you must believe that. But I also love Nicholas . . . Mr Kraven.'

Kraven started. Love? Never before had she spoken of love. She was an amateur, after all, overplaying her part, turning pathos to bathos, drama to melodrama. Where was the Stella of the bikini panties, the Stella who gasped and groaned and thrust, the Stella of mindless ecstasy. Well, that Stella could scarcely emerge here. But love? That was a subject he had learned never to broach with the Stella he knew. She would have hooted him off the stage.

'But neither Mr Kraven nor I matter in this.' There could be no doubt that she held them, had correctly gauged her audience. 'Whatever I tell Robert, my first thought is to spare him pain.' They were swallowing it, gobbling it down, this sentimental glop, this overcooked stew of clichés. And now she was turning to him, her eyes piercing in their sincerity. 'For some time now, Nicholas, I think you've wanted – whether consciously or not – to force me to confront our situation squarely.'

Kraven spluttered.

'No, no, don't protest, darling. What you want does you credit. Look *beneath* the surface. Think. What was the *real* reason you didn't wake me this morning?'

Because I thought you were dead, you sly bitch!

'Actually,' said Kraven, 'I didn't wake before ten myself. And you, you were sleeping so peacefully, so beautifully – '

'Robert says I sleep like a corpse.'

'Like an angel.'

She had written his part in this second-rate melodrama and he was playing it letter-perfect. She had bewitched them all.

'At any rate, it was already so late I thought you might as well sleep a little longer. At least until I came up with some course of action. Why wake you into panic? But then Early arrived, and after her, Rabbi Widerschein. There was nothing I could do.'

'Man wouldn't let me into the bedchamber, come high tide or low, said he clean it his own self.'

Stella raised Kraven's hand to her lips. She looked up at him with shining, adoring eyes. 'Darling, how noble of you, how gallant! A *beau geste* indeed! Your concern for my reputation has . . . I'm touched . . . you've made me so. . . I – ' Choking off her words, Stella turned her head abruptly away.

'Beautiful, jess beautiful.'

Stella rallied, smiling bravely through tear-filled eyes. 'I'm all right now. Look, everyone, there are four of us here, four heads and only one problem. Surely among us we can find the solution. Darling, what do *you* think I should do?'

'Well, to begin with, I'd like to say I agree with you absolutely about not hurting Robert, poor old fellow. But having said that, I must add that your reputation is also important. To me it's sacred.'

'Darling Nicholas.'

'Let's suppose you went out yesterday evening. For cigarettes, perhaps – '

'I don't smoke. You know that.'

'Well, for something, it doesn't matter what. You remember walking to Broadway. The shop was closed – there, that's a realistic detail, lends a little substance. And that's *all* you remember. Temporary amnesia. You must have been wandering all night. At any rate, you came to yourself half an hour ago, sitting on a bench, say. Be exact: near Columbus Circle, another detail. You took a cab home. *Et voilà!*'

Stella shook her head, smiling sadly at him. 'Is that the best you can do?'

'For a perfesser,' said Early severely, 'you kinda poor in smarts.'

'My sweet, you're an innocent. Believe me, it's not that easy to lie. I should know,' she added bitterly, 'I've been living a lie now for almost two years.'

Kraven felt queasy, un-Markolike, beyond his depth. Stella seemed to believe absolutely in the fiction she was creating before them. Could it be that the events of the past hour had unhinged her, had shaken her loose from the plane of reality and precipitated her into a scene from a three-handkerchief tearjerker of her impressionable girlhood? Was she some sort of schizophrenic? Did that delicious body harbour a host of differing personalities? The wild amoralist of his Thursday-night amours had long since given him reason to question her sanity. He had paid too little attention, perhaps.

Stella turned to Widerschein. 'Rabbi?'

Widerschein stroked his beard gravely. 'As I see it, we deal here with a question of adultery.'

Stella flinched.

'To solve a problem, first you must identify it. The Talmud says, "The man who calls a date a fig, except he wants to save a human life, is a no-goodnik." And Rabbi Gamliel comments, and again I translate, "Don't make hanky-panky with the truth." We're talking maybe from pinochle here? I don't think so. No, we're talking from adultery. You don't like the word is one thing, the truth is another. Listen, to make you feel better, Bathsheba probably didn't like it either. About her you know. So, any questions? No? Good. We begin.' He turned to Stella. 'You Jewish?' The question was punctuated by an upward corkscrew motion of the right forefinger.

'No, rabbi, I'm not.'

'Your husband, could be he's Jewish?' The identical gesture, now with left forefinger.

'No.'

'Okay, you were perhaps married in a synagogue, under a *chupa*, a rabbi officiated?' Both fingers at once now, spiralling upwards in complementary directions.

'No, no, and no.'

'Aha!' Widerschein smacked his fist into the palm of his hand. 'Then there's no problem.' He saw the puzzlement on their faces. The simplicity of these laymen! The simplicity, especially, of gentile women! He leaned forward, both hands open, palms upward, as if revealing something fragile and precious. 'Turns out, you're not married, don't you see? Not married, no possibility of adultery. No adultery, no problem. It's simple. You thought you were talking from a fig. Wrong. You were talking from a date.' He sat back, satisfied. 'Hoo boy, are you lucky!'

There was a moment of utter silence, and then Kraven began to laugh. Early cut him off. 'Rabbi, you as crazy as *he* is.'

'Thank you, rabbi,' said Stella. 'Mrs Byrd?'

'Honey, 'fore you does anything, you best choose up which of 'em you wants.'

Kraven's stomach began a slow churn complicated by delicate lateral flutters.

'I must tell Robert the truth.'

'Stella, don't react too hastily, for pity's sake. Have you considered – '

'I realize now I've been considering it for months, ever since I began noticing your little slips. For example, the time you phoned when he was still home.' It had been after eight. Poore-Moody should have been well on his way to Brewster by then. 'The time you had the bottles of wine delivered in mid-afternoon.' He had given a clear order that they not be delivered before eight-thirty. 'And today, not waking me up. That's what I was thinking about while I was inside dressing. I don't doubt, darling, that consciously you were motivated by concern for my honour. But subconsciously you were forcing the moment to its crisis. What you wanted from me was a decision. And that is Early's point too. She knows I must decide.' Stella stiffened her back. 'Nicholas, I can't, I won't, give you up.'

Early and Widerschein simultaneously released a sigh.

Kraven's stomach gave a sudden lurch. 'Stella, be very sure – '

'Darling, darling, I *am*.'

'Stella, I – '

'No need to say it, my precious one, my own dear Nicholas, I'm as happy and, yes, relieved as you are. In the long run, it's a kindness to Robert too.'

Kraven admitted himself baffled. This was a Stella beyond his ability to interpret. What was it she contemplated? Separation, divorce, remarriage? Stella, it seemed, adored him. Think of it! But did he love Stella? It was she who had squelched that possibility. He looked at her. Lord, she was beautiful. Arousing. But love? Whatever love was, *if* he was

51

capable of it then Stella was for him. He needed to rethink their relationship, that was all. It was necessary to dismantle the defences she herself had caused him to throw up around him.

But then she winked at him. What could it mean? No, she was playing a role, enjoying herself. *Did* she actually love him? Go know, Widerschein would say. Stella had created a little drama. Let it run its course. Meanwhile, there sat Widerschein and Early, knife and fork at the ready, as it were, eager to carve up and chew every word. There was time enough to learn of her actual intentions. For the time being, he would play along.

'Stella, I – '

'No, I know what you're going to say. But I must tell Robert alone, in my own way.'

'T'ain't right. Let him go with you, honey.'

'Er, yes, of course. You can't face this ordeal alone, Stella.' He looked at his watch. 'Good grief! I've a meeting with the College President and the Dean of the Arts in less than an hour. The hell with it! Give me a moment to phone and cancel.' Was Stella acting? If so, let her learn his mettle.

'But it must be important.'

'Well, in its way. But what is more important than us? The College is creating a new Institute of Medieval and Renaissance Studies. It seems I'm to be offered the initial directorship, God knows why.'

'He does,' said Widerschein.

'In any case, I'm sure they'll agree to meet at some other time, almost sure anyway.'

'Nonsense! Of course you'll attend the meeting. I'm not going to begin our life together by interfering in your career. What must you think of me? Anyway, I insist on talking to Robert alone.' She leaned towards him and kissed him on the lips.

'Of course, I'll honour your decision.' Kraven now felt

confident he had discovered her wavelength. 'My thoughts will be of you, my brave darling.' He must be careful. He too was beginning to overplay his part.

'When will you be back? Or can I phone you at the College?'

'Ay, there's the rub. I'm not supposed to know it, but Papa Doc – that's what we call Ari Papadakis, our chairman, darling – Papa Doc is giving a party in my honour directly after the meeting. My acceptance, you see, is taken as certain. But if I go to the meeting, I don't see how I can avoid the party. What the heck! Join me there, why don't you? I can give you the address.'

'I'll scarcely be in a mood for a party, darling, especially among strangers. Don't be impatient, beloved. Get in touch with me as soon as you get back, okay?'

They kissed, a delicious, lingering kiss.

'Before I go up to . . . to Robert, I think we could all do with a drink, something stronger than Early's excellent coffee perhaps.'

'A little *schnapps*. Wouldn't hurt, wouldn't be bad.' Widerschein patted his stomach.

'How about some cognac? Early, you know where it's kept. As for me, I must shower and change. But go ahead, enjoy yourselves.' And Kraven fled to the sanctuary of his bedroom.

* * *

DIGNITY HAD LONG TURNED A CALLOUS BACK to the Kravens. Only consider Opa: death had overtaken that marvellous old man as he sat filling out his pools coupon, trousers down, vulnerable to attack, a frail figure in the upstairs toilet. Not even Marko had cared to check whether Opa had written a winning column. And which of them had made a better end? Kraven was acutely aware of being the last of his line. The gods, or Onkel Ferri's demons, had one more chance to play before the game was ended.

And now Stella claimed to love him. Kraven looked at himself in the mirror: hair in disarray, hair growing perhaps a trifle thin, the odd grey thread in plain sight; a face somewhat gaunt, badly in need of a shave; bloodshot eyes from which depended bluish rings; the curving fullness of the Kraven nose. No, not an appealing sight. Still – he straightened his back – better at his present worst than Poore-Moody at his best. All in all, a shower, shave and change of clothing would work wonders. Stella was no fool.

Kraven selected a tie that might suggest at once the sobriety of the established academic about to confer with president and dean and the gaiety of the young (well, not old) bachelor whose mistress has just confessed to adoring him. Either Stella loved him because, simply put, she loved him; or because, caught *in flagrante delicto* and making a virtue of necessity, she had convinced herself she did; or because the shocking events of the morning had eliminated for her the line between the fantasies of *grand amour* she must secretly always have harboured and, to speak plain, the grunting sweaty carnality of a Thursday-night lay. Why involve Menachem Widerschein and Early Byrd in what was patently a private matter? Because she needed the co-operation of an audience in investing airy nothing with a local habitation and a name. The thing existed – not merely because Stella said so but because independent witnesses could attest to it. Their acceptance of Stella's truth would do more than corroborate Stella, it would also convince her.

Kraven remembered Marko's advice to the young Nicko, years and years ago: 'Lying's easy. You've got to say the first thing that comes into your head. Right out, I mean. It's no use stopping to think.' The lie thus spoken soon convinced even the liar of its veritude. It transformed reality, imposing the order of necessity on to the chaos of circumstance. This lesson was a large part of his inheritance from Marko.

Kraven put on his jacket. The sounds of revelry penetrated his door, a shriek of laughter. The cognac was working its social magic. It was time for them all to go about the business of the day, Early to her household chores, Widerschein to complete his rounds, Stella to face her Robert. And Kraven? A decent luncheon downtown, a walk in the spring sunshine, and then a visit to the Museum of Modern Art, which today was offering a film documentary on the life and times of Sarah Bernhardt. This evening he might drop in on the Papadakises. Once a year at their 'annual bash', as they called it, the chairman of the English Department and his wife paid off their accumulated social obligations. To him the invitation had been a bit desultory – they owed him nothing, after all – but he had told Stella he was going to a party and, good as his word, to a party he would go. He checked himself in the mirror. Not too bad.

Before leaving the bedroom he took from a drawer the *Tickety-Boo* file, leafed through it, and looked for a limerick, composed some time ago, that, as he remembered it, was singularly suited to the present occasion. Yes, here it was.

> Poore-Moody, a petit-point maven,
> Whose forebears in fame are engraven,
> Lost his wife to a chap
> With cojones on tap,
> And a name that is Nicholas Kraven.

Smiling, well pleased, he put it back in the file and returned the file to the drawer.

When he entered the living room Widerschein rose to greet him, a brimming glass of cognac in his hand. '*L'chayim!*' he said, spilling a little cognac on the rug.

'*Mazel tov!*' said Early.

'Darling!' said Stella.

55

THREE

KRAVEN TURNED UP Sixth Avenue from Fifty-third
Street and walked towards the Park. The documentary,
Quand Même!, had left him in a nostalgic mood. Satisfactory
so far as it went, it lacked something of the warmth of his
own feelings about Sarah Bernhardt. It might, too, have
benefited from access to the Kraven archives. Perhaps
he should consider bringing them to the Museum's attention.

Quand même! Even so! – Sarah's defiant motto, adopted by
his grandfather, August Alexander, in humble imitation and
fanatic adoration. How Opa had loved her! No, not love, love
was not the word to describe what the old man had felt for
Sarah Bernhardt, not even hopeless love, respectful and
distant. In his eyes she had been a being beyond the eliciting
of any mere human response, however exalted. She was
superhuman, supernatural, even divine, and Opa had ran-
sacked the metaphysical in search of metaphors to describe
her. He had been a moth to her great flame.

August Alexander had first seen her as Doña Sol in Victor
Hugo's *Hernani* on February 25, 1880. It was the fiftieth
anniversary of the play and Hugo himself was in the
audience. Opa had been twenty-one at the time – 'a young
Bock, Nicko' – and in Paris alone. From Doña Sol's first
appearance he had felt he was witnessing a celestial manifes-
tation. From her first words he had been possessed by a kind

56

of ecstasy. Throughout the performance he was utterly fascinated. He had walked back to his lodgings, in the rain, dazed, weeping, running a temperature. The following morning he caused to have sent to Mlle Bernhardt the largest bouquet of flowers obtainable in winterbound Paris. To this was attached a brief note: 'From the humblest of your adorers.' And that very afternoon he had himself photographed outside her house in the rue Fortuny.

'Go, Nicko, the album, the first one, over there.' Opa would settle Nicko on his lap and open the album. 'Here I am, a young *Bock*.' And there he was indeed. In his left hand he held an umbrella, with his right he held a small posy to his heart. One foot was set on the first step leading to the front door. He gazed up at a second-floor window, behind the curtains of which one could just make out a human shape. Sarah? Perhaps. Opa had thought so.

That had been only the beginning. Thereafter, the annual trip to Paris became a pilgrimage, a hegira, undertaken with the religious enthusiasm and awe of a zealot. Every year, except, of course, for the period 1914–18, he had had himself photographed, bouquet in hand, outside her house. In 1898, when Mlle Bernhardt moved from the rue Fortuny to the Boulevard Pereire, the locus of August Alexander's photographs changed accordingly. The pose did not alter with the passage of time; not so August Alexander, however, who gradually assumed the portliness of his middle years. The last photograph in the series, taken on an extraordinary visit to Paris at the end of March 1923, depicted Opa in deep mourning. The pose was different. He stood with his back to the house, his arms at his sides, his head bowed, in the attitude of a military guard at a state funeral. He was an old man now, greybearded. Scattered on the pavement at his feet were the flowers of a bouquet. This photograph Opa had had mounted and edged in black. Beneath the photograph in sober print appeared the following legend:

Over the years Opa had also had himself photographed outside the Odéon, the Renaissance, the Comédie Française, the Théâtre de l'Ambigu, and of course the Théâtre Sarah Bernhardt. In the end he had accumulated eight large albums filled with photographs of Sarah, virtually every one of the hundreds of postcards in which she figured, dozens and dozens of theatre programmes, posters, prints, reviews, knick-knacks, a fantastic collection, perhaps the most complete in the world. These memorabilia, transferred in haste to Hampstead when, one week before the Führer announced to history the return of his homeland to the German Reich, August Alexander fled Vienna, were now in Kraven's New York apartment.

The afternoon had waned. A chill wind, tinged with melancholy, blew in from the Atlantic. Kraven found himself more and more of late turning to memories of his childhood. Perhaps the phenomenon was a function of age. Approaching forty, he was himself becoming a figure of the past, towards which his thoughts quite naturally tended. He crossed Columbus Circle and began to walk up Broadway, stiffening his back and stepping out smartly.

* * *

KRAVEN REPLENISHED HIS DRINK at the makeshift bar and returned to the hubbub in the main room, the 'salon,' as Liz Papadakis called it. He had just spent a few ghastly minutes with Zinka Bleistift, the department's most militant pacifist and most conspicuously publishing scholar. She had attached herself to him like a suckerfish. 'Nickolino, hi! Haven't seen you in simply eons! Not avoiding me, you

sexy man? Tell me all about my new book, why don't you.'
She was a tall dark creature already past the half-century
mark, who possessed a huge nose that hung down limply
over fleshy lips. Over her left nipple this evening she wore
a brooch advising TRY GOD!, whether suggesting a new
course of holy living or urging the indictment of the
Almighty, Kraven was unsure. She had shaken him by the
hand but had failed to let go, paddling his palm with her
forefinger. 'I'm a woman of profound moral convictions,
whose strong sexual urges must be satisfied if I'm not to fall
into looseness.' With her other hand she had nervously
picked shreds of nicotine from her tongue, the glowing tip
of her cigarette almost burning her nose. 'I rather think I feel
a strong pulsation now! Yes, yes, that old black magic, Nick.
Here.' And she had conveyed his hand to her brooch,
holding him clamped in place. 'Tell me you feel it too.'

'Ari's looking for you. I think he went into the den.'

'No kidding?' She had released his hand immediately. 'I
think I'll toddle off then.' The rumours long circulating of
hanky-panky in high departmental places were perhaps true
after all.

The salon was filled with the usual Papadakis crowd,
mostly ageing colleagues and their mates, shrill faculty wives
or grunting husbands, accumulated in undiscriminating salad
days and not now abandoned in the sere and yellow leaf. In
a corner one of Papa Doc's graduate students, alone, earnestly awkward among such luminaries, pretended interest in
a gloomy gouache, petals on a wet black bough, the work of
Honoria, his hosts' teenage daughter. Baxter Gosson, the
department's only living Emeritus, stood with his back to the
fireplace, cocktail glass in hand, smiling vacantly and toast-
ing whoever passed across his line of vision. Milo Thaler,
resident poet, a young man who carried misery about with
him like an open umbrella, hovered over Aubrey Lubert,
music critic of a neighbourhood journal. Lubert was a

59

regular at the 'annual bash', perhaps because he lived in the building. Dressed this evening in a dark-blue velvet tuxedo and bright red bow tie, he winked at Kraven and mouthed a tiny kiss.

Alone for the moment, Kraven sank gratefully into quality time, and while there he composed in his head a rhyme in that tight, short, complicated form called *clerihew*, the name of his cousin Marko's college in London:

> On again, off again,
> A. Papadakis, the
> Speedy Gonzalez of old Mosholu,
> Fell on the floor atop
> Lush Zinka Bleistift and,
> Unzippered-trouseredly,
> Started to screw.

The heat and the noise increased. People were still arriving. John Crowe Dillinger, the medievalist, was making his way to the bar. Now here was a man well worth cultivating. Without question the most incandescent of Mosholu's luminaries, his appearance tonight was clearly something of a coup for the Papadakises. Dillinger was a meticulous scholar, a prolific author, who emerged from his study only to accept an award or to address some international symposium. The History Department did not require him to teach; it was enough that his name appeared in the catalogue and at the foot of a seemingly endless stream of first-rate publications. What on earth was Dillinger doing here?

Kraven, footing slow, followed the great man back to the bar.

'Unexpected pleasure seeing you here, John.'

'Eh?' Dillinger eyed him suspiciously.

'Kraven, English Department.'

'Ah, of course, yes.' He lowered his voice. 'God, how I

hate these faculty socials! Natter, natter, natter. No getting out of it this time, though. Diotima's here, inside there somewhere. Our masters designated me her escort, and that was that. Jesus Christ! In any case, you'll understand why I need this drink.' He took a lusty swallow of scotch. His eyes narrowed. 'She's not, I take it, a particular friend of yours?'

'Liz?'

'Diotima, the Kraut, my date.'

'I hardly know her.' In fact, he knew her not at all.

'Thought I might've put my foot in it.'

'Never fear, your secret's safe. Tell me, what've you been up to of late? Chipping away at some *magnum opus*, I'll be bound – or rather, *you* will be.' Kraven chortled.

'Rather outside the limits of your interests, I imagine,' said Dillinger coldly. 'You're a what's-his-name man, aren't you? The lunatic who sat around naked with his wife in the orchard?'

'Blake? No, I'm a Shakespeare man, actually.'

'Ah, yes, well. It's possible, then, that you've heard of Geoffrey of Monmouth's *Historia Regum Britanniae*?'

'Lots of good stuff there.'

'Precisely!' He took Kraven's arm in a sudden show of warmth. 'I've been working on the *Historia* – and the *Prophetae*, of course.' The great man winked and pulled at his ear. 'Not so long ago, you know, Geoffrey's writings were regarded as mere fabrication. Well, the tide's turned – thanks in no small measure to yours truly, to put it modestly. It's a matter of separating the wheat from the chaff. There's a harvest to be garnered in Geoffrey. He's a wily devil, though. You have to cross-check him, back and forth through the centuries. Gildas, Nennius. . .'

'The *Annales Cambriae*?'

'Why, yes,' said Dillinger, delighted. 'A bit late, of course, but frequently useful. I see you're something of a medievalist yourself.' Dillinger moved closer to Kraven and began to whisper, forcing him to bend over to hear his words. 'Just between the two of us, tell me this: in your reading of Geoffrey did you ever get any sense that Merlin was . . . well, of the Hebraic persuasion?'

Kraven's fingers, in the act of conveying a clutch of peanuts to his mouth, dropped their load into Dillinger's scotch. His legs felt drained of their power to hold him up.

'Feibelman!'

'What? See here, Kraven, are you all right? You look as if you've seen Banquo's ghost.'

Kraven rallied. 'It's nothing, the noise, the heat. I'm fine.' He held on to Dillinger for momentary support. 'The answer to your question, John, is yes. I'll go further. I've not merely sensed he was Jewish, I'm convinced he was.'

'Convinced? I don't think I'd go that far – although I can make out a pretty good case.'

'You know the *Apologia pro vita Grylli*, of course.'

'Yes, but not as well as I probably should. What's the *Apologia* to do with Merlin?'

'It seems that Gryllus actually met a Myrddin.'

'A common enough name in sixth-century Wales,' said Dillinger doubtfully.

'Ah, but he refers to this Myrddin as *poeta*, *vates*, *magus*. He tells us, moreover, that he was completely off the wall, bonkers.'

'The Battle of White Chapel,' Dillinger breathed.

'Exactly. But here's my point: Gryllus jots down one of Myrddin's spells.' Kraven paused. He had the great man now. 'Making reasonable allowances for Gryllus's faulty memory, John, for his mishearing, for his ignorance, Myrddin's "spell" was without question the Hebrew blessing over wine!'

'Jesus Christ!'

'There it is. Go take a look.'

'So I was right all along! D'you know what we have here?

Can you understand? Jesus Christ, this is bigger than the Dead Sea Scrolls!' Dillinger swallowed a half-tumbler of whisky in a gulp. Sweat beaded his brow. 'We can't sit on a thing like this. Look, the Royal Arthurian is meeting at Clerihew next month. London might be the place to go public.'

'I had thought of a monograph. . .' Kraven let his eyes grow wistful. 'But no, too many irons in the fire, spreading myself too thin. It's yours for what it's worth.' Here was true generosity of spirit; but here, too, was prudent foresight: Clerihew meant an almost certain encounter with Professor C.U.T. Quimby, an encounter he dared not chance. 'Anyone who'd given half a thought to Merlin's provenance might have stumbled on it. You yourself, after all.'

'That's very good of you, Kraven, very good. But the credit for the discovery's yours, I'll see to that. The hell with London, why wait that long? What about UCLA? I'm chairing the Arthurian section at the Institute of Med-Ren Studies, the seasonal chinwag. That's sooner. You're going, of course?'

'Inadvertently I allowed my membership to lapse.'

'The college will provide. I'll speak to our masters, they owe me for tonight.' He thumped Kraven heartily on the back. 'Well, I'm off. There's work to be done.' He paused, frowning. 'Damn Diotima! Look here, Kraven, you'll take care of her for me, won't you? Make my apologies, and so on? Remember, we're off to Los Angeles. We'll tell the world, my boy. My secretary'll make all the arrangements, give you the precise dates and so forth; the Dean'll speak to Papadakis. See you at JFK.'

Kraven beamed, his heart fluttering cheerily. An unexpected semester break on the West Coast, all expenses paid, had much to recommend it. Besides, a word passed from Dillinger to Pioggi to Papadakis would nicely boost his credit in the department. Of course, it might perhaps not be entirely cricket, actually to go to LA. An image of wheezing, sweating Feibelman presented itself to his inner eye. The old man *had* nudged Kraven towards the discovery, after all. He should not be entirely forgotten. Surely it would be possible to make some generous and offhand reference to a student of his who had clumsily and all-unwittingly stumbled on the truth.

Liz Papadakis bore down on him, cleaving through the press, drawing in her wake a rotund crone whose upper teeth preceded her as if gnawing out a passage. The crone wore an evening gown of moss green stained dark at the armpits, a gown like herself a relic of another era.

'Professor Dillinger's not leaving, I hope,' said the crone.

'You know, Diotima, don't you, Nick?' said Liz, 'Diotima von Hoden?'

'How d'you do,' said Kraven.

'You bet,' said Diotima von Hoden. She closely resembled the late Eleanor Roosevelt.

'Have you seen Ari?' said Liz.

'He's probably with Zinka. She was looking for him too. Splendid party, Liz.'

'Thanks.' Her eyes misted rapidly. 'Zinka, you said?'

'Well, possibly.'

'Look, if you see Ari, tell him from me to get his fat ass into the kitchen. We've got a fucking buffet to set up.' And Liz, gamely swallowing, dashed off, blowzy, stringy hair falling in her plump face, one thumb attempting in vain to conceal a twisted brassiere strap beneath the shoulder of her tight dress.

Kraven was thus left with Diotima, who had him wedged with his back to a corner. There was no way he might gracefully escape. This was the woman the slippery Dillinger had relinquished to his care.

Diotima was eyeing him through narrowed lids, her head cocked to one side, as if she were guessing his weight. 'We

were not fully introduced, such charming American infor-
mality. But I am at a disadvantage, so unfair. Mrs Papadakis
did not give me your final name.'

'Poore-Moody,' said Kraven, 'Robert Poore-Moody. My
friends call me Nobby.' How easily – too easily! – the
untruths nowadays slid off his tongue.

'Ah, but why then did Mrs Papadakis say Nick?'

'The Old Nick, an in-joke, too embarrassing to explain.'

'I understand. We won't talk of it.'

It was Kraven's turn again. Diotima was looking at him
eagerly. 'What is it you do, if I may ask, Fräulein von
Hoden? What, as Ari would say, is your area of special
competence?'

'Love.'

'No, I meant academically.'

'The European love lyric.' Her laugh was surprisingly
youthful. 'I'm a guest of your Comparative Literature Department. They sponsor my visit here. The famous Dick-
stein Lectures, you know. Five days in New York, three
public addresses. Then for me it is off to Russell Square for
a week of grinding at the British Library. Indeed, I hold a
Dozentur at Heidelberg.'

'Of course, I should have realized. Perhaps I know some
of your work.'

'Not much has been translated,' said Diotima doubtfully.
'But who knows? You read German?'

'*Aber natürlich.*'

'And speak it too. But the accent, so slight. . . Viennese?
You're not an American? No, of course not. Herr Robert
Poore-Moody is a man of mystery. Let me see. . .' Diotima
put a wrinkled finger to a recessive chin, held her head to
one side, and smiled flirtatiously. 'Poore-Moody, Poore-
Moody . . . hmmm. Poehr-Mutig? Of course, of course! The
old duke, one sees it in the nose. Turn your face, so, a little
more, yes, the profile. Wait, yes, and the Esterhazy chin.

One does not expect to encounter the best of the old aristocratic blood here in the New World. You are appearing incognito, your nobility?'

'Ahem.'

'Fear not, your nobility, I am mum.' She put a finger to her lips and then wagged it at him impishly. 'But I must find out all about you. The spirit of scholarly inquiry demands it. From which side of the blanket did Childe Poore-Moody emerge? What will I find in the *Alamanach de Gotha*? It is certain that you have a past.'

Kraven created on his face an expression to suggest hidden sorrows, private griefs. This in his view was one of his better expressions. The thing was to create a *formula*, that is, to visualize with the mind's eye a set of objects, a situation, a chain of events that evoked a particular emotion.

'Jesus, Nick, you look rum, must be something you ate. I keep telling Liz she puts too much ipecac in the dip. For that matter, watch out for the meatballs when they finally reach the groaning board. Trust me, it will not groan alone. Tabasco, that's the secret of the Elizabethan meatball. But don't let on I told.'

Solidly ursine, Aristotle Papadakis lumbered up behind Diotima and dropped a pale hairy paw on to her shoulder. His face looked as if it had been crudely etched on a bag of damp putty, or perhaps as if there were within the head some independent yeasty matter that, swelling after its nature, had minimized the definition of the external features. At the moment he had on the side of his neck what appeared to be a large fresh hickey.

'You're a sly son of a gun, Nick. You've found the prettiest girl in the room, and you're keeping her all to yourself.' Diotima fluttered her eyelashes madly. 'Missed your lecture today, Di, damn it. What was it again?'

'The Imagery of Self-Abuse in the Poetry of German Romanticism.'

'Right on!' Papa Doc rather liked such expressions, his use of which placed him, he thought, at the barricades with the seekers after a better world. (Earlier that evening he had greeted Kraven at the door with a manic 'Hey, man, what's happening? Gimmee skin!')

'Ari, my dear chap,' said Kraven, 'a message from the fair Liz. She has present need of you. Tell him, she said, to get his fat ass into the kitchen. Those were her very words.'

'Good fucking Christ! Can't she even put together a goddam fucking buffet without me!'

Papa Doc had exploded into a general conversational lull. Heads turned in their direction from every part of the salon. Over by the window Gosson, the emeritus, dribbling, raised his glass to them. 'Up yours,' he said amiably. Talk picked up again.

Shocked at his outburst, Papa Doc strove to recreate his earlier bonhomie. The fire was leaving his cheeks and, but for the hickey, his neck. The old familiar pallor was reasserting itself. 'We kid each other a lot, Liz and I. Don't want Di here to get the wrong idea. Hell, we've got more than twenty years under the bridge. A little kidding here and there, kinda keeps the juices flowing. Having a good time, Di? Right on! Say, better watch out for this guy.' Papa Doc winked at Kraven and gave him a chummy nudge. He was rapidly recovering his buoyancy, the stuff of which successful chairmen are made. 'Well, duty calls. I hate to leave you special people.'

'Right on, Ari,' said Diotima, a quick study. Papa Doc lumbered off. 'A charming couple the Papadakises, so *sympatisch* don't you think?'

'Absolutely,' said Kraven. 'They're everybody's favourites.'

The salon was less crowded now. People had begun drifting into the dining room; others were returning juggling paper plates piled high with food, plastic knives and forks, and styrofoam cups of wine. Liz, evidently unable or unwilling to wait any longer for Papa Doc's fat ass, had launched the buffet on her own. It was after eleven. The salon was a wreck. Ashtrays were filled to overflowing; empty glasses and dishes, spilled drinks, crushed potato crisps, wayward globs of dip, soiled napkins cluttered the surfaces. The smoke hung at eye level.

'Shall we get something to eat?'

'Not for me, thank you. I'm watching my figure.'

'I've been watching it all evening,' said Kraven gallantly.

'Ach, you naughty boy,' said Diotima, delighted. 'Now I must be on my way. I think, a pity, no? But the hour is so late; the jet makes a horrid lag, yes? Do you know where in the world is Professor Dillinger?'

'Home with his books, I believe. A flash of inspiration that has cast the last decade of the sixth century into a strange new light.'

'Then my escort has abandoned me?'

'I am your escort, Fräulein von Hoden.'

'But I am an abandoned woman, nevertheless!'

'I sincerely hope so.' The spirit of chivalrous uncles lived on in Kraven. 'You have been left entirely in my hands.' He spread them, as if to accommodate a 38C. The spirit of cousin Marko smiled.

'In this case, let's go!'

* * *

THEY WALKED TOWARDS COLUMBUS AVENUE. A large but nervous member of the family *Belostomatidae*, Gregor Samsa perhaps, skittered shiny-backed across the pool of lamplight at their feet and leaped desperately into the gutter's garbage. A foetid stench blew in gently from the river on a seasonal zephyr. An old checker cab rattled down the avenue towards them. What luck! Kraven hailed it and quickly bundled Diotima inside. The cab gave off the melancholy smell of long-forgotten urine.

'Where to, man?'

'Where are you staying, Fräulein von Hoden?'

'The Hotel Koh-i-Noor.'

'Hotel Koh-i-Noor, please, driver.'

'Where's that at, man?'

'Er, where *is* the hotel exactly?'

'Brooklyn.'

God save the mark!

But the Hotel Koh-i-Noor proved something of a pleasant surprise. The cab dropped them there after a wild lurching drive through and around the byways of Brooklyn. Once over the Bridge the cabbie had cheerfully admitted that he knew the Borough not at all. Moreover, he would ask directions only of his black brothers. Diotima, however, was delighted with the turn of events. 'A quest! An adventure!' Her enthusiasm succeeded in thawing some of Kraven's irritability; each wrong turning, each misdirection, became a stimulus to hilarity. She was a spritely old girl. Another juddering stop. 'Hey, brother, you know where the Cohen-Whore's at? Shit, no, it's a *ho*-tel.' It appeared they were parked outside.

The hotel stood on a quiet tree-lined street. It had obviously been built in a more generous age, in the second half of the last century, probably before the then proud and wealthy city had thrown in its lot with crass New York. Architecturally it might have graced the Midi in its heyday, not one of the better known hotels perhaps, but one of the quietly opulent, the regally discreet, the very sort of place at which the Prince of Wales in mufti might have passed the tea-and-crumpets hour with the Divine Sarah.

Within the vast lobby all was gloomy elegance, marble, cool travertine, polished oak, mahogany, great velvet hangings, faded brocade. In the middle stood a circular tufted banquette. It was high backed, and from its centre huge ferns thrust upwards towards the vaulted ceiling, shrouded now in darkness. The reception desk, heavy and ornately carved, was the principal focus of light at the rear, but that focus, inadequate to the illumination of the whole, was augmented by scattered minor foci, old Tiffany lamps throwing soft warm pools of light, here on a decorative screen, there on a studded chesterfield, and over there on an ancient rug. Of India there was no sign, apart from two giant elephant feet, umbrella stands, one on each side of the revolving doors as one entered, and at the far end of the vast expanse the man at the reception desk himself. The night clerk was in the full dress uniform of a Sikh sergeant major in the days of the Empire, turban, campaign medals, puttees, waxed moustaches and all.

Diotima approached the Sikh, who snapped to attention, his back ramrod stiff.

'My key, please, sergeant major. Suite 69.'

The Sikh swung around, removed the key from a hook, swung back, but seemed reluctant to hand it over. He looked with great suspicion at Kraven, twirling a waxed moustache the while. 'You want I should call you a cab, mister,' he said at last. 'At twelve-thirty in the morning, they ain't exactly cruising around.'

'My brother accompanies me to my room,' said Diotima blithely. 'But he will certainly require a taxi later.' She extended a hand for the key.

The Sikh shrugged. 'Sure, sure.' He grinned, revealing a gold tooth, the last nugget of an exhausted lode. But he retained the key. 'Brother is *one* thing; hanky-panky is another.'

Kraven flushed. Did the fool really imagine that he and Diotima. . .? that he could possibly wish to. . .? 'Look here, you're insulting my sister. Moreover, we have family matters of the gravest importance to discuss.'

70

The Sikh whirled on him in triumph. 'So how come you *talk* different?'

'My brother and I were separated during the war,' said Diotima. She took a ten-dollar bill from her purse and placed it on the counter. 'He escaped to England, I was hidden on the Continent.'

'Them Nazi bastards, you should pardon the expression!' exclaimed the Sikh, his face reddening, his lower lip trembling. Faster than Kraven's eyes could follow it, the ten-dollar bill disappeared from the counter and into the folds of the turban. Diotima received her key. 'No offence,' he said to Kraven. 'You should understand, this is a respectable establishment, a nice class people we got here. Drunks and bums and *hooliganim* we don't need. Deep throat neither. You wouldn't want your sister should have it any other way.'

And the Sikh, once more at attention, saluted after the British fashion, his right hand oscillating into place before his temple. 'Room service will get you a cab. All you do, you just ring down when you're ready.'

Diotima's suite had a sitting room that might have added lustre to an intimate corner of Versailles and beyond this a bedroom, approached through carved double doors, one of which stood partly open. All the woodwork in the sitting room was painted white and trimmed in gold leaf. Huge paintings after Gainsborough and Watteau hung in ornate frames upon the walls. A bust of Marie Antoinette, in the manner if not necessarily by the hand of Houdon, graced a marble pedestal in a far corner. Here was a fine escritoire, there a japanned cabinet.

'Please to sit down,' said Diotima, indicating a love seat. 'You would like a drink? I have a bottle of vodka, genuine Russian, very good, duty free.'

'I think not, Fräulein von Hoden. I must be going.'

'So formal! Diotima! We are friends, true?'

'Diotima.'

'So much better. And I must call you Robert. I have your permission?'

'Of course. And now. . .'

'Sit down in any case. I want to give you my book, a reward for being a good boy. It will take me only a minute to dig it up.' She pointed again at the love seat and winked knowingly. Kraven sat down while Diotima went to the bedroom. For an ancient tub of a woman she walked with a remarkably girlish spring to her step.

He looked around him. A fantastic hotel, a fossil, perfectly preserved. ('I stay at the Koh-i-Noor whenever occasion takes me to New York. An extraordinary relic. Bit of luck finding it, actually, but that's another story. Yes, in Brooklyn of all places!') Such things were good to know.

Diotima returned, book in hand. She sat down beside him.

'You have a pen, please? I must inscribe it.' She scribbled on the flyleaf. 'Here you are, my dear friend. It is my fondest hope you will enjoy it and even – who knows? – perhaps learn from it.' Diotima flung her hand expressively on Kraven's upper thigh and kept it there.

The woman must be pushing seventy. The gesture meant nothing, no more than academic camaraderie, totally sexless. He turned to the title page. *Die Leiter*, von Diotima v. Hoden. 'What's it about, Diotima?'

Diotima moved her hand an inch higher. 'Didi, please. And you are Nobby.'

How to stop her without drawing attention to what she was doing and thereby embarrassing them both?

'You ask a good question, what is it about? How shall I answer you? Well, it is about love, of course. But, no, it is not a philosophy, not a theory. A handbook? No, not that. A discipline, then? Yes, yes, a discipline of love.' The hand moved higher. 'Here is what I write about. Love is a *Leiter*, a ladder, a series of graduated steps. The steps make an ascent from the remote to the near, from the simple intellec-

72

tual formulation rising ever upward to the complex physiological response.'

'Fascinating.' She was flicking his genitals, for pity's sake!

'We begin at the beginning. The pupil steps on to the first
rung of the ladder by the simple conceptualization of the
abstract Truth, who, as we all know, is also Beauty and
Love. The abstraction, naturally, is vague, is nebulous; it
lacks definition, as is its nature; it lacks light.'

Kraven was interested in spite of himself. 'Well, I've often
thought of Truth as standing at the top of a "huge hill,
cragged and steep".'

'Excellent! Begin by visualizing the hill, but focus on its
peak. There stands Truth. You see her?'

'I see her.' Not actually, of course, but Kraven was for the
time being willing to go along.

'She is also Beauty. Is she not beautiful?'

'Yes.'

'Very good! We climb to the next rung, still somewhat
clouded, still very much of the intellect. Favourite abstract
paintings, perhaps; music, Wagner, for example. Here is
Truth! Here is Beauty!'

She rose to her feet and began to pace before him. Sunk
in thought, she held her hands stiffly before her. Her
movements were mesmerizing.

'We climb higher. We enter the world. The surf, the
wooded land, the desert plains, vineyards, valleys. See the
panther crouch! See the dolphins leap! There an eagle falls
to his crag like a thunderbolt! You see them? There is
enough light? Once more you see Beauty and Truth, but
now as they exist in all creation.'

Diotima paused in her pacing and approached him, wild
eyed. Startled, he drew back, but she seemed not to notice.
'We approach the summit,' she said, and resumed her
pacing. 'From the beauty and truth in all living things to
beauty and truth of creation's noblest creatures we move.

Man and woman. Picture them as Praxitiles must have seen them, or Leonardo, or Bouguereau. See their sinuous grace. Adam and Eve in the Garden of Eden, Hero and Leander, Antony and Cleopatra, the Duke and Duchess of Windsor. Slowly they approach one another. They sink down upon a flowery bank. They embrace. What are they doing? No need to ask. Truth! Beauty!'

She sat down once more beside him; once more she touched his thigh, this time gently, featherlight. Kraven made an effort to stand, but she caught him by the arm and pulled him down again.

'Only two rungs remain. Concentrate. To the particular we now ascend. Up, up, we go. From the truth and beauty of all mankind to the truth and beauty of one. I am Eve, you are Adam. From multiplicity to oneness we have come, one and one. I look at your beauty, Nobby, and see it is true.'

'And the last rung?' In seconds the ordeal would be over. In minutes the Sikh would find him a cab. In an hour, at most, he would be home.

'Ah, the last rung? Impatient sweetheart.' She laughed her girlish laugh and bit his ear lobe. 'On the last rung we find the total concentration of *all* the senses in one member, yes, *the* member, Nobby, the catalyst of the intellect fully engaged, the ecstatic expression of the act itself, the ultimate insight.'

Kraven sighed. Diotima raked him with her eyes, held him with them. It had been a long time since he had felt himself to be more Nicko than Marko. He was out of his depth, and he knew it. Longing to be gone, he felt powerless to move, as if hypnotized. Like a schoolboy in the headmaster's study, he waited for permission to leave.

'Tell me, Nobby, what do you know about aphrodisiacs?'

She was making strange fluttering motions with her fingers, which she held at the level of her bosom. Her eyes flashed. She took him by the arm, lifted him to his feet, and began to walk him slowly around the room. Her grip was firm. He could not resist.

'Aphrodisiacs, love potions, they have an interesting history, most interesting. Do you know they are common to every human culture? All over the world and in every age? Do you know that recipes appear on the earliest Egyptian papyri? *Jah*! I have seen them, Cairo, Berlin, the British Museum. Of course, there is a lot of nonsense too, a lot of ignorant superstition. But it's not all nonsense, my Nobby, not all superstition.'

She paused in their wanderings, but kept hold of his arm.

'In recent years I have limited my researches to fungi, particularly to the *Basidiomycetes*. You know about fungi?'

'Hardly anything. Well, I *have* heard of *Aminita muscaria*, of course.'

'Tsk-tsk-tsk.' She shook an admonitory finger at him. 'Stay away from it. Too unstable, too unpredictable. No, sweetheart, *Aminita* is not for you.'

'Good lord, I don't mean I've actually taken any!'

'But *I* have, you see.' She began once more to escort him around the room. 'I have lived among so-called primitive peoples, among ancient cultures where fungi are still in use, today as always in the past. I have made my experiments. I have travelled the world, Nobby. I've lived in ways our sophisticated colleagues would call savage. What I have seen! What I have done!'

She struck her forehead with the palm of her free hand and enjoyed a moment's reverie. Kraven watched her carefully. In spite of himself, he recognized a gesture and an expression he could use.

'*Basiomycetes* are the answer, and of these, only three. But soil and climate are important. Of the essence. They must be sought out *in situ*. From the Matto Grosso, *Mutinus giganticus*; from the southwestern slopes of Kilimanjaro, *Ithyphallus torosus*; from Tampasak, *Dictyphora incrassata*.'

She began to run her hand up and down his arm, feverishly clutching, as if seeking something she had lost.

'Cooked in the traditional native way, any of these is a powerful aphrodisiac. But I have found my own way, I have combined all three. Yes, Didi's Love Potion. What have I found, Nobby? You ask what I have found? An aphrodisiac without equal. What have I done? I have brought together what cruel Mother Nature keeps apart, separates by vast oceans, continents. But you will see. Wait there, sweetheart, wait, my treasure, only wait.'

She released him and ran to the bedroom, stopping for a moment at the door and turning her wild eyes on him. 'Don't move.' And she disappeared.

Kraven remained where she had left him, rooted by her command.

'Here it is, Nobby, as I promised!'

Diotima. She stood at the door to her bedroom waving triumphantly aloft a cork-stoppered test-tube, a large phial filled with a khaki-coloured liquid. Kraven stood transfixed, horrified. Diotima wore not a shred of clothing. Her iron-grey hair, frizzled, hung wild and loose to her shoulders. Her large round stomach protruded and hung low, mercifully screening her pudendum. He noticed that her thighs were mottled and comically thin. She wore a feral grin.

'Here I come!'

She ran towards him, leaping, her huge half-empty breasts flapping against her stomach. Head down, she charged him, knocking him off his feet and on to the floor. He fought for breath. With her knees she pinned down his upper arms and held him immobile. Her pudendum radiated heat on to his chest. She unstoppered the test-tube. She pinched his nose. 'Bottoms up!' she giggled, pouring the liquid into his gasping mouth. Choking, gagging, he was forced to swallow.

Warmth immediately suffused his body. He ceased his struggling, no longer knew why he struggled. Sensing the change in him, Diotima shifted, swinging around nimbly until, maintaining the same position, she was facing the other way. He was looking at her raised buttocks. He saw the stretch marks, the drooping deadwhite skin, the bluish discolorations, the wiry hair; he saw her parted vagina, glinting and foam flecked, saw the dingy beard. And yet he was filled with a pleasurable excitement, a steadying delight. Diotima was panting. She was struggling with his belt, unzipping his fly. He felt himself grow magnificently stiff.

And then the world faded and disappeared, along with his consciousness.

FOUR

KRAVEN STOOD within the chthonic fastnesses of the Brooklyn Bridge subway station. The muttered directions, reluctantly divulged, of the sergeant major's morning relief, a swarthy corporal, had led him from the Koh-i-Noor not to the promised Clark Street IRT subway but eventually, after nervous meanderings, to Borough Hall. His stomach rumbled, and well it might. Since lunchtime yesterday he had not eaten. Oh yes, a few peanuts last night at the Papadakises, an olive or two, but no real food. Certainly he had drunk too much. An excess of alcohol was far more likely to have caused him to pass out in Diotima's room than the foul potion the old witch had poured down his throat. The conscious Kraven mind shied nervously away from the tale the Kraven memory insisted on relating. Had it happened? Surely not. He was reluctant to recast that grotesque figure in the role of naked nymphomaniacal Valkyrie. As for what followed her attack upon him, over *that*, fortunately, the Kraven memory drew a kindly veil. Yet an image persisted, ineradicable, of vaginal dewlaps. No, far better to attribute what he thought he had seen to sottish nightmare.

He had awoken that morning alone in the tousled bed, alone in Diotima's magnificent suite, alone (thank God!), vigorous, and unusually alert – alone and sporting an erection of colossal proportions. Nor had it been the familiar matutinal index of a full bladder. He knew the difference well enough. No, this had been an erection of rampant lust, and yet one curiously divorced from sexual desire. He had sat up in the bed and admired it. With his forefinger he had depressed it to the level of the sheets, but it had slipped sideways from beneath the pressure and sprung up again, buoyant and free. He had got up and stood before the mirror, turning sideways, first this way then that. Why, it exceeded the full straining span between the tip of his little finger and the tip of his thumb! There it had stood, swaying gently, curving grandly upward, majestic. Excelsior!

The astonishing erection had lasted through the shower, had responded eagerly to a brisk towelling. Kraven had returned to the bedroom, the independent baton, the magical stick, enthusiastically pointing the way. It leaped and jounced, it dipped and perkily swayed.

He saw that Diotima had folded his clothing neatly over a chair. A note had been pinned to his shirt: 'Always an old violin plays the most beautiful melody, is not this true? Until next time, your Didi.' Could there be some truth to the shocking images now teasing the outer edges of his consciousness?

> Hocusing-pocusing,
> Didi von Hoden,
> Wagnerian temptress and Circean witch,
> Shimmied and shook herself
> While she was wearing, e-
> Rotomaniac'lly,
> Nary a stitch.

Kraven shuddered.

He had had to wait half an hour before it was possible to dress. Indeed, only after he had taken matters personally in hand had the mutinous member, albeit reluctantly, slowly submitted, crestfallen, its pride humbled, but at last at one with the rest of his body again.

The platform was crowded. A train was pulling in at last. A diminutive woman, her hair done up in large plastic curlers, elbowed her way deliberately in front of Kraven. Familiar with the strong territorialism of regular subway riders, he gave ground. But when the doors opened before them he raced her for the only available seat. She won, fortunately for the vestiges of Kraven gallantry, and winked up at him saucily. He winked back. Here was subway goodfellowship at its very best.

Strap-hanging, jerked rudely by the train's fits and starts, Kraven closed his eyes and found himself listening to the fairy tale a plump lady beneath him was reading to the child curling sleepily on her lap. 'At that moment the little tailor ran from his shop into the street, waving his fly swatter above his head. "I killed seven with one blow!" he shouted. "Think of it! Seven with a single blow!" All the people in the street looked at him in amazement. . .'

When Onkel Koko broke the dreadful news to Opa, the old man said simply, 'So it was no use, all for nothing the escape from Vienna. They found them anyway.' That was before he fully understood the magnitude of his loss.

In the early hours of 2 November 1941, a lone German bomber, separated from its squadron during a raid on the East End docks and wandering off course, flew over Hampstead and jettisoned its remaining bomb. Nicko, Mummy, and Opa were living in the big house in Harrogate by this time. They had been in the north for almost a year, ever since Nicko's father had decided that London wasn't really safe enough any more. Daddy would come up to see them on weekends and holidays, whenever he could, and usually he had brought a Kraven or two with him. Sometimes Grandpa Blum and Aunt Cicely came too, but never on the same train as the Kravens. On this particular weekend Onkel

Koko had brought cousins Tillie and Marko for a visit. But by then Daddy had been eight months dead. He had reached for a rose in the Harrogate garden, and . . . and then he had died. Crumbs of soil stuck to the blood on Daddy's face, where the thorns had scratched him as he fell.

For the first few weeks Nicko had had to share with Opa the huge double bed in the first-floor back bedroom. It was this very bed that now stood, thanks to Marko, in Kraven's New York apartment. Not that Nicko minded sharing. It was super to sleep with Opa, who had a million midnight stories to tell.

The train pulled into Astor Place. Damn it! In his sportive eagerness to race for a seat, Kraven had mistakenly boarded a local. The winner in that contest, meanwhile, had got up to leave. Kraven sighed and sat down. He was still far from Grand Central, where he would change trains. Next to him the child had fallen asleep on his mother's lap, his dirty sneakers rubbing from time to time against Kraven's trouser leg.

He was still sharing the bed with Opa when Onkel Koko brought the news of the bombing. They had believed Nicko was asleep and they talked in strangled whispers. He did fall asleep after that in terror. But he awoke once briefly in the night to hear Opa sobbing beside him.

In a way it was Daddy's fault, although as always his intentions had been of the best. In the autumn of 1939, before there had been any thought of moving his family to the north of England, Felix Kraven had had an air-raid shelter built at the foot of their Hampstead garden. Such private shelters were springing up all over suburban London, although the real terrors of *Blitzkrieg* were as yet unimagined. Theirs had been the first in Beauchamp Close.

It was a small square structure of double brick with a reinforced concrete roof. 'Safe as 'ouses, them there', the builder, a man of nice irony, had assured Daddy. 'Stand anything bar a direct 'it. Y'might try a bitter camouflage,

81

just t'be on the safe side. Most do.' 'Do you think so?' 'Yerss. Frow up an 'ill all round, just the door showing. Plant it, 'erbaceous borders, that sorter thing. Rock gardens is popular. Don't take much to confuse the 'un.' He glanced at Daddy. 'No offence, sir.' 'And none taken, my dear fellow', said Daddy, who prided himself on his colloquial English.

Mummy had bunk beds moved into the shelter, a table, some kitchen chairs, lamps, an oil heater. It was quite cozy, just the place to play ludo or snakes-and-ladders. Meanwhile, Daddy busied himself on the roof, periodically arranging and rearranging an assortment of branches. 'Why are you doing that, Daddy?' Nicko had asked once, awed by his father's perilous acrobatics. 'To confuse the Hun, of course. Doesn't take much, you know.'

But Felix had reckoned without the Kraven demons.

When the sirens wailed in the early morning hours of 2 November 1941, Tante Carlotta, Tante Erica, and Onkel Gusti zipped themselves into their siren suits and made for the air raid shelter. They took with them a large thermos flask of tea and a tin of sandwiches.

Onkel Ferri, helmet on head, gas mask over his shoulder, binoculars around his neck, was at that time some five miles away at his post on the roof of an office building. He was an air raid warden and proud to be doing his bit. On the roof with him was Vice-Admiral Bunny Mayhew, retired, VC, a fellow watcher of the skies.

Many years later Ferri admitted to Kraven that he had actually heard the lone bomber fly over, had even started to telephone the local anti-aircraft battery on his observer-post telephone. Mayhew had stopped him.

'Plucky beggar. Must be separated from his chaps. Goin' it alone, don't y'now.'

'But it's a German bomber!'

'Don't need *you* to tell me it's Jerry. They'll get him

82

before he reaches the coast, poor blighter. Give him a sportin' chance, old boy.'

Onkel Ferri had replaced the receiver.

Meanwhile, in the air raid shelter at the foot of 15 Beauchamp Close, Onkel Gusti and Tante Erica sat playing gin rummy. Tante Carlotta had just poured three mugs of tea from the large thermos flask when the bomb struck the shelter, blowing it to pieces. It had been a direct hit. Curiously the mugs of tea survived undisturbed. A charred scrap of paper found in the rubble showed that Tante Erica's famed luck at cards had held to the end. The house itself had sustained almost no damage, merely a broken window-pane or two.

But why had Onkel Ferri, now transformed into the Compleat Mourner, failed in his duty? Had his yearning to be accepted as a sporting Englishman softened his resistance to Admiral Mayhew? It was shortly after his release from the asylum that the Compleat Mourner revealed his theory about the anti-Kraven demons.

The train came to a skittering halt. Metal ground on metal and howled. It was Fifty-first Street. Kraven had missed his station.

* * *

IT COST HIM ANOTHER TOKEN to reach the down-town platform. Perhaps there had been something in the witch's potion, some mind-diverting ingredient, say, that prevented him from focusing on the simple task of getting home. Then too, the ugliness of his surroundings surely prompted a sensitive concentration to flee, thoughts to turn defensively inward. The New York subway system, after all, had succeeded in granting contemporary incivility a formal expression.

On the tracks at the entrance to the tunnel a signalman

idled, whistling to the spirit ditties of no tone. Over his clothes he wore a bright orange tunic, and he held a lantern in his hand. He was there to warn his fellows, out of Kraven's line of vision but presumably working in the tunnel at the other end of the platform, of a train's approach. A pleasant enough sort of occupation, Kraven mused, but for its location almost pastoral in its simplicity. At the end of another grateful day, Corin would cease his whistling, twitch his orange mantle, and be off: tomorrow to fresh tracks and stations new.

Kraven retired from the edge of the platform. It made him nervous to stand there. One always feared the shove from behind that would send one teetering over the edge and into the filthy well, sprawling amid the unutterable disjecta of countless subway riders, the oily soot, the rat faeces, one's head coming to rest in the Stygian trickle that ran ceaselessly between the tracks, one's leg fetching up against the live rail, the death rail.

From the distance came the rumble of a train. Corin courageously faced the sound and began to swing his lantern before him, left, right, left, right. Three unnerving siren blasts answered his signal. He turned and faced the other way. Once more he swung his lantern. Satisfied, he turned again and walked boldly into the tunnel's mouth. It swallowed him up. The train clattered into the station emitting angry blasts. It was gaudily disfigured but relatively empty. Kraven got into the last compartment and sat down. A faulty fluorescent light flickered on and off. A copy of the *News* was scattered the length of the floor, twisted, torn, much trodden on. The doors closed but the train remained in the station.

Evil Eddie, Ducky 128 and Shaddow 19 had been in the compartment before him and had not scrupled to leave clear signs of their passing. The cognoscenti, Kraven knew, claimed for such effusions of the People the lofty status of

Art. Academicians and literati, instant diagnosticians of the *Zeitgeist*, saw in such optical migraines the efforts of the in-articulate to articulate, the longing of the oppressed, the nameless and the alienated to assert their selfhood. Shaddow 19, Ducky 128, Evil Eddie, the epigraffiti of the damned. Alas, alas, Kraven searched his heart in vain for under-standing.

With the sound of a snapping femur and a mighty shake that sent him sliding down his seat, the train at last began to move. When it re-entered the tunnel, Kraven peered through the grimy window. There, each in his individual cubby carved out of the tunnel wall, each wearing the distinctive orange tunic and carrying his tool, stood Corin's fellows, all secure.

So *that* was how it was done. Poor Koko, had he but known!

Oskar Kraven had been Nicko's favourite uncle. Indeed, he was a universal favourite. Tall, handsome, charming, he possessed a chivalric grace that dissolved all opposition. Women melted at his glance, men found him a jocund companion. Tillie and Marko, his children, had from their infancy supposed him a fool, which perhaps he was, but had also fiercely defended him as a lovable fool. He was Tante Carlotta's despair and joy. His fecklessness, inordinate even in a Kraven, was a constant worry to her, but, as she had once admitted to Felix, had he been more responsible he would have been less Koko, and that was unthinkable. He gambled too fondly, drank too enthusiastically. But Lotti was proud simply to be seen with him. And indeed they made a fine pair, Onkel Oskar, elegant, swinging his cane, his hat angled just so, a fresh boutonnière in his lapel, and Tante Carlotta, still a lovely woman in her forties, short but liberally endowed, her delicate hand resting gently on his arm.

She worshipped him. After twenty years of marriage he loved her deeply, warmly, but no longer passionately. His passion he reserved for a series of mistresses. But he chose discreetly and well, for he would not have hurt Lotti for the world. Infidelity is too harsh, too narrow a word to describe Koko's . . . what? peccadillos? adventures? amours? He and Lotti enjoyed a marriage of mutual contentedness and kindliness, in the middle years an idyllic state.

Then came the German bomb, assembled in a cursed hour and blasting to smithereens the shelter at 15 Beauchamp Close. Koko endured the death of his beloved Lotti by the simple expedient of refusing to acknowledge it. She was away on holiday, it would do her a world of good. He would join her as soon as he could get away.

Probably no one will ever possess all the facts having to do with Koko's violent death. Precisely what followed his ill-timed arrival on the platform of the Tottenham Court Road station and preceded his ill-fated interference with the smooth-running of the Northern Line will almost certainly always remain shrouded in mystery. The official facts, however, are these: (1) 'On or about eleven o'clock on the night of 12 September 1946,' Oskar Kraven, widower, womanizer and poker player, had purchased a ninepenny ticket at Tottenham Court Road underground station; (2) at eleven twenty-three he had been overtaken in the tunnel, within eight hundred feet of Goodge Street, by a train already slowing down for the station approach; (3) according to the Medical Examiner's report, 'deceased was discovered to possess in his bloodstream a level of alcohol far in excess of what might be expected from convivial drinking.' Deceased, in short, as the Medical Examiner had added when pressed by the Coroner for clarification, had been 'blind reeling drunk'.

This last 'fact' Onkel Ferri, the Compleat Mourner, had dismissed as a caddish insinuation, a vile affront to the memory of his fallen brother. In Ferri's reconstruction of the melancholy events, Koko had probably peered over the edge of the platform in a vain search for some sign of his train. He had been struck from behind 'by a person or by persons unknown', – the Kraven demon(s)! – who had seized this opportunity of catching a Kraven in so defenceless a position. His assailant(s) had immediately fled into the night.

The anti-Kraven forces, as the Compleat Mourner saw it in that far-off time, were still legion in the world. Flushed with their successes of 1941, the malevolent demons had struck again. The recent defeat of Nazi Germany had not diminished their fervour or ingenuity. Pity the poor Kraven who let down his guard!

Koko had perhaps lain on the tracks for a short while, momentarily stunned. But then he had pulled himself to his feet, dusted himself off as best he could, and with typical Koko-esque insouciance had decided to return home on foot. He had set off into the tunnel's black mouth, no doubt swinging his cane.

* * *

KRAVEN'S TRAIN SCREECHED INTO BLEECKER STREET. Once more he had overshot his station. This must stop, and now. He was becoming a Pynchonian yoyo. The human brain, he had read somewhere, began daily at age thirty to shed particles in shocking quantities, a kind of galloping intelligential dandruff, the seborrhea of the mind. He ploughed today through drifts of such stuff as once his dreams were made on.

Kraven got off the train right there, at Bleecker Street. The pattern must be broken before it gelled, before it became a way of life. How many of the ancient derelicts he had seen over the years and at all hours, male and female, sitting sometimes in their own urine on platform benches, pawing through refuse bins, shunned like lepers of an earlier time, left alone to their haunted dreams, their fitful catnaps, how many of them, he wondered, had been caught long ago as he had almost been caught today in a Moëbian nightmare, a goetistic spell, the lifetime shuttle? Fanciful, no doubt. But he left the platform for all that.

Climbing to street level, he found himself in a neighbourhood of factories and gas stations, an area of converging dirty streets, a place of giant trucks and honking automobiles. The streets hummed with noise and activity. Large, heavily muscled men in T-shirts and Levis, stomachs bulging with beer, shouted at one another, kidded, cursed. Kraven walked quickly towards Houston, hailed a cab, and got in.

'Where to, Mac?'

'Home, please.'

'You kiddin me? Where's home, mistuh?'

'Oh, sorry.' Kraven told him.

The driver soon found the heaviest traffic and contrived to stay with it. He aimed his cab unerringly at the larger potholes, even when to do so threatened bloody collision. A neatly printed sign on the rear of the driver's seat advised passengers to 'Sit Back And Relax.' Kraven watched the meter tick away.

About an hour later the taxi drew up just short of Kraven's building. The fare was witheringly high. Kraven stepped, right foot first, out of the cab. As the foot took his weight, he felt the ground beneath it momentarily subside and then hold slippery-firm. He had never developed the specialized antennae of the native New Yorker. 'Oh, shit!' he said, with perfect accuracy.

FIVE

RING-RING! KRAVEN'S TELEPHONE, sounding its shrill summons, reminded him abruptly and cruelly of unfinished business. Almost certainly it was Stella. The events of yesterday morning flooded back to torment him. Into what snares and befuddlements had Stella carelessly led him? *Ring-ring!* He could not cope with her now. She must allow him time to think, a minimal courtesy to the victim.

He walked through to the living-room windows and shifted the blinds slightly. A huddle of loutish youths across the Drive were staring up at him. Was that Princip, the SDS champion of his Shakespeare class, among them? The costume and the scoliotic posture were all too familiar. They seemed to be arguing among themselves, gesticulating. One of them pointed at his window. Instinctively Kraven pulled back. What were they up to? Princip gave a clenched-fist salute. Immediately below, the doorman from the next building was in neighbourly conversation with his own doorman, Clarence. We are not safe, Clarence; we are not safe. The phone meanwhile had ceased its importunings. Kraven turned from the window. Princip and his fellows, whatever their fancied intentions, were the least of his concerns.

The apartment comprised, essentially, four large rooms. The dining room, across the gallery from the living room, he had transformed into a study: book-lined walls, reading lamps, easy chairs, the sanctuary of the scholar. The living room could easily accommodate the dining table and chairs; in any case, he took most of his meals in the kitchen, a large and forbidding area of exposed pipes and gauges, a turn-of-the-century Engine Room of a transatlantic steamer. In view of their size, living room and bedroom might seem to the casual eye sparsely furnished. Kraven's purchases had been a couch, two easy chairs, a coffee table, and some rugs, Persian in type if not in provenance. All the other furniture, large items and small, had come from the house in Hampstead. Here were the pieces that just before his planned departure for New York Marko had claimed as belonging to his own branch of the family in Vienna. As it turned out, Marko's destination had been not the New but the Other World. When that unhappy fact became known, the furniture itself had already been long upon the high seas, obedient to the established westward yearning of Kraven destiny. It was Nicholas not Marcus Kraven who had reclaimed it from dockside storage.

For the last twenty years of his life Onkel Ferri had served in the dual capacity of Compleat Mourner and Keeper of the Record. As Keeper of the Record Ferri had had in his possession a century's collection of Kraven documents, letters, photographs, knick-knacks of all kinds. After Opa's death the collection had become swollen with the old man's vast hoard of Sarah Bernhardt memorabilia. Our Kraven had become the Keeper in his turn. It was an obligation that he took very seriously. The walls in his living room, bedroom, gallery and entrance hall were covered with photographs of the Divine Sarah, the earliest dating from 1869 (*Le Passant*) and the latest from 1920 (*Daniel*). There were also numerous framed prints, among them a rarity from her first American tour, Sarah Bernhardt, unimpressed, standing upon the back of a whale in Boston harbour. There were, besides, four original Mucha prints in mint condition, *Lorenzaccio*, *La*

Samaritaine, Gismonda, and *Tragique Histoire d'Hamlet*. It was a cheap modern reproduction of this last that decorated Kraven's Mosholu office.

Mixed in at discreet intervals among these relics of the incomparable *tragédienne* were photographs from the general Kraven collection. All the Kravens he had heard of or knew were represented at least once, some many times, especially Opa, who had loved to be photographed. His mother, however, appeared only twice on the walls: in one (*circa* 1922), in her late teens and ravishingly beautiful, Mummy was dressed in the costume of a Spanish dancer. She was striking an attitude, inspired no doubt by a moving picture of her idol, Rudolph Valentino, and biting on a rose. In the second photograph, taken after the last wave of Kraven immigration from Vienna, his mother was alone in the midst of the entire Kraven clan. The picture had been taken in the Hampstead drawing room. The focus of attention, naturally, was Opa. The rest of the family had disposed itself around him. All the grown-ups looked grim – unsurprising, in view of what they had recently fled from. Only Tillie was smiling. Marko and Nicko sat on the floor at Opa's feet, Marko biting his nails and Nicko rubbing his eyes. Felix was not in the picture, from which fact Kraven deduced that his father had been the photographer.

This curious blanketing of the walls might well strike the unprepared visitor as weird. In Stella's view, it was 'creepy'; the apartment, she said, looked like 'a mausoleum'. On those Thursday nights spent in his apartment, she preferred the illumination of candles. Candlelight softened the mood, she maintained. It was 'sexier'; more important, it caused the offending photographs to disappear into a devouring gloom.

Over in a corner, stuck in the earth of a glazed clay pot, was Opa's magic stick. The stick had been his first purchase in England. He was never without it. It was a long shaft of ebony with a sharp metal point at one end and a double handgrip at the other. 'It's a magic stick,' said Opa. 'It's a shooting stick,' said Nicko's mother flatly, 'that's all it is, Nicko.' But that was silly, thought Nicko. It couldn't shoot anything, not possibly. Where was the hole for the bullets? 'I wouldn't be so vexed if he just used it outside, but he uses it indoors. Look at my floors, look at the holes and scratches! Take a good look, for heaven's sake, at the carpets!' 'He's an old man,' said Felix, 'he needs a stick.' 'But must it be *that* one? My father also needs a stick, but his has a sensible rubber tip.' 'He likes that one, that's reason enough. Not another word, Victoria. Remember whom you're talking about.'

Meanwhile, in the Hampstead garden, Opa demonstrated to Nicko some of the extraordinary stick's properties. 'Look at its point: hoopla, it's a sword!' He assumed a fencer's stance and made a few passes in the air. True, he staggered a little and held his free hand to the small of his back. But in Nicko's eyes this was a creditable performance. 'Look at it now!' Opa stuck the point into the earth. 'Hipsy-pipsy, it's a chair!' And he opened the handle and sat down. Oh, it was magic, all right.

The phone was ringing again. Kraven went to his window and peeped out. Princip and company had gone. He must remember to get in touch with Nimuë. The phone stopped ringing. Kraven returned to the couch.

He sorted the morning's mail on his coffee table, bills, advertisements, and – what was this? – a letter from England, from Aunt Cicely, no less. What could have prompted her to break silence? He felt a vague, inexplicable disquiet. It seemed an ill-omened thing. His hunger returned with increased force. He would have something to eat, and then, thus strengthened, he would see what the old girl wanted. It was lack of food, surely, that caused the hand carrying the letter into the kitchen to tremble.

Aunt Cicely was his mother's younger sister. Dry and cold, there was no juice in her. As a young woman she had not wanted for beaux, but she had never much wanted them either. They came and went, evanescent. She had never married.

Still, she had nursed her mother, her sister, and her father through their last illnesses with commendable skill. She was good at plumping pillows and changing bedpans, at administering pills and charting temperatures. In the sickroom she displayed a brisk and bracing manner, a cheerful no-nonsense determination. She thrived on the ill-health of others.

Cicely lived frugally, rattling around in the damp house in Hendon, once her father's, now hers. In winter she confined herself to the kitchen, where she set up a bunk bed, considerably reducing thereby her fuel bill. She made all her own clothes and ate, in her own phrase, 'not enough to keep a squirrel alive'. Certainly she had the hoarding instincts of a squirrel, for Aunt Cicely was undeniably rich. Not only had she her own fat savings and shrewd investments over many years but also Grandfather Blum's, the fruit of a long lifetime of parsimony and thrift. There was even Kraven's old house in Hampstead, which he had sold her for a piddling sum before leaving England, eager to be rid of it and, a Kraven to the end, unwilling to haggle over price. She must by now be receiving a handsome rent on that.

He had no expectation of inheriting her wealth. Aunt Cicely would know that a Kraven could be relied on only to fritter away the money.

She was his only living relative. They had never cared much for one another. Infrequently, very infrequently, they exchanged cards. But now this letter. Kraven had finished his sandwich, had drunk down the last drop of his coffee. Gingerly he picked up the envelope, slit it open, and took out the letter.

Dear Nicholas,

I imagine you're very surprised to hear from me after so long a time. The truth is, I've been thinking about you a lot lately, and *a very good friend of mine* said, go on, write to him, for heaven's sake, get it off your chest, he won't bite you, and hence this letter. I have discovered that I can *always* rely on the advice given me by this *particular friend*.

Do you think your affairs might bring you to England in the near future? Many's the time I remember the jolly romps we had together, Nicko, years ago, when you were a little boy. Such fun! Wouldn't it be nice to sit over a cup of tea and a digestive biscuit and chat about those days?

I have certain, *private* family matters that I want to discuss with you, matters that it would be *unwise* to *commit to paper*! Better have a chinwag with him, says *my friend*, whom *you do not know as yet*!

Do try and come soon, my dearest Nicko.

> Your loving
> Aunt Cicely

The letter took Kraven somewhat aback. He scarcely recognized his aunt in its sentimental tones. In her old age, she had rewritten their past. Jolly romps, indeed! And who was this mysterious friend? Some old hag, no doubt, who had latched on to Aunt Cicely as on to a good thing. As for the private family matters, Kraven knew well enough what they were. She had obviously decided to tell him at long last about the cloud hanging over his birth.

One dark day in childhood Marko had come to him with a postcard found by rummaging through drawers forbidden to him. It was written by Grandfather Blum and posted from Blankenberg on 18 August 1935, eleven months after Nicko's birth. It was addressed not to Mrs Felix Kraven but to Miss Victoria Blum:

Dear Victoria,

Beg to inform you weather good. Prices somewhat higher than anticipated. Will make holiday bookings henceforth with 'Seaview' in Margate, as always hitherto. Please note address hereinunder indicated.

Trust 'all goes well' with you.

Greetings,
Dad

'Seems you're a bastard, Nicko.'

'It's not true at all! You rotter, Marko, you beastly rotter!'

'*Bah*-stud! *Bah*-stud!'

'It's not true, I tell you!' Nicko began to cry. 'I'm telling Onkel Koko what you said.'

'*Bah*-stud! *Look* at the stinking *bah*-stud!'

The question of his legitimacy had haunted Kraven's childhood. Had he been born out of wedlock? Was the diabolic Marko right? He looked at his mother with different eyes. He felt a nauseating insecurity, as if he walked on ground shifting from a seismic shock. Perhaps his mother had eloped with Felix, had married his father secretly, unknown to Grandfather Blum. No, she could scarcely have concealed her pregnancy, to say nothing of his own arrival and his continuing existence for eleven months before the damning postcard had come. Besides, it had been addressed to the Kraven house in Hampstead. Nicko had agonized for years.

And now Aunt Cicely was prepared to tell him all about it. Her mysterious friend had perhaps warned her of the psychological damage she had unwittingly done him. Kraven crushed the letter in his hand and tossed it into the wastepaper basket. Well, she was a quarter-century too late. At the age of fifteen he had betaken himself to Somerset House, and there with relatively little trouble had found the evidence of his parents' marriage.

Kraven, in need of cheering up, decided he would without delay phone his budding poetess, his Nimuë.

* * *

NIMUE'S POEM SAT UNDER THE TELEPHONE, her number exposed. Kraven dialled, heard the ringing in the Bronx, cleared his throat, and waited.

'Yeah?' Heavy breathing, slightly catarrhal.

'Er, yes. May I speak with Nimuë, please?'

'Who?'

'Nimuë. Miss Berkowitz.'

'I get it, sure, you mean Naomi, right? Hang on a second, fella.' The voice was a gravelled monotone. It receded into the near distance, began to bellow.

There followed a grunt, a tiny shriek, a pause, then: 'Yeah?' It was her own darling voice.

'Nicholas Kraven here.'

'Gee.' The darling voice became suddenly sharp: 'Just a minute.' A gentle hand now on the receiver: 'What you grinning at? Like this is a *private* conversation. *If* you don't mind. Yeah, that's what I said, *private*. Why-n't you get lost?' The hand was removed. 'Sorry about that.' Here was his sweet Nimuë.

'I'm phoning about your poetry tutorial. Bit of bad luck there, I'm afraid. Not a free hour anywhere on my appointments calendar, booked solid through the rest of the semester.'

'O gee.'

'Couldn't agree more, but there it is. What's to be done? I've taken another look at your poem, Nimuë. In fact, I've got it here in my hand. Yours is a talent to be carefully nurtured, a new and exciting voice in American letters.'

'O wow, when you say things like that, it makes me, you know, I kinda get all, I dunno, like gooey all over.'

Kraven's heart felt a tremor. 'Perhaps if I referred you to a colleague? I'd hate to do it, but the week, alas, has only five days.'

'Well, maybe . . . Hey, I wouldn't wanna use up your free time, but y'know the weekend, well, maybe sometimes . . . the week, y'know, it's got seven days, not five, and hey.'

'Good heavens! The weekend, of course! I should have thought of it myself.'

'O wow!'

'Now next weekend's no good, I've been asked to give a paper in LA, "Whither American Poetry?" Hmm, that involves a delay, at least a fortnight. Of course, there's always tomorrow, Sunday. But perhaps you have other plans?'

'Tomorrow's great! What time?'

Such eagerness in the pursuit of learning was all too rare in today's young. 'Two o'clock? We can have a late lunch and get right to work.'

'All *right*!'

He gave her his address. 'You think you'll be able to find it?'

'I got friends.'

'Two o'clock, then. Remember to bring your other poems.'

'Far out!' She hung up.

Kraven picked up Nimuë's poem and read it through. The purple words danced on the page. His voice, it seemed, made her gooey all over. Far out! But what could she have meant that she had friends? People familiar with the bus and subway system, probably. When he got up tomorrow, he would change the sheets on the bed.

* * *

OVER THE YEARS KRAVEN HAD PRODUCED the requisite scholarly articles. 'The Brothel and the Paradise

Garden: Shakespeare's *Pericles* Revisited'; 'Below the Salt: Plebeian Resentment in *Coriolanus*'; 'Desdemona's Wedding Sheets: A New Interpretation.' These were but to scrape the surface. He had, moreover, published a book, well received, as such things go: *The Womb, the Tomb and the Loom in Shakespeare's Major Tragedies*. One might even say that early in his career he had written with enthusiasm, certainly with enjoyment.

But the world around him, alas, had changed. For whom, Kraven wondered, was he keeping alive the lamp of learning? For a Princip? True, a Dillinger might alter the world's view of the Middle Ages. Perhaps that mattered. But a Kraven? Yet another arcane article to be read only by other drudges like himself? No, that was finished, done. Kraven's 'light verse' parodies, usually of poems, sometimes of songs, provided him now with a luxury, a private entertainment divorced from any practical goal. His stuff was unpublishable, he knew, but that fact bothered him not at all. What mattered was that writing it gave him pleasure.

He removed *Tickety-Boo* from its hiding place and leafed through its pages. Here, for example, was a lyric he had written one morning shortly after Stella had left him to return to Poore-Moody:

To Stella,
On a Friday Morning

In nought but panties thou art clearly fairer
Than Botticelli's pallid Primavera,
And Trojan Helen, reft of all her clothes,
Cannot assume a more enticing pose.
Salt Cleopatra, nude, is second best
To thee, beloved, who art scarcely dressed.
Why then delay, why cause me so much anguish,
Why leave me on our mutual couch to languish?

Come, Stella, come, for Venus' laws condone
The revelation of thy fragrant zone.
To see, to touch, to sniff, to taste – egad!
The thought alone doth drive me raving mad!
Thou knowst that pecker in the morning's light
Far stronger is than pecker in the night.
Why poinst thou at the clock, thou timid mouse?
A fig I give thee for thy wretched spouse!
Remove thy panties, leap into the bed,
Forget this once that thou art elsewhere wed.
Thou art my love! There can be nought amiss
If thou and I once more achieve our bliss.
Alas, alas, our pleasures thou wouldst mar:
Why put'st thou on thy breast-concealing bra?
What's this? Thy pantyhose? O, evil chance
That I should be tormented with thy dance!
Thy blouse, thy skirt, and now thy jacket too –
What use my plaints, what though my lot I rue?
To think my dame her duties thus should shirk:
Her duties owed to me, not to that jerk!

Kraven refiled the poem. No, publication clearly was impossible. *Tickety-Boo* amused him, and that was enough.

SIX

BY ONE O'CLOCK ON SUNDAY AFTERNOON Kraven had readied his apartment to receive Nimuë. The light layer of dust, accumulated since Early's Friday whisking, had vanished. In the bedroom the window blinds were drawn together and the resulting gloom dissipated in the area of the great bed itself by the soft warm light of a bedside lamp. In the kitchen the coffee pot, primed, had only to be plugged in; while on the dining table in the living room was spread a tempting selection of Zabar's delicacies: cream cheese and chives, smoked salmon, chopped herring, Greek salad, various cheeses, Danish crackers, pumpernickel, bagels – not the food of poetry perhaps, but food conducive, in Kraven's experience, to feelings of well-being. Casually placed on the coffee table was *The Enthusiast's Guide to Sexual Fulfillment*, a volume boasting 'more than 100 full-color photographs and many easy-to-follow diagrams'.

By two o'clock Kraven had brushed his teeth for the third time since arising. He had also emboldened the after-shave splash of Dunhill, whose strength was by then disappearing, with a liberal douche of Zizanie. By two-fifteen he had determined, this time with assurance, to favour an open-necked sports shirt without benefit of silk scarf, whose dash, he now saw, was rather too affected. By 2:35 he was wondering whether some of the more easily perishable of

Zabar's offerings should be returned to the refrigerator. His anxiety was mixed with a scruple of irritation.

But at 2:55 the house phone rang. The voice of Clarence, rendered sepulchral in its journey along the wire, announced the imminent ascension of a visitor. It could only be she, his Nimuë. A knock at the door, and there she stood, enchanting, clutching a sheaf of papers to her bosom.

'Gee, I guess I'm late, huh?'

'Not to worry.'

'First it was my old man, wouldn't let me out. Where my going? Who lie be with? And like that.'

'But here you are. That's what counts.'

'Like I'm over eighteen, hey.'

'Ah.'

'Then we have this accident, in the Heights, y'know?'

'Your *father* brought you?'

'No, Gabe. He was going to this Anti-Nuke Puke-in in Washington Square, see.'

'You mean Gabriel Princip? You came with him?'

'Yeah, Gabe. He's got this great new Mongo Demon, y'know, the motorbike, the Mark III? So he's giving me this ride in, and like in the Heights we go over this pothole, and his rear tyre blows, I mean it's like Gonzo City, and we're stuck in the boonies. You think he worries about me? No, he's worried about his Mongo. I coulda been killed, and he starts screaming and yelling like maybe it was *my* fault, for Chrisakes. I mean, Jesus! So I told him what he could do with his fucking Mongo, and I took a bus. That's why I'm like late.'

'And you left Princip in the Heights?'

She smiled. 'Yeah, hey.'

'Well, never mind. Do come in.'

Kraven followed her down the hall and into the living room. She had exchanged her adorable jeans for a denim mini-skirt. The blouse appeared to be the one of their first

101

encounter. On her stockingless feet she wore sneakers, dingy grey and frayed. Kraven's heart thumped in its cage.

'Hey, what a great apartment! Gee, all them pictures!' She ran over to the wall and examined the photograph of the Divine Sarah in *Le Passant* (1869). 'A relative?'

'My mother. She was a great actress.'

'That's definitely cool, I mean that's beautiful.' She scanned the wall, whirled around to take in the rest of the room, spotted the dining table and leapt gloriously towards it. "Look at all that stuff, will ya? Cream cheese and chives, wow! Howja know?" A forefinger by Praxiteles plunged into the bowl and conveyed a generous dollop to her exquisite mouth. Her eyes closed in ecstasy. "M-m-m-m-m." The tip of a delicate pink tongue emerged and licked her lips, trembled for a moment and disappeared. Kraven supposed the thumping of his heart audible and raised a hand to still it.

Nimuë's demeanour underwent a change, a curtain closed across the source of light. She walked shyly towards him, her head bowed, and thrust into his hands her sheaf of papers. 'Here's all my stuff, my pomes, and that.' She took a step backwards, blushed, and the world grew roseate.

'Good, good. I'm eager to read them.'

He sat down on the couch, but Nimuë stayed where she was, her head still bowed, refusing to look at him.

'Why don't you sit next to me?'

'Okay if I like move around a bit? Just while you're reading, I mean?' She spoke in a small voice and addressed her sneakers.

'If that's what you'd rather.'

He watched her wander, pause now before this photograph, now before that. She held her hands behind her, resting them on firm love-apples, luscious fruit of the new Hesperides. She stepped back before the *Lorenzaccio* print ('Your mother! O wow!'), then resumed her wanderings. She left him and made for the bedroom. His heart leaped up. He heard the screech of curtains pulled back on unoiled rollers. His heart sank.

Kraven began to read the uppermost of the papers he held in his hand.

'Fathership (I)'
by
Nimuë Berkowitz

For as long as I've known you, you've always been true,
As firm as the Rock of Gibraltar.
Trusting and kind, like the Red, White, and Blue,
Hey, you've never been known to falter.
Ever our pal, both in gut-ache and health,
Respect from your family's your lot;

Whether in poorness or yet in wealth,
Even so, it is honor you've got.
Low in IQ? Sure. But high grades in love.
Only for us you have striven.
Very determined to earn from Above
Each buck of an honest day's livin'.

Yes, I mean YOU,
O dear father, so true.
Unto you we will all stick like glue.

Curious sounds were emerging from the bedroom: *Sproing*, a pause of perhaps three heartbeats, *spuh-roing*, another pause, *spree-oing*, pause, *sup-a-roing*. Kraven hurried to the bedroom, poems in hand, and stood at the open door. Nimuë rose from the bed, majestic, legs together, arms held out. She executed with awesome grace, her head flung back, her body arched, a backwards mid-air somersault, her tummy almost grazing the ceiling, and returned with perfect balance to her feet. *Sproing*. She bent her knees, tightened the muscles up her perfect legs, articulated her pelvis, her tummy, then pushed off, and she was up again, over, down. But now she saw him standing entranced in the doorway and so permitted herself, in an exquisite series of diminishing bounces, to come to rest.

'Wow, that's great! I've never seen a bed this size. D'you get sheets made special?'

Nimuë dropped on her back and sinuously, using elbows and rump, made her way to the top of the bed. She leaned against the pillows, near leg bent under, right arched pyramidally over it. In this position her mini-skirt afforded Kraven a view of her panties, a delicate Aegean blue, a surprisingly wide strip between her legs. He hurried into the room and sat beside her, an intrepid Argonaut in search of the Golden Fleece, his prow ostent and seaworthy.

'I've read "Fathership (I)," Nimuë, and I'm impressed. It takes a courageous writer nowadays to attempt acrostic verse, a difficult device, one usually fatal to poetry. But you've pulled it off. And with no loss of sincerity or sense. Where have you been hiding? The English Department's your proper milieu.'

Such was his enthusiasm that he grasped her near leg on the inner thigh, within centimetres of the Aegean. Undisturbed by his gesture, perhaps as unaware of it as he, she leaned towards him, bringing the Aegean all but to his hand. He felt the warmth of the south, even a stray tendril of the Fleece itself caressing his thumb. Much hoped he to travel in the realms of gold.

'Hey! I mean, you liked it? O wow! And like I'm what you said, a poetess?'

'Nimuë,' said Kraven fervently, 'you are yourself a poem.'

The bedside phone began to ring, shattering the mood of intimate revelation upon whose brink he had believed himself poised.

O Stella, how like you!

But could she really have known?

'Gonna answer it?'

He picked up the receiver. 'Kraven.' His tone was surly.

'Yeah. Gabe Princip. From your Shakeshit class.'

'Perhaps you are unaware, Princip, that an unsolicited phone call from a student to a professor in his own home is bad form, to put it kindly. I maintain office hours. They are posted. Use them.'

'Is that Gabe?' Nimuë, her eyes alight, leaned forward, plunging Kraven's bent thumb into the Aegean itself.

'*Cool* it, man,' said Princip. 'I mean, *maintain*. Like, why you always *hassling* me? You *listening*, man? I mean, you *hear* me? You think hassling's all you gotta do, right? Talk *muscle*, right, and you'll make out with the chicks? I know where it's at. I'm not bugging you; I'm talking nice and polite. So how come right away you take a crap on me?'

'Was that you lurking about my building yesterday, you and a gaggle of hooligans? Next time, I assure you, I'll call the police.'

'You gonna need more than the pigs, motherfuck.'

'Princip, you attend one lecture in three. At the moment you're carrying a C- in the course, a grade laughably above the actual value of your work. Your contribution to class discussion is virtually nil. And now you have the temerity to phone me in my own home, to utter vague threats, to insinuate distasteful innuendos, to insult me in any depraved way that occurs to you. Are you making a special effort to fail the course?'

'I didn't even wanna speak to you, asshole. Nome Berkowitz is there, right? Yeah. Well, I was phoning *her*, so like I say, *maintain*. But seeing as how you brought it up, my grade and shit like that, I'm no English major, man. All you gotta do is give me a Pass, y'know what I mean? I don't need no

105

grade, just a Pass. Then I can tip. Nobody's hurt. All you gotta do is play it cool.'

'The Dean of Students will be fascinated to learn of this conversation. Like me he might wonder whether your presence on campus adds much to the lustre of Mosholu.'

'Yeah? You kidding me, right? Well, try this on for size: you think he's gonna be fascinated to learn that one of the perfessors is humping his students? I mean, we gonna talk *lustre*, we gonna have to talk *faculty*. *I* know this particular perfessor can't even get it up, but the thing is, will *he* know? I mean, will the *Dean* know? Like, what about these *private* sessions in this particular perfessor's *pad* and all? Where you right now? The bedroom? You ever tried it on the kitchen table? Man, when Nome pops on the kitchen table, you *know* you had your ashes hauled.'

'It *is* Gabe.' Nimuë snatched the receiver from Kraven's hand. 'Let *me* talk.' She frowned, scratching with her free hand in the area of her left nipple. 'You fixed your bike yet? Where the fuck you calling from? . . . No kidding? . . . Aw, *c'mon*, Gabe, you can pick me up. . . I dunno, an hour maybe . . . All you gotta do, you just like *stay* there. . . Gee, you know what that does to me, when you talk like that. . .' She looked at Kraven and giggled. 'Who, *him*? You gotta be kidding. . . Yeah, I dig . . . sure. . . No, just reading my stuff . . . For fuck's sake, Gabe. *Jee*-sus! . . . Okay, okay. . .'

She returned the receiver to Kraven, who replaced it in its cradle. They sat silent for a while, immobile.

'So Gabe is in your class, gee. . . You shoulda heard what he said about you. But he won't hurt you really. He's kinda nice when you get to know him. Okay, so he's a jerk, but he really turns me on. All the way, I mean *all*. Like, y'know, he's a piston, pow-pow-pow! The trouble with Gabe, he don't understand a Plutonic relationship.'

'*Pla*-tonic,' said the teacher faintly.

'Huh?'

'*Pla*-tonic.'

'We say *Plu*-tonic in America.'

Nimuë, shifting slightly on the bed, became aware of Kraven's hand still trembling in her crotch. She looked at him with wonder, with curiosity, and then with startled understanding. Her eyes lifted now to his. Mouth agape, hovering on a shy little smile, she looked down at his hand again. 'Gee. . .'

Kraven removed his hand and sighed. He placed it over his eyes and inhaled willy-nilly her perfume. Alas. Posed now like Rodin's Thinker, his panic scarcely gave him leisure to philosophize constructively. Princip was a source of danger to him, perhaps of violence . . . Nimuë was reduced to an aroma on his fingertips.

But what was she doing squirming about on the bed? He peeked at her through his pensive fingers. Arching her body and giving her weight to her shoulders and heels, she had hitched her thumbs into her panties and was even now engaged in rolling them down.

'I never had it off with an old guy before.'

Kraven leaped to his feet and backed away from the bed, blushing. On her face he thought he saw that mixture of irritability, pride, lightly veiled disgust, and, yes, pity he had often seen on the faces of other pretty young girls when men of a certain age sought to charm them, daft old peacocks, shorn of all but the dingiest plumage, striving nevertheless to spread a show. Never before had he been the recipient of such a look. Thanks to Princip, of course, he had long since shrunk. Now he felt the last tickling relaxation of the scrotum.

'Look, Nimuë, I'm afraid I'm going to have to cancel your, um, tutorial today. I've just remembered that, um . . . well, I'm sorry to have brought you down here for nothing. It's just that, um. . .' In desperation he plucked gratefully from Papa Doc's trendy vocabulary a word he knew she would understand. 'The vibes, you know. The vibes aren't right at all. No point in going on.'

There was a savage, a maniacal pounding at the front door coupled with the insistent ringing of the doorbell. The hateful expression disappeared from Nimuë's face; she placed a protective hand over her venereal tuft. At the same time, the racket eased Kraven out of his shame and into a comforting anger. 'If that's your boyfriend out there, he's in more trouble than he realizes.'

Anger sustained him as he made his way to the door but quickly abandoned him as he opened it, scampering off at the sight of a mightier anger. For there stood not Princip but Stella, a Stella haggard and furious. Her eyes were swollen. She seemed not to have changed her clothing since last he saw her. She pushed him aside and stormed into the apartment. He could only follow.

'Where've you been, you rotten swine? I've been trying to reach you since Friday night. If I hadn't gotten a busy signal just now, I wouldn't even have known you were in. I'll bet you were holed up in here all weekend, letting the phone ring, having a little laugh at stupid Stella, while I've been going out of my mind up there. . .' Suddenly noticing the dining table with its careful arrangement of delicatessen offerings, she stopped in mid-stride and whirled on him. 'Expecting someone?'

'A student's here. For a tutorial.'

'Since when do you give tutorials? And what about the food? You're feeding students all of a sudden?'

'For pity's sake, just some odds and ends I found in the refrigerator.'

'I *know* the odds and ends you keep in your refrigerator, remember? You must have kept this stuff well hidden. Anyway, where is he?'

'There's absolutely no need to shout. It's a she, actually. She's in the, um, bedroom.'

108

Stella laughed bitterly. 'Should I ask what she's doing in there?'

'Making a phone call. Private, I suppose.'

Nimuë, clutching a scrap of Aegean blue nylon in her hand, chose this moment to appear. She waved it shyly at them.

'Oh, hi! This your wife?'

'This is Mrs Poore-Moody, a friend and neighbour. Stella, this is Nimuë Berkowitz, a Mosholu poetess.'

Stella crinkled her nostrils. 'Nicholas, I've got to talk to you.'

'Nimuë, I'm sure you'll understand. An emergency, you see. Dreadfully sorry about the tutorial.'

'Gee,' said Nimue, wiping her nose with the scrap of the Aegean.

'I'm going to put you in touch with Smilow Thirkell, our Resident Poet. I think you're ready for him.'

'O gee, but –'

'And once again, my apologies.'

'But where's my pomes and that?'

'Ah yes, I'll get them.' Avoiding Stella's eyes he went to the bedroom. When he returned Nimuë was stepping into her panties. Stella, her back to the room, was staring out of the window. He thrust the papers into Nimuë's hands. 'Here they are. Excellent. Keep up the good work.'

'Great meeting ya, Stell,' said Nimuë politely.

'Nicholas,' said Stella. Her voice was grim. She kept her back turned.

Kraven hurried Nimuë up the corridor and out of the door.

'Off you go, then.'

'Have a nice day.'

He closed the door and, experiencing a moment's vertigo, leaned his forehead against it. And now for Stella. Taking a deep breath, he returned to the living room. Stella was pacing, clenching and unclenching her fists.

'Not that I care, darling, but just to satisfy idle curiosity, could you explain why Miss Bitchertwit had her panties off?'

'God, I don't know, Stella. The girl's clearly unstable. She must've taken them off when I let you in. Talking to her boyfriend on the phone, you see. Perhaps they get their jollies that way.'

'No doubt.' Stella's voice dripped acid.

'But what happened with Robert? You can't imagine how worried I've been.'

'No, in fact I can't.'

'I could hardly get in touch with *you*,' said Kraven reproachfully.

'But I might've with you, if I could've found you, you crud. Where've you *been* since Friday?'

'Stand still for a minute, you're making me giddy.' He held out a hand to her, but she slapped it angrily aside.

'Well?' At least she had stopped her pacing.

'I didn't get the position, Stella, it collapsed under me. The President was very polite about it. We've been a little too precipitous, he said. The budget crunch, and rot of that sort. He said that before founding an Institute of our own we ought perhaps explore the possibility of becoming an East Coast wing of the one already in place at UCLA. Even in the Ivory Tower, he said, we have to heed the warnings of the crass accountants. Christ, it's not as if it was *my* idea.' Kraven was beginning to believe in the imaginary Institute. He felt hurt, even angry.

Stella's eyes softened. She placed a comforting hand on his arm. 'Oh Nicholas, I *am* sorry.'

'He's sending me to LA in a week or so to sound them out. Something may yet come of it.'

'I hope so.'

'Are you going to tell me about Robert, or aren't you?'

That was a mistake. Stella resumed her pacing. It was apparent she was restoking her fury. Damn, damn, damn. Kraven stood by helplessly.

'But after the meeting, then what? Jesus Christ, that was forty-eight hours ago!'

'Yes, it was. Well, I went to the party anyway. Remember, I told you. How could I avoid it without looking even more of an ass? Thought it best to face the bastards down, you know. The truth is, I got drunk, totally pissed.'

'No, don't tell me, let me guess. Afterwards you wandered the streets, a victim of amnesia, and came to yourself this morning on a bench near Columbus Circle.'

'That's most unfair, Stella.'

Stella stopped short and faced him, her fists tight-clenched at her sides. Her eyes filled with tears. 'Oh Nicholas, you're such a liar. And now you're all I've got. I suppose I deserve you.'

She fell sobbing into his arms, clung to him, buried her face in his chest. He felt his shirt grow wet. She shook against him. He held her tightly, trying to comfort her. They swayed together for a little while, until her shaking stopped and she pulled back, turning her bruised eyes to his, the tears still streaming down her cheeks.

'He's left me.'

'What!'

'He's gone.'

She collapsed on to the couch behind her and began again to sob, quietly now, her head up, ignoring her tears, twin rivulets ceaselessly flowing. He sat down beside her, drew her to him, gently kissed her wet cheek, her earlobe, her neck, lifted her hands clenched primly on her lap, took them to his lips, gently, gently. After a while her sobs subsided, ceased altogether.

'I'm sorry,' she said in a small voice.

'No need, no need,' he said. 'But if you can, if you feel calmer, tell me what happened. You told Robert about us. Then what?'

She looked at him, puzzled. 'Told Robert *what* about us?'

'About leaving him for me. Try to pull yourself together, darling. You remember, Friday morning, your decision to go upstairs and tell him?'

'Oh God!' Stella began to laugh, hysterically, grotesquely, her eyes still swollen with tears. Not knowing what else to do, he thumped her on the back. She stopped abruptly. 'You're serious, aren't you? Oh Nicholas, whatever we mean to one another, and I don't pretend to understand what, you couldn't have supposed I'd leave Robert for you. When have you ever. . .? All right, I admit I've wanted you, ached for you. Even, damn it, wept for you. Perhaps I love you. But leave Robert for you? You didn't actually believe, not *really*?'

'No, no, of course not.' And, as a gallant addition, he offered, 'Wishful thinking. It's just that you *did* say. . .'

'Well, what *was* I to say? What would *you* have said if you'd come in like that, starko, and the room full of people, one of them a rabbi? I said whatever I thought would sound plausible.'

'Quite.'

'I've been so miserable, and I needed you so desperately. I don't know what to do. I've been frantic.'

'Didn't Robert say anything?'

'I never saw him. He must have slipped back to drop me the note on Thursday night, but of course I was down here by then. We were. . .' She looked at him shyly. 'It was good, though, wasn't it, Nicholas?'

He would never understand her. 'What note? Really Stella, you're beginning to babble.'

'The note he left on my pillow.' She reached dramatically into her bosom and withdrew a crumpled piece of paper.

'Here, read it, it concerns you too.' Her eyes were filling with tears again. 'I've got to find him, I can't bear it.'

Kraven smoothed out the note.

Stella, my darling,

By the time you read these words, I will be far away. No, don't try to find me. There's no point. Meanwhile, your absence downstairs gives me the opportunity to write to you.

Do not be alarmed, or ashamed, or suppose that my leaving has anything to do with your charming little affair. You were always discreet and considerate. Indeed, I began my Thursday night trips to Westchester in order to give you a measure of certitude, a space of worry-free time, however brief. You are a young and vigorous woman. Because I have never doubted your love for me, I have never been troubled by jealousy.

But I am now 65, my dear, and my thoughts are turning inward. You know I have never been religious, certainly not in any formal or doctrinal sense. But as I enter my last years (months? days?), I find myself thinking more and more about that spark of life which animates our weak flesh. I cannot believe it extinguished when the flesh itself no longer can feed it.

'Where's the rest of it? There must be more.'

'Oh yes, there is.' Stella reached into her bosom once more, felt around, frowned, stood up and shook the skirt of her dress. Two crumpled pieces of paper fell to the floor. Kraven picked them up. God, even now, at such a moment, her every movement, her slightest gesture, aroused him. Stella sat down again. He turned from her ravaged face back to Poore-Moody's maunderings.

Well, I grow philosophical and fear I bore you. Enough of that. Let it suffice to say I go to find a love greater even

113

than ours, perhaps a metaphysical love, certainly a love
that transcends the flesh and embraces the spirit, the
source, as I think, of the spark. Yes, I go to seek peace and
truth, and I trust that in the time left to me I shall find
them. My search begins among the Cistercians. I pray that
it may end there.

'The silly old bleeder's becoming a monk!' The words
leaped to Kraven's lips unbidden and issued into the attentive air. Stella wailed. He comforted her, absentmindedly
caressing her thigh, eager only to read on. 'There, there.'
She quieted down.

My affairs, I think, are all in order. Blount, DeWinter
and Grobstock have agreed to represent me. They will tell
you that I have liquidated one quarter of my assets for my
own use. The rest is to come to you as capital after the
spark departs this flesh.

But now I must say goodbye. I think I love you more at
this moment, if that be possible, than in all of our married
life.

Robert

'Incredible,' said Kraven. 'He's clearly a nutcase.'
'What am I to do? I'm at my wits' end.' And indeed,
strained and blubbered as Stella was, her hair wild, even now
wiping an errant tear from the tip of her nose, he could well
believe her inability to cope.
'You have two options. Have him committed on the
strength of this letter or let him become a monk. In either
case he's institutionalized and out of harm's way.' What
Kraven saw was the extension of Thursday night into the
rest of the week.
'Oh Nicholas, how can you be so callous? We're talking
about Robert. Please, it breaks my heart.'

114

'What would you say was a quarter of his total assets? More than a million?'

'How can you be so crass?'

'You want him back, you'll have him back. From this moment forward I'll devote myself to it.'

'I *knew* I could rely on you.' She sniffed fetchingly. 'Thank you, darling.'

He was touched by her simple gratitude, touched and aroused. In removing the letter from its hiding place she had accidentally opened the top buttons of her dress. Her glorious bosom rose and fell. The declivity beckoned. But Kraven had a strong sense of occasion. Not for him the route of the cad.

'But my dear, it's Sunday afternoon. Absolutely nothing can be done on a Sunday. Tomorrow morning, first thing, I'll begin to make enquiries. Meanwhile, my love, it's pretty plain you haven't slept much since Thursday night. You're exhausted, you need rest. What good will you be to Robert if you make yourself ill?'

'How can I sleep? It's impossible.'

'But you can, of course you can. I'm looking after things now. Be a good girl and do as you're told.'

'All right, Nicholas.'

'Go upstairs and take a warm bath. Have some Ovaltine or hot milk. Remember, I'll be on it first thing in the morning.'

'Yes, Nicholas.' Stella rose, obedient, prepared to go. 'Only, do you think I could perhaps stay down here? At least until the waiting's over? The apartment's so empty without him.'

Kraven gave her request a moment's serious thought. But no, no, he would not take advantage of her in her weakened state. He needed time to work out his feelings for this woman. Why had he felt so devastated, for example, by the sudden non-existence of their engagement? Could his Stella ever feel for him what Robert's Stella felt for Robert?

'There's nothing I'd like more. How can I let you go? But you should stay by your phone. He might try to get in touch, you never know.'

'Oh yes, you're right, I'll go now.' And she ran from the room. He followed her to the door. She turned and took a step towards him. 'Thank you, darling. Without you, I'd be totally lost, ready for the nuthouse myself.'

So she had accepted her husband's insanity. He held her in his arms, felt a familiar stirring, kissed her, but let her go. Kraven had much to think about.

* * *

HE BEGAN HIS THINKING almost immediately, over a very late lunch, the sight of his table laden with delicacies awakening a sudden appetite. Happily, Nimuë was already almost interred, buried under a new understanding of events. She, poor child, still wallowing in the swamp of her humid adolescence, had mistaken his kindly interest in her creative strivings for the bellowings of male lust. Kraven had half-convinced himself of this. Biting into a buttered bagel heaped with chopped herring, he shook his head with mature understanding. A self-centred generation, hers.

But Stella was another matter, Stella, who only moments before had clung to him, looked up at him with her tortured eyes. Her image danced and swayed before him. His groin ached. He yearned towards her. She loved him, she had said, or had come closer to saying so than at any time in their stormy affair. And he? Poore-Moody was gone. Kraven began to reconstruct the hopes and feelings she had once so wantonly smashed with her brash laughter.

When the telephone rang he supposed it was Stella and ran lightly to answer. If she was to be confined to her apartment, could he not join her there? Yes, my darling, yes!

'Ah, Nickolevio, Ari here. Not torn you from your type-writer, I trust?'

'As a matter of fact, you have.'

'Sorry to bother you on a Sunday, Nicko, but I've got a favour to ask.'

'Splendid party, Ari. Had a wonderful time.'

'Yes, it went rather well, I think. Got some good vibes. You made quite an impression on Diotima, you rascal. Saw her at the Prez's levee yesterday. You were all she could talk about, so handsome, so aristocratic, so *sympatisch*. Kept calling you Nobby, for some reason. I didn't know whom she was talking about until she said she was in on the joke, knew all about the Old Nick, and there you stood revealed in all your known splendour. Obviously some Krautish error in translation, hardly worth correcting, so I didn't. Knew you wouldn't mind, fella. A Kraven by any other name, and so on.'

'I must have you and Liz over here one of these days. It's a bit difficult for a bachelor, of course. But the pressure's beginning to build towards a Kraven cocktail party. Next month, perhaps. Well, I'd better be getting back to work.'

'Hey, hold it, wait a minute, man.' Papa Doc chuckled. 'You're pretty slick, I'll grant you that. Hell, it's not that big a favour, y'might even enjoy it. You're a Clerihew man, right? Wrote your dissertation for Cecil Quimby? Well, guess who's flying in from Merry Old in a couple days. Yup, your good buddy from London U, Ceece himself.'

The back of Kraven's neck prickled.

'You're strangely silent, guy.'

'Bit of a surprise. I thought he was dead. I *know* he retired. What brings him here?' Kraven saw on the horizon a little cloud.

'Pio Nono.' Pio Nono was Papa Doc's pet name for Malcolm Pioggi, Dean of Faculty and Humanities. 'The lecture series. Quimby has the same deal Di von Hoden got

117

last week. Three public lectures, we wine 'em and dine 'em, then we pour 'em back into their jets, a cool three thou ahead. Jesus, those guys've really got it knocked! Anyway, you and Ceece will have a lot to talk about, old times and so on, how you're coming along, star pupil of the bush league makes it in the big time, crap like that. Pio Nono thinks you should go out to the airport and pick him up. I volunteered you to make the opening remarks at the first lecture, introduce your good buddy to the attentive throng.'

Kraven was aghast. It was all beginning to unravel. He stood trembling and at bay, staring about him for some starting hole, some temporary refuge. He and Quimby must not meet. For him that would mean disaster, the end of everything. Equally obviously, Dillinger had not yet been in touch with Dean Pioggi. Papa Doc, at any rate, knew nothing of the conference in Los Angeles. Was there hope then?

'What d'ya say, Nick?'

'My pleasure.' The problem was how to prevent his name from coming up during his absence.

'Right on. Come in and see me tomorrow morning. We'll work on the logistics, plan a strategy.'

'Um, Ari, I ought to warn you. The old boy's frightfully forgetful. Must be pushing eighty. Even when I knew him he'd begun dribbling down his chin. I'm surprised he's on the lecture circuit. Even in his glory days he was no great shakes. But the point is, chances are, he won't remember me at all.'

'Come off it.' Papa Doc chuckled deep in his throat. 'Modesty doesn't suit ya, fella.'

'No, honestly. At my orals, for example, he turned up late, looked about, said excuse me, sorry to disturb, and was about to take off again. They had to haul him back and explain to him what he was supposed to be doing there.'

'See me tomorrow, Nick. Meanwhile, get back to your typewriter. Oh, and thanks.'

God, what a day! He was a simple enough man, demanding little, expecting less, wanting only to be allowed to go his own way in peace. And now Quimby! The Kraven curse, the familial demons, were in hot pursuit. He would have to get out for a while, if only to safeguard his sanity, if only because Stella might in fact call. What he desperately needed was quality time. But his apartment was under attack from all points of the compass.

SEVEN

KRAVEN SAT ALONE at one end of the long bar in Donovan's Amsterdam, brooding over a whisky and soda. Near the windows at the other end, but behind the bar, stood Donovan himself, short, mean eyed, his shirt sleeves rolled, idly turning the pages of *Midstream*. There were no other customers.

Kraven liked Donovan's. He liked its appalling seediness, the dull khaki linoleum on the floor, pitted and rent, the soot-soiled peeling wallpaper, the gloom – above all, the gloom. Donovan never switched on his lights before what he called 'lighting-up time' in the late afternoon. As a consequence, the room's only illumination was furnished by whatever daylight could fight its way through the top half of the grimy street windows. The lower half was masked by an emerald green curtain strung on a brass rail. Still, the daylight bounced gaily enough off the nicks and scars of the polished long bar, it winked and gleamed on the rows of bottles along the bar wall, it shone dully on Donovan's bald pate. There was light and enough. The room exhaled a sour smell of stale beer, disinfectant and sawdust.

Stuck to the mirror above the bar a year-old poster advised that only two weeks remained in which to catch Dolly Divine and her Erotic Ensemble, a Smash-Hit, at Spinoza's World-Famous Burlesque, 'Come One, Come All!' Kraven squinted at the photo of Dolly Divine on the poster.

He could not remember ever having seen anyone seated at one of the booths in the rear of the long room or at any of the little square tables scattered untidily about the floor. In fact, in all the years he had been coming to Donovan's, admittedly infrequently and always of an afternoon, inevitably when the world pressed a trifle too heavily upon him, he could not recall another customer. Donovan himself was no genial mine-host-of-the-tavern. He served Kraven with surly reluctance, carefully moving the bowl of pretzels out of convenient reach. Street sounds barely penetrated Donovan's, and then they lost all distinction, automobile horns, pneumatic drills, insane laughter or cries for help all reduced to a uniform 'Bummm-m'.

Kraven took a sip of his drink, moved over to the next stool, and reached for a pretzel. Donovan rattled his pages angrily. What was to be done about Princip? Princip was an explosive mine that must be deactivated. He was a destroyer, a tearer-down, an avatar of unreason, who mocked with every action of his being the symbols of peace that he flaunted. What, Kraven wondered, would the Divine Sarah have had to say to a Princip? What had Art to say in the face of Chaos? Opa liked to quote an aphorism remembered from the days when he still read books: History is merely the record of satin slippers descending the stairs as hobnail boots go up. The Gabe Princips of the world were ascending, their victorious banners unfurled. A Kraven could hope to win only an occasional skirmish or remain in place on the staircase for no more than a very short while. Was he doomed meekly to give the vile Princip his Pass? There was that within him that whispered no. But how, how?

And what of Nimuë, whom he had innocently sought to help? He knew her now to be in league with that very Princip. No, it was not a matter of her having misconstrued his intentions. That was mere bluff. It was clear enough now

121

– one had only to think of Princip's phone call – that she had been a plant. By now she must have described to Princip the supposed lurid happenings on Opa's great bed. Princip had his ammunition all right. He had already shot across Kraven's bows; he stood ready now to hit him broadside. Could Kraven, his pinnace in direst jeopardy, do other than surrender?

It passed belief. To think of Nimuë coming out of his bedroom this afternoon waving – by God, actually waving! – her panties at Stella and him! To think of her actually stepping into those panties in Stella's presence! What had happened to young womanhood in this dreadful age? Whither had fled discretion, the maidenly blush? There was no instinctive feeling among them that virginity was itself a virtue; or if indeed it was *not*, then that at least the *appearance* of innocence should be the face a young girl presented to the world. They did not scruple to share the shameful secrets of their most intimate activities with whoever would offer a willing ear. 'When Lovely Woman Stoops to Folly' was a poem it was impossible to teach them nowadays. They simply couldn't understand what all the fuss was about. No wonder, then, that Nimuë had fallen in with Princip's plan, the common moll of Princip and his gang of louts.

Another sip, another pretzel, another angry rattling of *Midstream*'s pages. Donovan listened in on Kraven's privacy. Indeed, he looked at Kraven with deep suspicion.

And now C.U.T. Quimby, Cecil, the Rouged Roué of Clerihew. The image of that thin, stooped figure, lips pursed around the point of his acidic tongue, white hair hanging in greasy locks over his threadbare gown, fingertips drumming together as if in nervous prayer, was sharply etched in Kraven's inner vision. Quimby posed a threat to peace beside which the practices of a Princip were little more than gnat bites. He could reveal all. Kraven sipped his drink and peeped furtively at Donovan. There might be a prison term for that.

* * *

AFTER KOKO HAD FALLEN VICTIM, just short of Goodge Street, to anti-Kraven forces, it was discovered to everyone's surprise that that ordinarily improvident charmer had possessed a life insurance policy. His beneficiaries, naturally, were his children, Tillie and Marko. But Tillie, taking only her manicure kit and a small bag of needments, had eloped immediately after VE Day with an American soldier, a Corporal Minelli, and disappeared into the vastnesses of the New World, another Kraven pioneer to have felt the *Drang nach Westen*. Inquiries undertaken by the insurance company produced shocking news. Not three months into her adventure and driving with neither licence nor skill, she had got the worst of an encounter with a steel pillar on the Queens side of the Fifty-ninth Street Bridge. The car had sustained little damage, the pillar none at all. But Tillie had broken her neck and died on the instant, another Kraven victim. As a result, Marko, then a boy of fourteen, became the sole beneficiary of his father's surprising foresight.

Victoria Kraven, Nicko's mother, was Marko's legal guardian. She needed advice. Opa, much enfeebled with age and accumulated traumata, had by now tuned out the mundane. And so she turned of necessity to her own father, Grandpa Blum, who told her whom to see and what to do. Marko suddenly had great expectations.

Meanwhile, he continued at grammar school, one year ahead of Nicko, who at age twelve was already in the second form. Marko, alas, was not a good student. Moreover, he was always in trouble. He was caught puncturing the tyres of his Latin master's bicycle; he was caught stealing gooseberries from the school's Victory Garden, a wartime holdover; he was frequently caught smoking; and, worst, he was caught peeking through a hole he had scratched in the black paint coating the window of the girls' lavatory. For this last offence Victoria Kraven was summoned to the school. 'He's a refugee boy who has lost both parents and his sister in tragic circumstances. Surely he deserves another chance.' Marko got it, and another, and another. Frequent canings served only to increase his cunning: he was caught less and less. In the fifth form he took up with one Monica Scrod, a plain, overgrown girl with a bovine face and irregular teeth, who nevertheless enjoyed a certain popularity among the boys for her willingness to pull down her knickers: 'Thruppence for a look, a tanner for a feel.' Marko, it was said, received one-third from every transaction.

At the end of that year Marko was to take the General Schools Certificate Examination, in his view a waste of time since he planned to leave school anyway.

'But surely you'll go on and complete sixth form, Marko,' said Victoria. 'If you matriculate, you can go on to university.'

Marko shrugged. 'It's no use, Aunt Victoria, my mind's made up. No more bloody school. It's the grown-up world for me.'

In fact, he *was* quite grown up, almost six feet tall, already shaving, his razor regularly bloodying a severe case of acne. For hours on end he would stand before the bathroom mirror squeezing pustules and spurting their contents on to the glass. The concentration involved in such close work eventually caused him to become slightly cross-eyed. This, curiously, was an attractive feature, for it gave him an aloof, quizzical expression. His square teeth, like his fingers, were already badly stained with nicotine.

But Victoria still had a card to play.

'If you *were* to go to university, I should see to it that you began to receive your annuity then and there. You wouldn't have to wait until you're twenty-one. But, of course, it's the GSC and the sixth form first.'

Victoria had found the sole chink in Marko's armour of happy-go-lucky ignorance. Now, at the eleventh hour, he began to study, enlisting Nicko as his tutor.

'It's not fair, Mummy, I've got my own homework to do.'

'Try to find time for both. We must help Marko if we can. He's only got us and Uncle Ferri in the whole wide world.'

Marko passed his GSC – barely, to be sure, but he passed. His surprise was exceeded only by that of his masters. Yes, he was on his way to his annuity.

But the early enthusiasm that had carried him out of the fifth form was quite gone by the time he entered the sixth. He had discovered poker, at which he was soon adept, and this entertainment, along with pornography – he was already a familiar figure in the sleazier emporia of Soho – became a passion. Yet the school year continued with unperturbed pace along its course.

One day Marko came upon his cousin bent over his books at the kitchen table.

'I'll not matriculate, nipper.'

'Not at this rate, you won't.'

'It'll be such a disappointment for poor old Aunt Vic, that's what bothers me. Hurting your mum, I mean.' Marko looked woeful.

'Start studying now, then. You pulled it off last time.'

Marko shook his head. 'Never, not a chance.' He sat down at the table and reached for Nicko's ruler, with an end of which he began to scratch musingly at his pustules. Suddenly, he slammed the ruler on to the table. 'Good lord, I've just had a super idea! What if you sat for me?'

'You must be barmy, I'm not a cheat. Sit for you? It'd be no better than lying.'

'Lying's easy,' said Marko. He spoke as one who, having reflected on the experiences of a long and varied life, was prepared upon request to formulate a philosophy, a guide for the perplexed. 'You've got to say the first thing that comes into your head. Right out, I mean. It's no use stopping to think. Grammar school was useful for something. I can make anyone believe whatever I want. 'Course, it takes practice.'

'God, what an unutterable swine you are! Besides, I'd get caught.'

'No you wouldn't. There's hundreds sitting for the exam, maybe thousands. All you'd have to do is fill in my name. That's not even lying. I'm Marcus Nicholas, you're Nicholas Marcus. It's the same thing, really, only you're back to front. Besides, we'd be doing it for your mum, remember. It'd be our secret.'

Nicko shook him off. 'Well, I'm not going to. If you fail, it's your own bloody lookout.'

Marko sighed sorrowfully. 'And you call yourself a son. Don't blame me if it kills her.' He sat down again. 'How'd *you* like to go to university?'

'Fat chance. We're not all stinking rich.'

'Ah, well, you see, that's why you're lucky you've got me. If I could get into university, I'd come into my annuity. Then all I'd have to do would be to push some of it your way – and Aunt Victoria's, too, of course. But if you're not interested . . . well, I think it's a bloody shame.'

Nicko stared at him in amazement. 'You'd never do that, not really.'

''Course I would. Good lord, we're cousins, aren't we?'

Nicko felt a wild elation. He sprang to his feet and thrust out his hand. 'I'll do it!'

The cousins shook hands gravely.

So Nicko prepared for both examinations. He went with little sleep, was reluctant to leave his books even for meals, developed headaches, grew pale, his eyes dark ringed. He had a perpetual cold. Marko played poker, palpated breasts and squeezed pustules. In the event, Marcus Nicholas Kraven was matriculated with distinction; Nicholas Marcus Kraven passed his GSC with a score sufficiently high to exempt him from next year's matriculation examination.

Victoria was jubilant. 'How marvellous! How wonderful! Two such brilliant boys!'

Next morning the cousins were playing cricket at the bottom of the garden. The wicket was chalked on the door of the potting shed. Marko was batting and Nicko bowling. After a while Marko called a halt and paced with a heavy step towards his cousin, his pitted face lugubrious in the extreme. Nicko dropped the ball and put out his hand for the bat. But Marko's expression had nothing to do with giving up his favoured place at the potting-shed door. The older boy placed a comforting hand on the shoulder of the younger.

'I've got bad news for you, chum.' Marko retained the cricket bat and used the knob at the top of the handle to scratch at a pustule on his chin. 'The fact is, cobber, I'm not going to be able to send you to university after all.'

Nicko recoiled from his cousin's grasp. 'You absolute rotter! You beastly liar! You never intended to help me, not ever!'

'Steady on, old chap, I most certainly did. But the case is altered, you see. Last night your mum told me the details of the bequest. The annuity's not as much as I'd supposed, and I can't lay my hands on the capital before I'm twenty-one. There's only enough for me.'

'But you promised, you took a solemn oath, we shook hands on it! You stinking bastard!'

'I'd watch who I was calling a bastard if I were you.'

'You . . . you . . . bugger! You sod!' Nicko bit hard on his lower lip, but he would not cry in front of Marko. He turned abruptly on his heel and ran into the house. Upstairs, slamming the door of his attic room behind him, he threw himself upon the bed.

* * *

THE DOOR TO DONOVAN'S OPENED. Startled, Kraven turned round. In the doorway he saw the shapely silhouette of a woman, her head surmounted by an Afro that the street's backlight presented as a halo of massed blonde curls. She closed the door behind her and took a few paces into the room, where she stood in the dimness for a moment as if dazzled by popping flashbulbs, smiling, looking about in response to the silent applause of an invisible multitude. To Donovan she blew a kiss. Then she shrugged, smoothed her dress about her hips, tossed her curls, and bumped and ground her way to Donovan's end of the bar.

'Hey, Dolly!' Donovan actually smiled. He folded his copy of *Midstream* and placed it beneath the bar. Leaning towards her, he closed his eyes and puckered his lips.

'Hey, yourself!' Taller than Donovan, she bent forward and kissed him on his forehead, leaving there a mark in vivid carmine.

'So how'd it go?'

'Looking good, Donovan, looking good.'

'You mean the old guy came through, you got your angel?'

'Could just be.'

'No kidding!'

'Europe, here I come. Whee-ee!'

Donovan glanced at Kraven and frowned. He and Dolly put their heads together and continued their conversation in whispers.

Kraven took another sip of his drink. He glanced again at the poster, and then as recognition dawned, at the woman talking to Donovan. Of course, Dolly Divine! She was heavily and carefully made up, a most attractive eyeful. Her pert bottom merely kissed the barstool as she leaned forward in conversation. If only. . . But present problems overwhelmed libidinous fantasies. Kraven sank once more into his thoughts.

* * *

AND SO MARKO HAD GONE TO LONDON UNIVERSITY, specifically to Clerihew College, just off St Giles Circus. From the day of his admission until the day of his doctorate almost fourteen years would elapse. But then, Marko was in no hurry. To his surprise he discovered that university life agreed with him, he rather liked it – not the academic side, of course, but most assuredly the social. The university provided him with a seemingly endless stream of girls, all submitting sooner or later, usually sooner, to his blandishments. Although lacking his late father's good looks and elegance, he had managed somehow to master the paternal technique.

From time to time a girl would persuade him to move into digs with her, but Marko usually tried to avoid even limited cohabitation. He found it poisonous to an affair. It was a nuisance to be asked about his comings and goings; it was disgusting to find evidence of female necessities and feminine weaknesses all over the place. Bickering led to full-scale arguments, arguments to tears, and tears to Marko's departure. He would drift back to the house in Hampstead and reoccupy his old room. Another girl, he knew, was waiting in the wings, eager for him to beckon her on to centre stage.

But Marko also enjoyed, after his fashion, the intellectual ambience of the university, the knowing talk of politics and the arts, the all-night drinking sessions with his fellows. Over the years he picked up a smattering of quotations, of quips, of positions and issues, of ideational attitudes, all that his father Koko had mocked as 'boonk'. *Kultur* came to him as a scattering of petals on a vast expanse of rough gravel. Sometimes, alas, a petal would blow away before he had noted its beauty. Here a petal might be ground underfoot, there another might wither and die. But by and large he was able to maintain among the roaring boys the reputation of a wit. He knew better than to allow himself to be drawn into a sustained debate.

Then, too, the university gave him leisure. There was seldom any need actually to *do* anything. He was attending university, and that, in his and the world's view, was doing quite enough. The very fact of his attendance was in itself elevating, or at any rate distinguishing, tending to dissolve the rigid class and ethnic barriers that in those years would otherwise have limited his social mobility. He moved with ease among all manner of men and women. He developed an indefinable *ton*. He belonged.

Nicko, meanwhile, had left school at the end of his fifth-form year. He began work as a stockboy in Dindan Frères, a French firm of cloth wholesalers with offices just off Regent Street. When his employers discovered that he possessed an excellent command of German and an adequate ability in French, he was promoted to a very junior clerkship in what the firm called its Foreign Office. Victoria had been proud of his rapid preferment.

During the years in which Marko with halting steps pursued his several degrees, Nicko advanced through various clerkships to the exalted post of Foreign Office Chief. He despised his work, but he knew no other. Indeed, he had become almost a recluse, spending most of his leisure hours alone, either in the Library at the British Museum, in the balcony at Covent Garden, or at home with his books and his gramophone. He had few friends, none close. His relationships with women were sporadic and unsatisfactory. He

130

was awkward and shy with them. An anachronistic, romantic gallantry masked his wretched sense of inadequacy.

'It's no use, Marko. I never seem to meet anyone I can really talk to, there's the rub. Where could I find her? The women I meet know nothing of anything that interests me. There's no hope of a halfway decent conversation.'

'Decent conversation, you silly sod? Good lord, what's that got to do with fucking?'

But Nicko derived some pleasure from Marko's years at the university. From first to last Nicko did all Marko's written work for him. This was a mutually satisfying arrangement. For Nicko it meant direction and purpose in his reading and the challenge of professional criticism for his work; for Marko it meant increased leisure time and a halfway decent academic record. Because Nicko's interests lay in English literature, Marko had elected to read in that discipline; as Nicko narrowed his focus to the Elizabethans and Jacobeans, Marko perforce did likewise; and when, towards the end of his cousin's career, Nicko became interested in the parent-child relationship in Shakespearian drama, *The Parent-Child Relationship in Shakespearian Drama* became Marko's doctoral dissertation.

One evening in late January 1964, Marko dropped in on his cousin at the Hampstead house. Opa was long since dead; Victoria Kraven had died in 1955, her last years, thanks to Nicko's advancement, what she herself had called 'comfortable'. For the past several months Marko had been living with Sybil Bowen, a graduate student in nutrition, in rather squalid rooms in Praed Street. Nicko had seen little of him. His arrival was announced by the slamming of the front door and a cry of 'What ho, me old cock!' Nicko, sitting reading by the living-room fire, shivered.

'There you are! Good-o!' Marko stood for a moment in the doorway and tugged at his forelock in mock servility. He was brimming with good cheer and excitement. The grinning

131

vigour of his irruption had caused the gramophone needle to skip from its groove. 'Not scratched, I trust.'

Nicko sighed. 'Shut the door, can't you. There's a hell of a bloody draught.'

Marko made straight for the cabinet and poured a large whisky for himself. 'Arses up! Ah, yes, that's better.'

Nicko got up and closed the door. He turned off the gramophone. So much for the '*Porgi amor*'.

'Thank God that screeching's off.' Marko went over to the fire and stood with his back to it, screening Nicko from the warmth.

'Take off your coat if you're staying.'

'In a minute. I'm bloody frozen.' Marko spread his coat tails around his buttocks. 'That's the ticket.' He raised and lowered himself on his toes for a moment. 'Notice anything about my face?'

'You're a bit yellowish.'

'No, you twit, it's the acne, it's clearing up.'

'Ah.' This was an old story, and Nicko knew better than to protest. In fact, but for the occasional eruption of a tiny pustule or two, Marko's acne had long since cleared up, leaving his face unscarred. But he was obsessed with what he regarded as his disfigurement. In the mirror he still saw the pitted and pimpled face of his adolescent self, and tried whatever remedies came his way, from vinegar baths and anchovy paste to hypnosis and faith healing.

'It's all thanks to Sybil. Took one look and told me my trouble was lack of vitamin A. The old body's starving for it, simple as that. I've been pumping the stuff into the system ever since, carrots, pills, the lot. Rather like it, as a matter of fact. Made an enormous difference, as you can see.'

'Good for Sybil.'

'Mock on, old chap. But she's the first one to be of any earthly use, apart from fucking, in all these years. Not that I've anything to complain of there.'

132

'And so you dashed over here to tell me all about it?'

'Er, no, not exactly.' Marko looked momentarily crestfallen, but he swallowed a mouthful of whisky and rallied. 'How's our dissertation coming along, old son?'

'*Our* dissertation is virtually complete.'

'No need to twist the knife.'

'I'm polishing up the last of the footnotes.'

'Bang on!' Marko was clearly on the verge of some great announcement. He took a steadying swallow of whisky, his yellow eyeballs gleaming, the hand around the tumbler trembling in his excitement. But he contrived a casual tone. 'You remember, of course, I applied last November for a lectureship in America? I told you about that, didn't I? No? Yes, there was an advert in the *TLS*. You never know, I thought. Nothing venture, nothing gain, that sort of rot. Posted off my credentials, had the Quim put in a good word for me. The thing is, old boy, I've got the job!' Marko no longer strove to mask his elation. He pulled from his overcoat pocket a thin envelope edged in red, white and blue and waved it triumphantly aloft. 'It arrived this morning. Trouble is, the appointment's contingent upon the completion of the degree. I've got to arrive "degree in hand". You'd think it was a bloody wanking contest. Anyway, it's a relief to hear the dissertation's done. No need to say how grateful I am, I suppose.'

'Congratulations.' Nicko, smiling, tried hard to swallow his envy. 'What college?'

'Mosholu. Odd name, what? Has a sort of Jewish flavour to it, pious offspring founding a college, that sort of thing: In Memory of Our Beloved Parents Moshe and Lou Katz.' Marko rubbed his hands together in glee. 'It's in the Bronx, wherever that is. Somewhere near New York, I'm told.'

'Marko, have you pictured yourself behind the lectern? Do you honestly think you're capable of teaching college students?'

'They're bloody Americans, you bloody sap. It'll be bloody money for bloody jam. What the bloody hell do they know?'

* * *

THE DISSERTATION WAS ACCEPTED. Professor C.U.T. Quimby had found it a trifle eccentric, Marko reported. The great scholar had pursed his lips around the tip of his tongue. 'Surely not *every* encounter between father and son, dear boy, reproduces the meeting of poor Laius and his burly offspring on the road to Thebes. You have quite succumbed, I fear, to the Hebrew melodies of your co-religionist, that naughty little doctor from Vienna.' Still, he had admitted that the dissertation was cogently argued and adequately substantiated, possibly even commercially publishable. He had held out a thin cold hand. 'So you're off to the former colonies, eh? Perhaps our paths will cross there. Good luck, dear Marko.' Quimby had turned his face away, a tear trickling down his rouged and hollow cheek. 'Ah, Marko, Marko!' The old man had been quite overcome.

Marko turned up in Hampstead again to make a selection of Kraven furniture for shipment to New York.

'My God, Marko, you're turning a frightful colour!'

'Been using a sunlamp, actually.'

'You should see a doctor.'

'But I *am* a doctor, old chap.'

'What does Sybil say?'

'Sybil says, "Do it again, Marko! Don't stop!" That's what Sybil says.' He winked and made pumping motions with his hips.

One month before Marko's planned departure, Nicko flew to Paris to confer with his opposite number at the main branch of Dindan Frères. He was gone three days. Upon his return he was greeted by a phone call from the Compleat Mourner.

'I've got tragic news, Nicko. You'd better brace yourself.'

'What is it?'

'Marko's dead, run over in Oxford Street early yesterday evening.' The Compleat Mourner had, through long practice, a manner of saying such things that somehow softened the meaning of the words. Nevertheless, this was a shock.

'I can't believe it!'

'I know, I know. You two were very close. The funeral's tomorrow, the usual place. I've made all the arrangements. It had to be delayed, you see, because of the rum circumstances. He was bright yellow. There's been an autopsy, of course. I'll pick you up in the car at nine-thirty.'

'But you said he was run over.'

'He was, after a fashion. It seems he collapsed in the path of a bus, a number 113. The driver swerved to avoid him, but he was too late. There were plenty of witnesses. It wasn't the driver's fault. Marko held up traffic for forty-five minutes, according to the wireless. Lucky it wasn't rush hour. You see the pattern, don't you, Nicko? There'll be another inquest, just as there was for poor Koko.'

The coroner's inquest in due course found that death had been caused by 'carrot-juice addiction'. The court heard evidence that in the last ten days of his life, without regard to his earlier known habits, the late Marcus Nicholas Kraven, PhD, had taken eighty million units of vitamin A. In addition, he had drunk during that period about ten gallons of carrot juice. Dr Gerard Barker, the pathologist who performed the autopsy, testified that the effect of so vast an intake of vitamin A from carrots and tablets was virtually indistinguishable from alcoholic poisoning. 'It produces the same result,' he said. 'Cirrhosis of the liver. The man was dead before the bus struck him.'

The funeral was sparsely attended. At the graveside, apart from Nicko, the Compleat Mourner and Aunt Cicely, stood Sibyl Bowen, Dr C.U.T. Quimby, and a brusque young rabbi, eager to get it over with. The wind blew strongly out of a low, smudged sky, whipping the pages of the rabbi's prayer book and moulding to her body Sybil's black dress. Undoubtedly pregnant, Sybil stared unseeingly through eyes red and swollen. Nicko took her by the arm to steady her; she seemed on the point of collapse.

They all stared down at the coffin, the Compleat Mourner with equanimity, Aunt Cicely sourly. A spattering of rain came and went. Quimby stood slightly apart from the other mourners, holding a large, dirty handkerchief to his nose, blowing, wiping, blowing. He seemed genuinely sorrowful and watched the young rabbi with hungry attention. Later, he shook hands with the family members. 'Reft of my dearest pledge,' he mumbled, and blew his nose. 'Tragic, an inestimable loss.' He turned to the rabbi. 'Care for a lift back into town, dear boy? I've a comment or two on the ritual you might find interesting.'

The Compleat Mourner, dragging a reluctant Aunt Cicely with him, took the opportunity to visit a number of familiar grave sites scattered about the cemetery. His was the smooth and cheerful manner of the professional cicerone, eager to point out to the traveller the local antiquities and curiosities.

Nicko accompanied Sybil back to her waiting taxi. She was quietly weeping. 'I killed him,' she said.

'Whatever you'd like to keep for remembrance. . .'

'He was all right until I told him about bloody vitamin A. I should turn myself in. O God, Marko darling! O Marko!'

Nicko helped her into her taxi. He stole another glance at her midriff. 'I suppose he had already made his final arrangements. One forgets that he was about to leave anyway.'

'Leave?' She was looking *at* him now, not through him.

'For America, his teaching post.'

Her large eyes, beautiful, brimmed with tears. 'Oh please, Marko said nothing about America. Why would he go there?

He'd have had to tell me, wouldn't he? I'd have to get ready myself.'

'Absolutely. Forgive me, I'm confused. Look, if something should come up. . .' He felt in his jacket pocket. 'Here's my card. Get in touch with me, don't hesitate.'

She did not respond. Her eyes had lost their focus. She held the card rigidly in her hand.

'You know the address, driver? You'd better take her home.'

He never heard from Sybil again, of course.

It was while he was writing a letter to Professor Aristotle Papadakis, Chairman of the English Department, Mosholu College, explaining Marko's inability to take up his new post in the autumn that Nicko conceived his brilliant idea, an idea at once breathtaking in its audacity and terrifying in its implications. It was a very simple idea. Why might he not go to America in Marko's place? Who would know the difference? If this Papadakis was prepared to receive a Marcus Nicholas Kraven and a Nicholas Marcus Kraven presented himself, verifying diploma 'onanistically in hand', would he even question the inversion of names? Why should he?

But no, there must be a flaw in it somewhere. Nicko, of all people, would never get away with it. Bravura on a grand scale was hardly his forte. He resumed his writing.

But the brilliant idea refused to go away. It nudged and teased his concentration, drawing his mind away from the letter. The academic degree was much more certainly his than it had ever been Marko's. How splendid if he were able to devote his life to literature, to scholarship, to the pursuit of Truth! How inexpressibly wonderful if he were to become a torchbearer in the dark night of ignorance and kindle the flame of learning in eager young minds!

America, to the west, offered unlimited hope, a *vita nuova*. The natural leaning of the Kravens tugged at him. But could he – *he*, law-abiding, diffident Nicholas – pull off so grand a deception, so terrifying a fraud? And would he dare? Absently, he plucked an imaginary pimple on his cheek. Only if he were to become Marko in fact, not merely in fancy, could he burst through the iron gates of his prison into the bright lights of freedom.

Kraven was on his way.

* * *

'CHEER UP, GUY. She didn't mean it. And if she did, well hey!'

'What?' Kraven looked up to find Dolly Divine at his elbow, smiling encouragingly, her drink in her hand.

'It's never as bad as it looks.'

'To me it looks very good indeed,' said Kraven gallantly. 'You're Dolly Divine, aren't you?'

'Yeah,' she breathed. Her broad grin showed her delight in his recognition. 'You a fan?'

'I'm Martin Chuzzlewit,' said Kraven. 'I'm a freelance journalist.'

'No kidding? D'you read what the *Wall Street Journal* said about my act? I was a smash hit at Spinoza's. You ever do reviews, Marty?'

'Books, sometimes. Look, may I buy you a drink?'

She swirled what remained of the drink in her glass. 'In a bit, maybe. Let's go sit over there by the window. I'm waiting for my sisters.'

Donovan, behind the bar, disapproving, took out his copy of *Midstream* and turned its pages.

Dolly Divine rolled on a calm full tide across the room towards a window seat. Kraven, his troubles forgotten, followed her admiringly. They sat at opposite sides of the table.

'So what didja like best about my act, Marty?'

138

'Ah, well. . .'

'My "Stormy Weather" number, right? Yeah, that always brought the house down. I used to think it was the tassels. You remember the tassels, Marty? They loved "Stormy Weather" at Spinoza's.'

Meanwhile, the door of Donovan's had opened and closed. Dolly looked up and waved excitedly. Coming towards them were a brunette and a redhead. Kraven got to his feet.

'So how did it go, Dolly?' said the brunette anxiously.

Dolly gave a thumbs-up sign.

'No kidding! You gonna tell us, for Chrisake?' The brunette put her hand to her left breast, as if to slow her heartbeat.

'Later. But don't worry. You're in like Flynn, too. Sit down, why doncha, the both of you. You too, Marty.'

They sat.

'These're my sisters,' said Dolly. 'Sugar Plum. . .'

'Please t'meecha,' said Sugar, pushing one shoulder forward and looking up at him beneath lowered lids. The tip of her tongue briefly caressed her upper lip. She was the brunette, her hair descending softly to her shoulders, a fringe covering her forehead. Like Dolly heavily but expertly made up, her face was rather thin, and she was perhaps slightly less well endowed than her sister. For all that, she was striking.

'. . .and the baby, Candy Peaches.'

Candy, who, despite the hard, unfriendly surfaces of Donovan's captain's chair, was stretched out so that only her shoulders and coccyx touched it, said nothing. But she nodded to Kraven, grinning, and gave him an inexplicable, complicitous wink.

'I'm Martin Chuzzlewit,' said Kraven.

'Marty's a fan,' explained Dolly. 'Besides that, he writes a column. That right, Marty? He was just telling me how he was wowed by my "Stormy Weather" number. So I was thinking like maybe he'd like to write up about today. I mean, y'know, an in-depth interview? Lucky us meeting like this.'

'May I buy you ladies a drink?'

Dolly downed what remained in her glass. 'You bet.'

'My pleasure,' said Sugar Plum.

Candy winked once more.

'Barkeep!' called Kraven sternly and snapped his fingers. Donovan looked up, sighed, put down *Midstream* and shuffled over. 'Hi, Sugar Plum. Hi, Candy.'

'Well, ladies,' said Kraven expansively, 'what will it be?'

'Daiquiri, straight up,' said Dolly.

'Vodka gimlet,' said Sugar Plum. 'Heavy on the ice.'

'Stinger,' said Candy.

'And I'll have another scotch and water. Got all that?'

Donovan raised his eyes to the ceiling and shuffled back to the bar.

'Your tastes in tipple are as different as your looks. Each of you is uniquely beautiful.'

'Momma moved around a lot,' said Sugar Plum.

'And you're all in show business?'

'Dolly's the real *artiste*,' said Sugar sadly. 'I'm the oldest – not that I'm *old*,' she added hastily, 'but, like, y'know, I was born *first*. Jeez, someone's gotta be! – but anyways, I never made it into the big time, never got the breaks. And Candy here has barely started.'

'That's pretty good, Sugar,' said Candy. ' "*Barely* started" is good.'

Sugar Plum looked puzzled.

'Never mind, honey,' said Dolly, leaning forward to pat her older sister on the knee. 'You'll make it. You gotta believe, is all.'

The drinks arrived, presented by Donovan with an extravagant flourish to the sisters and with an irritable grunt to Kraven. They sipped, the sisters ruminating on the vagaries of show-business success.

'Dolly ain't just a stripper, Marty,' said Sugar Plum. 'Bobby – that's our angel, Bobby – he says she's dizzy-assed.'

'An *Ecdysiast*, for Pete's sake!' Candy gave Sugar Plum a lovingly playful punch on the shoulder.

'Who *is* Bobby?'

'He's a mult-eye millionaire,' said Sugar Plum. 'He's gonna make Dolly an innernational celebrity.'

'Okay, Sugar. That's enough,' said Dolly hastily. 'Listen, Marty. I know you'll understand. Things're kinda in the balance right now. We've got this backer, see? This angel? But nothing's finalized. He don't want his name mentioned just yet. But since you're a friend, I can tell you: things're looking good.'

'You're putting on a show in Europe,' said Kraven. 'Sorry about that, but I heard you talking to Donovan.'

'Exploring the possibilities, y'might say,' said Dolly, playing it close to her bosom. 'Checking out the options. *You* know: nothing definite. The sons-a-bitches get a whiff of the rolling green and the prices take off. You buy one little dress, it can cost anywheres up from seven hundred and fifty. And ostrich feathers? Forget it!' The road to the big time was strewn with boulders. 'You know what my costumes're worth? Wanna take a guess? Twenty, maybe twenty-five gees!'

'How did you meet Bobby?'

'I was doing a private party up in Westchester, couple maybe three years ago, my "Scheherezade" number. Bobby liked my act. I don't remember, did I do my "Scheherezade" at Spinoza's? You remember, Marty? Anyways, Bobby and me got to talking, found we had a lot in common. You know how it is. He's a sweet old guy.'

'And you're all going to Europe with him?'

'Dolly is,' said Sugar Plum. 'We're going along with Dolly.'

'I think I detect a romantic entanglement.'

'For the record,' said Dolly with a mischievous grin, 'you might say we're just good friends.'

141

'Another round, ladies?' Kraven snapped his fingers at Donovan, pointed to the table, and made a circular motion with his finger.

'I always wanted to go legit,' said Dolly.

'You could do it, too,' said Sugar Plum.

Candy, grimacing, rolled her eyes ceilingwards.

Donovan placed the second round on the table and with a flourish removed the empty glasses.

'It ain't easy to change your image, break outta burlesque, open on Broadway maybe, Hollywood even.' Dolly fell silent before the enchanting possibilities. The big break was happening to someone every day.

'You could do it, Dolly,' said Sugar Plum again. 'She could too. Go on, tell him about the show.'

Dolly looked at Kraven dubiously.

'He's okay,' said Sugar Plum. 'You won't spill any a this, will you, Marty?'

'Mum's the word.'

'Well, I got this idea for a show, see, a show with class. . . You really innerested in this, Marty?'

'Fascinated.'

'I figure, y'know, to kinda ease into legit. I figure, I make my reputation over there, I can write my own ticket back here in the States. So I gotta get me a different kinda audience, not just a lot a guys who only wanna look at your whatsis. Oh sure, there'll still be plenty of naked girls on stage, three maybe four strippers, a comedienne, a couple of gymnasts, an all-girl orchestra, and like that. See, what we'd do, we'd do these scenes from Shakespeare.'

'What a terrific idea!'

'Yeah,' said Dolly modestly, 'not too bad. I even got this title, Candy give it me, some kinda Follies. What was it, Can?'

'*Bardic Follies.*' Candy, shifting in her seat, sipping her drink, crossed one magnificent leg over the other.

'That's probably just the shot in the arm the legitimate theatre needs,' said Kraven. 'An all-female Shakespeare company. *Bardic Follies*. I like it.'

'Candy's been to college,' said Sugar Plum proudly. 'She's a bachelor-girl.'

'I even got this scene worked out,' Dolly went on. '*Hamlet*. You know the play, Marty? Well, Candy was telling me about this book she read, and I saw the possibilities right away. It was by this shrink, a buddy of Frood.' She snapped impatient fingers at Candy.

'Jones,' said Candy agreeably, 'Ernest Jones, a limey disciple.'

'This is the way I see it. The curtain goes up. The stage is dark, just one spot on Gertrude. That's me, I'm a queen. I'm wearing just this black negligee, very tasteful, of course. I'm sitting on a throne, maybe fixing my hair. Then the music starts, Ravel's *Bolero*, soft at first, sorta dreamy and sad. That's Hamlet's theme, see; he's my son. Another spot picks him up. He comes in, dancing slow. He dances over to me, and then he sorta goes down on his knees and holds my hand, feverish, you can tell he's upset, but kinda wistful.'

'Act three, scene four,' breathed Kraven.

'Yeah, right. Anyways, that's when Hamlet's old man comes in, my first husband. A third spot picks him up. Oh, I didn't tell you: he's dead. What he is, he's a ghost. So he's got white paint on all over and he's wearing this white robe. Now his theme begins, "The Anniversary Waltz". See, what I've forgotten is today's our anniversary. Slowly he takes off his robe; but he does it with dignity, being as he's a king, and from the Other Side. Then his theme takes over, getting stronger all the time. He begins to sorta dance towards me, in time to the music. Like I said, he's got this white stuff all over him, even on his you-know. You can tell he's royal. He's moving his hips, rubbing his hands up and down his thighs. "O. How we danced. On the night. We were wed.

143

Dee-*dum*. Dee-dee-*dum*. Dee-dee-*dum*. Dee . . . dee . . . *dummm*." You with me so far, Marty?'

'All the way.'

'Okay. So now the Ghost kisses me. And when he moves back, I sorta rise from the throne, my lips still glued to his. Then he slips off my negligee, kinda sad, kinda regretful. Y'see, he's only a ghost, so what can *he* do? We go into our dance number, slow and easy, suggestive but tasteful. Anyway, Hamlet's been watching us all this while, still on his knees. You can see he's mad. He gets up. Then *his* theme starts in again, getting louder all the time: "BOOM. Baba-baba-baba-BOOM, baba-BOOM." You can hardly hear "The Anniversary Waltz" any more. Then he dashes over and pulls me from the Ghost's arms. The Ghost's spot goes out. He disappears. Then me and Hamlet begin this dance. He takes off his shirt, still dancing. Then he reaches for his tights. Lights out. Curtain.' She paused.

'Terrific!' said Kraven. 'But I thought it was to be an all-girl show.'

'Yeah, well,' said Dolly. 'There's still a few bugs need ironing out.'

Kraven eyed Candy with real interest. 'You thought all this up yourself?'

'The basic idea.' Candy created on her delightful face a mock *moue* of chaste pride. 'Of course, the full treatment is Dolly's. She's the *artiste*.'

Dolly nodded in modest agreement; Candy winked again at Kraven.

Candy, Kraven was ready to acknowledge, was no bimbo. This stunning young woman whose slovenly posture was itself a thing of beauty had a sense of irony that matched his own. *Bardic Follies* could take its place honourably alongside *Tickety-Boo!* Were he not already so fearfully entangled, he might be tempted to get to know her rather better. As it was, he had better go. Besides, he did not have enough cash on him to pay for another round of drinks.

'The hour cometh, and now is,' said Kraven. 'Alas, I must go. But it's been an enormous pleasure meeting you all.' He got up. 'Good luck with *Bardic Follies*.'

'Here, Marty,' said Dolly, taking a card from her purse and handing it to him. 'My agent. You can always get in touch.'

* * *

KRAVEN LEFT DONOVAN'S and made his way towards home. His spirits were lifted. Whisky and soda and the hermetic peace of Donovan's had played their part, to be sure, but the most effective tonic had been the encounter with Dolly and Sugar and Candy. Candy is dandy, thought Kraven, modifying the familiar aphorism, and quicker than liquor.

Had America proved to be the answer to the Nicko problem? America had served him well; he had prospered. He had left behind the retiring, diffident, ineffectual Nicko, had assumed with his new role rather too much, perhaps, of the caddish Marko – to the point that, at fleeting moments of shaming introspection (but moments lately of increasing frequency), he believed himself to have out-Markoed his cousin. He had donned the mask of Marko, and now he feared it had grown to his flesh. 'Oh Nicholas, you're such a liar,' Stella had said to him today. He had no wish to continue as Marko, but could not countenance a return to the Nicko of old. Could not the best of Marko be joined to the best of Nicko? Alas, only Marko, not Nicko, could deal with the current crisis.

At worst, he had only to give Gabe Princip his Pass and let him go. As for Stella, well, he would lie low for a while. Let her suppose him hot on the trail of Poore-Moody. But did he love her? And Quimby remained a problem. He must not be permitted to reveal what he knew. But how to prevent it? There must be a way. Kraven rallied; he would find it.

EIGHT

ON MONDAY MORNING Kraven went back to Mosholu in a mood more cheery than usual. The problems that had seemed so insoluble only yesterday were already meandering, as if under their own volition, towards solution. One had merely to accept the advice an ordinary cab company offered: Sit Back and Relax. A good night's sleep had made all the difference. Meanwhile, he would be able to cancel the balance of this week's classes, perhaps even dismiss his students early, today. Yes, while the divinity busily shaped, Kraven would stretch out poolside in the Californian sunshine.

On his way to his private cell he stuck his head into the departmental office and called out a hearty good morning. Typewriters stopped their busy clatter and three Bronx mommas, the secretarial staff, distinguishable one from the other only by superficial details of dress, lifted peroxided heads from their work. They replied in chorus, their voices twittering with identical inflection, 'Good morning, Nicholas.' Mrs Trutitz, their stern directrix, required a more personal, a more intimately concerned greeting. Accordingly, she kept her eyes on her work and remained silent.

'How's it going, Bella?' said Kraven gallantly.

Bella Trutitz indicated an area between the tip of her altered nose and her frowning forehead. 'We've been up to here all morning.' She rapped sharply on her desk. Her girls must get back to work. The typewriters resumed their clattering. 'I dropped a note in your box, Nicholas. Ari wants to see you as soon as you have a moment.'

Kraven had never been able to accustom himself to this familiarity of address. He winced, offended in his sense of hierarchy, of degree. 'How about right now? Is he free?'

'I think so. Just a minute.' She got up, banging her knee on the desk as she did so. She shot him a look of mingled agony, disappointment and reproach but limped courageously to the Chairman's door, whereon, well mannered in spite of it all, she knocked before entering.

Kraven spent the few seconds of her absence humming a private hum, '*La donna e mobile*'.

The door opened and Mrs Trutitz reappeared. 'It's okay, you can go in. Only, do me a favour, don't keep him too long. He's got a full schedule today.' She let out a sudden groan, bent over to clutch her knee, and in that awkward position hopped the necessary paces back to her seat. 'My God, I think it's swelling!'

'I'll just toddle on in then,' said Kraven cheerily. 'Mustn't keep the Benign Despot waiting.'

Papa Doc was stretched out on his chair, his hands clutching one another behind his neck, his sneakered feet, raised and crossed, resting on his desk. He looked like a large sack of potatoes carelessly dumped there and turned into a crude effigy, at its top a white mask upon which some unskilled child had smudged features in coal dust, at its bottom filthy sneakers to suggest feet. Also on the desk were a mug of coffee, a half- finished danish, and, turned towards the visitor, a colour photograph of wife and daughter smiling inanely.

'I told you the impression you made on Diotima, right? Right on, guy. Can't hurt to have the hallowed name of Mosholu carried back to the Old World's seats of learning. You really turned her on.'

'Bella said you wanted to see me.'

'I've already had two phone calls about you, one from Dillinger, the other from Pio Nono. I'll say this for you, Nick, no one can accuse you of being too communicative.'

'Ah, you mean Los Angeles. It all seemed rather iffy, or I'd have mentioned it to you.'

'No hard feelings, Nikos. Christ, I'm tickled pink.' The lower part of Papa Doc's mask opened to represent a smile. 'Congratulations. According to the Dill, you've made the discovery of the century.' He leaned across his desk and gave a damp paw to Kraven, who shook it briefly. 'I didn't know you were into the Middle Ages.'

'I try not to be too narrow in my focus.'

'Right on, my view exactly. Anyway, Pio Nono's hot to have another *vexilliarus regis* marching westward, expects departmental co-operation, secretarial help should you need it, whatever. Now, is there anything I can do to speed the scholar on his way?'

'Not a thing, Ari.'

'You sure? Speak up, Nick, now's the moment. This is the thin edge of the wedge, you know. You're my precedent. We'll get our finger in the pie yet. We're an active department but, hell, let's face it, largely invisible. Until now. The limelight's beginning to turn in this direction at last, and with the limelight comes the gravy. The vibes are good, Nikos, very good. You need anything, you got it.'

Kraven shook his head.

Papa Doc struggled to his feet, indicating the interview was at an end.

'About Quimby, Ari.'

'No problem, fella, Pio Nono already thought of that. You're off the hook.' Papa Doc poked himself in mid-gut. 'Ol' Ceece Quimby is gonna be introduced by Papadakis himself.'

'Splendid. Er, listen, Ari, d'you suppose you could avoid saying anything about me to the old fellow?'

'Why the hell should I do that?' Papa Doc's eyes narrowed.

'No *good* reason. I just thought I'd like to surprise him with a phone call. Sentimental rubbish, I suppose. It was Dillinger's idea, actually. He thought the old man might get a kick out of a transcontinental call from a former pupil, out of the blue, as it were. He said Dean Pioggi agreed with him. Still, if you think otherwise. . .'

'No problem, guy, that's a great idea,' said Papa Doc hastily. 'But what if he asks after you?'

'Well, in that case. . .'

'No problem. Anything of a personal nature you can tell me about him, anything that might punch up my opening remarks? You know, like what he likes?'

'He likes parsnips, the raunchier passages in Marlowe's *Hero and Leander*, and young plump male buttocks.'

Papa Doc's grin was sickly. He walked Kraven to the door, his arm around his shoulder. 'You know, Nicko, I have a dream . . .' His voice trembled. 'I have a dream. . .' He paused at the door, his hand on the knob. 'Fella, there's a helluva lot riding on you, I want you to know that. Don't screw up.'

Kraven went on his way humming a cheerful hum. The Shaper was busily shaping. Sit Back and Relax.

* * *

KRAVEN ENTERED THE LECTURE HALL BRISKLY, but he broke step when he saw waiting before his lectern the venerable Feibelman. The old man was brimming with excitement, his spirit irrepressible. He stood rocking backwards and forwards as if in prayer, his knees bent, his back curved, his eyes closed. But when he heard Kraven before him, he popped his eyes open and straightened his back. There was a grin on his face that Kraven found disturbing.

'Perfessor, you could maybe spare me a minute?'

Kraven looked at his watch. 'Sorry, no, it'll have to wait. Find your seat, Mr Feibelman.'

Despondent, the old man turned and slouched off.

Kraven, at his lectern, surveyed his class. A representative sampling. Antonia Anstruther was in her place, impassive and exposed as usual. Over there sat the wretched Hakim, a plagiarist, neatly attired in a suit of quiet grey, his rich silk tie a paean to elegant taste. Princip, as expected, had not shown up. As Kraven's wandering gaze passed over Giulietta Corombona, she raised an inquisitive eyebrow and shrugged. His eye moved on without pause.

Kraven looked at the grinning faces before him and knew that today's class would not last long.

He told them of the Institute of Medieval and Renaissance Studies, of the unexpected call to address an august assemblage, of his commitment to scholarship and to their alma mater. He regretted the necessary cancellation of classes but knew that they would understand. When the trumpet sounded its brazen call, they would expect to find him in the van. They would all meet again one week from today, in any case, by which time they would have read *Macbeth*. Unhappily, he would have to cancel the balance of today's lecture, last-minute arrangements requiring his attention. 'Are there any questions?'

Mr Feibelman raised his hand.

Kraven nodded and pointed.

'Before you go, sir, you should be so good: what was it Lear saw on Cordelia's lips?'

'Ah yes, our little cliffhanger of last Thursday. Good for you, Mr Feibelman.'

'Nu?'

'I'm inclined to let that crucial matter hang, if only to make sure you all return next Monday.' He paused for the expected titter and was not disappointed. He created a warm smile. 'But I'll leave you with a clue. Cordelia was hanged, remember. What problem for her soul would her constricted throat create? Ah, I see that for some of you the light has turned on.' Kraven saw nothing of the kind.

He gathered together his precious lecture sheets and made for the door. Feibelman and Giulietta, trailing after, met him there. Kraven paused for his petitioners. 'Please make arrangements with Mrs Trutitz to see me immediately after my return, but as for now, I'm afraid I must be off.' And Kraven fled, panting for a blessed moment of quality time in the privacy of his tin cell.

* * *

THE SOOTHING CLUTTER at once embraced him. The blinds were drawn, the lighting dim. A mild aroma of book decay from the burgeoning shelves gently tickled his nostrils. The chaise longue beckoned, it yearned towards him, but he wanted first to sort through the bundle of mail he had picked up on his way back, and so he sat at his desk, rapidly discarding, piece by piece, the mass of college junk that always accumulated, unsolicited, unwanted, in his mailbox. At last he came to a fat manila envelope from the History Department. Ah, Dillinger had been as good as his word. Here was his ticket of leave. He weighed the envelope in his hand. It was a masterstroke of the shaping divinity that he should be absent during Quimby's visit. If Papa Doc could be relied on to hold his tongue, then the last of the Kravens had weathered another demonic tempest, flags flying, the proud vessel tacking gaily to port.

He opened the envelope and found within it a thick brochure of the Los Angeles Conference, maps of Westwood and environs, an application for optional side-trips to Disneyland, the Getty Museum and the Columbia Pictures studios, a voucher for a round-trip airline ticket, and a cheque to cover incidental expenses. There was also a brief note: 'You were right about the Gryllus, of course. Tamara Grieben, my secretary, is taking care of the details of the trip. By the way, we're staying at the Bel-Air, not those tacky hostelries in the brochure, so pack your grip accordingly. Let Tamara know if there's anything you need. See you in LA. John.' One must take his hat off to Dillinger. The man knew how to parlay scholarship into *la dolce vita*.

Idly Kraven turned the pages of the conference brochure. Here was the Arthurian Section. Mosholu's Dillinger was to open with 'New Light on Camelot'; Harvard's Terence Hill was to respond with 'Old Wine in New Bottles?' Kraven flipped on. 'The Babylonian Captivity and Proto-Protestantism: A Reassessment,' 'The Maid of Orleans and the Limits of Medical Inquiry,' 'The European Market for Levantine Manuscripts, 1300–1450'. All this beneath the Californian sun and within a stone's throw of the Pacific.

The air-ticket voucher, falling from the travel kit, caught his attention. He picked it up. What was this? Destination: London, England. Purpose: Conference of the Royal Arthurian Antiquities Institute, Clerihew College, London University. Bloody hell! Dillinger's efficiency extended no further than his secretary, who had got him down for the wrong conference. The Royal Arthurian was to meet in the following week, as Dillinger himself had told him. Had it not even occurred to Tamara Grieben that a brochure for Los Angeles and a ticket for London were incompatible?

He had long since abandoned hope that life could be simple. But why must it be daily twisted and knotted by the well-meaning interference of the feeble-minded? If he hoped to straighten out this particular stupidity, he would himself have to go to the History Department. Yes, he would have to make the trek across campus and confront Mrs Grieben with the irrefutable evidence of her idiocy. It was fortunate indeed that he had caught her error in time. England in April? Not while the warm sunshine, the palm trees, the luxurious pool at the Bel-Air beckoned.

There was a knock at the door. Kraven, upset and not yet thinking clearly, called out, 'Come in.' The door opened. A grinning Feibelman stood there. 'Yoo-hoo, it's me.'

Kraven had almost convinced himself that he alone had discovered in Gryllus the proof that Merlin was a Jew. But there still remained a small and dwindling area in his mind that acknowledged Feibelman's primacy. The old man deserved a hearing. 'As you see, I'm quite busy, Mr Feibelman. But I can spare you a couple of minutes. What is it?'

'What I wanted to tell you this morning, Perfessor, was you wouldn't see me any more this week.' Feibelman advanced into the room and sat himself upon the chaise longue. 'But after what you said in class, looks like I'm gonna see you after all, in Westwood yet. How about that?'

Kraven's stomach gave an unpleasant lurch. 'What do you mean?'

'Have I got a son-in-law! You wouldn't believe. A big person in Boston, a doctor, a specialist, ear, nose and throat, my daughter Sharon's his wife. And he has a patient. Who should he be? Perfessor Terence Hill, the Harvard man, Mr Middle Ages, I don't have to tell you.'

Kraven began to drown beneath Feibelman's grin. In his stomach there burned a poisonous mineral. 'Go on.'

'A long story short, Morris happens to mention to Perfessor Hill my theory. Poor feller, he's got inflammation of the inner ear, which, you can imagine, is painful. No problem, don't worry, Morris knows right away what to do. What happens? This weekend Morris arranges on the telephone a three-way conversation, me, the perfessor, and Morris and

153

Sharon.' Feibelman frowned. 'I don't want you should take offence. In scholarship there's room for many opinions. But in Harvard it's possible Merlin is a Jew. So Perfessor Hill suggests maybe I should fly out to the conference. When it's his turn to speak, he's gonna give me a few minutes of his time. In particular, he says, he wants Perfessor Dillinger to hear what I have to say. So what you think? Not bad for an old man.'

Kraven, pale and in a cold sweat, feared he would puke.

'Sharon, meanwhile, is calling all over LA, making sure I get kosher meals. If I tell her my own perfessor's gonna be there, don't worry, she's gonna look out for you too. Listen, kosher food's not so bad. Anyway, I thought you should know.'

Kraven swallowed bile. 'Congratulations, Mr Feibelman.'

Feibelman got up. 'By the way, naturally I'm interested, what you gonna talk about? That I don't wanna miss.'

'Mustn't tip my hand,' said Kraven. 'Wait and see.'

'Looks like you got yourself another customer,' said Feibelman at the door. 'Hiya, kid.'

The voluptuous Giulietta Corombona stood waiting.

'I'm sorry, Miss Corombona,' said Kraven in a modulated tone, 'but I meant what I said. No conferences until I return.'

She grinned warmly at him and sashayed to the chaise longue. She was, thought Kraven, a casting director's dream of Carmen, dark, damp, seductive, impudent, confident of her power. He sighed and closed the door. He would save more time by listening to her than by attempting to get rid of her.

'Be brief, Miss Corombona.'

'I'm kinda worried about my grade inna course.'

'That's scarcely surprising. In your place, so would I be.'

'I'd do anything to get an A, know what I mean? Anything.' She winked.

154

'An A is perhaps rather out of your reach at this point, my dear. What is it so far, two Fs and a D? But it would help if you started to read the plays, perhaps contributed your mite to class discussion.'

Giulietta ran her hand slowly up her leg, taking with her enough of her skirt to reveal a wealth of thigh. 'No, I mean you just like tell me what you want, Vietnamese massage, round the world, leather and whips, nursery romp. . .' She parted her legs slightly, winked once more, and inflated another pink sphere. 'Shit, I know education's important. Last term I made the fucking Dean's List. All you gotta do, you tell me how you like it.'

'I think, Miss Corombona, you had better leave.'

She sat up smartly, offended, and began to dig around in her school bag. 'You know what this is?' She held in her hand a scrap of Aegean blue. 'You're nothing special. Gabe told me about you and Nome Berkowitz yesterday. This is from Gabe's personal collection. He told me to bring it along. You gotta use it, he said, use it. Now all I gotta do is rip my T-shirt, yell "Rape!" you'll be outta here so fast you'll think you slipped on vaginal jelly.' She put Nimuë's panties back in her bag. 'I just bet, one way or another, my grade's gonna zoom, right?' She closed her eyes and kissed the air.

A good commander knows when to call retreat. Kraven sighed. 'Perhaps we can hope for a better grade by the end of the semester. We'll talk again after my return from Los Angeles.'

'I'll be waiting for you.' She reached for her bag and stood up.

The door closed behind her. Kraven collapsed into his chair.

How had it happened? Only minutes before, he had been en route to Los Angeles, his fingers as good as curling around an icy plastic tumbler, the first drink of his flight.

What folly, what utter folly! He had paid too little heed to the cryptic warnings of anti-Kraven forces, had believed himself safe from demonic hostility in the New World. Hubris had brought him down. His eyes stung; he flushed; he gulped. What trick, what device, what starting–hole canst thou now find out, to hide thee from this open and apparent shame?

He picked up his travel voucher, intending to tear it in pieces, this bitterly ironic icon of his lost world, when he experienced a sudden epiphany. Oh, Kraven of little faith! Was it not likely that the Shaper himself had shown his hand in the apparent error of Tamara Grieben? He struck his forehead after the admired manner of Diotima von Hoden. And was not the Shaper's hand resolved into a finger pointing to London? Likely? No, it was certain.

What a fool he had been! Looked at from his new vantage of understanding, the last few days had presented him with a series of promptings, of urgings, each a little stronger than the last. Kraven was able to see, albeit dimly, a hint of the Great Artificer's plan. In the deep backward and abysm of time, something was shaping. His destiny called him; he would not shrink. Gallant Kraven would run to meet his future as another into a lover's arms. Tonight. There must be no hesitation.

Airline voucher in hand, Kraven left his office. Eastward ho!

Part Two

London
Mid to Late Spring, 1974

NINE

TO OUTWARD APPEARANCE AT LEAST Aunt Cicely's house was unchanged from the days when it was her father's. A wooden gate bisected precisely the tall, well-trimmed hedge that marked off the property from the public pavement. From the gate a crazy-paving path snaked its way towards the arched front door. A robust English lawn on either side of the path led to border flowerbeds and rockeries and again to tall, well-trimmed hedges, these hiding Grandpa Blum's front garden from the unwanted admiration of neighbours. The house itself was massive, three storeys, not counting the attic floor, and it was built in mock-Tudor style, white stucco over brick, non-functional aged beams between the floors, a plethora of quaint brick chimneys, leaded-light windows.

Kraven stood at the door and rang the bell. Of the rain that had greeted him at Heathrow there was no longer a trace; the sky, a lively blue, was punctuated here and there by friendly puffs of white cloud. He rang the bell again and heard footsteps. The door opened.

'Hello, Aunt Cicely.'

There was a small shriek. 'Nicholas! Is it really you? I can't *believe* it! Come in, come in, do!'

This was his Aunt Cicely all right but a Cicely strangely altered. In the decade since last he had seen her she had shed ten years. She had put on weight; she was almost plump.

159

And what had become of the wild mop of grey hair combed before breakfast and then allowed to follow its will? Cicely's hair was now a rich reddish brown, modishly cut, and softly shaped. She was wearing cosmetics. Instead of the shapeless 'sensible' tweeds of yore, she had on a dress of colourful heavy silk.

'You look absolutely spiffing!'

'Ah, you rogue,' she said, clearly delighted, 'just like your father.' She hugged him. 'But what on earth has brought you here like this, so unexpectedly? Oh, no! *Not* my letter? How thoughtless of me! There was nothing urgent, nothing at all. I'm getting on, you know, and so there were things I wanted to talk about.'

Ah, but the letter had been one of the Divine Shaper's promptings. 'Not to worry. I've plenty of work to do at the British Library. I would have come anyway in the summer. Your letter merely focused my attention. Why wait? I thought. Luckily, a junior colleague was able to cover my lectures.'

'It's worked out well for you, then, this American adventure?'

'Pretty well. We can't expect total success. You remember Onkel Ferri and his demons?'

'Indeed I do. A kindly man, if a bit *odd*, like *all* your lot.'

'Look, I don't suppose you could put me up for the night? I'll book into a hotel tomorrow.'

'No trouble at all. One of the spare bedrooms is all right. A bit damp, I expect, but if it's only for the night, it'll do. We can have it airing all day. Mr Fishbane's in Grandpa's old room, or you could have that.'

'Mr Fishbane?'

'How silly of me! You don't know, how could you?' For a moment she giggled, her hands held girlishly over her mouth, her eyelids lowered. 'I have a boarder now, what a *lark*, eh? An elderly gentleman, by your standards, I suppose. We hit it off the moment we met, you know how such things sometimes go. And so you see, I've got a boarder.' She lowered her eyes modestly. 'He's not *actually* a boarder, of course. No, he's my friend, is Mr Fishbane, my special friend. It's made *such* a difference.'

'Well, perhaps it's too inconvenient. . . .'

'Nonsense, won't hear of it, not to worry. Besides, you're here because of my letter – with Mr Fishbane's connivance, as you've probably already guessed. But come along, you simply *must* meet him. You'll like him, I know. Well, anybody would.' She took her nephew by the hand and led him to the back of the house, through the scullery and into the kitchen.

In a rocking chair before the fire sat Mr Fishbane, old and diminutive, eating from a bowl of porridge that he held hugged to his chest, his head bent, the tip of his beaked nose almost in the milk. He wore a black waistcoat, unbuttoned, over a striped shirt whose detachable collar was elsewhere. A tartan shawl draped over his shoulders and tartan slippers depending wanly from his toes proclaimed him at once a Campbell and a McTavish. As they entered the kitchen, he looked up from his bowl: a thin sharp face from which red-rimmed eyes glittered oddly, as if covered in translucent webbing.

'Percy, you'll *never* guess! Look who it is. My nephew Nicholas, come to pay us a visit. Our letter certainly did the trick, didn't it?'

'Hiya, kiddo!'

'Mr Fishbane lived in America for many years.'

'Lewissohn Stadium, Third Avenue El, Ebbets Field,' said Mr Fishbane. 'Know New York like the back of me hand.'

'Sit down, Nicholas, over there, at the table. Did you have a good flight? You must be exhausted. I'll get you something to eat.'

161

'Don't trouble, I'm not in the least hungry.'

'Rustle him up some toast. *And* a pot a tea.' To still all protest, Fishbane held one hand with the flat of the palm towards Kraven. 'No trouble, none at all.' With his other hand he offered his empty bowl vaguely in the direction of Aunt Cicely, who took it from him, smiling proudly, and carried it off into the scullery. He had not once taken his glittery eyes off Kraven. 'Okey-dokey, so you're fresh in from the good old Hew Hess of Hay, right, mac?'

'Aunt Cicely's letter suggested urgency. . .'

'Course, they did put down the Atlantic Cable a few years ago, or I miss my guess. A tootle on the blower would've done, would've done nicely.' Fishbane removed a cigarette from its hiding place behind his ear and placed it between his lips, from which it hung limply and soon wetly.

'Besides, I have the odd item to check at the British Library. . .'

'I suppose you know the famous Karl Marx chair? You haven't actually sat in it, have you?'

'There *is* no Karl Marx chair, in point of fact. It's something of a myth.'

'Ah, yes, well,' sneered Fishbane. 'Something to keep the proletariat quiet, no doubt.' He grinned in the manner of a debater who has scored a most telling point. 'Ever been to Highgate Cemetery? It's not far from here, worth a visit. He's buried there, y'know – unless that turns out to be a myth too.'

Into the kitchen came Aunt Cicely, bearing tea and toast. Fishbane placed his gnarled claws on the arms of the rocking chair and shot himself energetically to his feet. Once on these he exercised his elbows for a moment, strutted like a bantam rooster to the table, and hopped on to a chair opposite Kraven, to whom he said courteously, 'Everything jake, bub?'

'Oh, quite.'

162

Thus assured, Fishbane bent over his toast and began to gobble.

'I'll leave the two of you to a nice chat,' said Aunt Cicely. 'Nicko's room needs airing, Percy. I'm putting him in the one next to yours.'

Fishbane, busily chewing, waved his knife at her, as who should say, by all means, not to worry on my account.

They ate in silence, or, if not in silence, then without words.

Kraven looked out of the window. It was beginning to cloud up again. Low black clouds against a background of higher grey were racing in rapidly from the west. The leaves on the trees had begun to stir in anticipation of a weather change. And yet the sun still shone from the faultless blue that filled the rest of the sky. Rain or no rain, he would have to go out. He felt himself to be an intruder in the established domestic arrangements of others.

The old man pushed away his plate and opened the trouser button at his waist. 'All right,' he said, 'let's hear from the intellectual élite, let's have the view from the academy.'

'On what?'

'Don't give me that. We know all about the protests here, the peace marches, the sit-ins. You've got a society on the verge of collapse there, feller. Well, anyone with half a brain knew it was coming. You can't go on beating down the bleeding masses year in year out and not expect an explosion.'

'I've rather kept my nose out of politics.'

'Have you, indeed? No doubt, no doubt. Not all of us were so lucky. Yours everso truly ain't been back in more'n twenty years. Got my bleeding arse out while the going was good. Used to write a column for *The Workers' Trumpet*, you've heard of that democratic organ, no doubt. Last of the dailies to tell the unvarnished truth?'

'What made you leave? Homesickness?'

'Un-American Activities Committee. Remember the fucker with the shit-eating grin? The Feds were after my ass.'

'Good lord, what on earth for?'

'That would be telling, wouldn't it?' Fishbane placed a horny finger at the side of his nose and gave a conspirator's wink. 'I won't say I carried a certain card, but I won't say I didn't have a card at all.'

'I see.'

'Oh, you do, do you?' said Fishbane angrily. 'The bleeding Feds thought they saw too. You can't carve up a man's life like it was a salami. What I was looking for was justice, that's all. That's why I wrote for the *Trumpet*. We didn't want to overthrow the bleeding guv'ment. All we wanted was a fair shake for the ordinary stiff.'

'Good for you.'

'Ah, yes, well,' said Fishbane, mollified.

Sounds from the scullery told them of Aunt Cicely's return. Fishbane, never moving his glittery eyes off Kraven, moved his mouth to the scullery side of his face and raised his voice: 'That you, Ciss?'

'Here I am,' said Aunt Cicely genially, joining them.

'Interesting feller, your nephew, Ciss, very interesting. Course, he doesn't have the commitment you and me's got. He doesn't say much, either, but I can tell he's got a lot on the ball.'

'I opened the window a bit and put on the electric fire, Nicholas, but I don't think the bed should be made up yet. If you need to lie down, you'd better use my room, at least until yours dries out.'

'Thanks awfully, Aunt Cicely.'

'Thenks hawfully, Ornt Cicely,' mouthed Fishbane *sotto voce*.

'I'm not tired, actually. Thought I'd walk around London for a bit.'

'La-dee-da,' mouthed Fishbane.

'But, Nicholas, we've oodles to talk about.'

'Aw, there's plenty of time for that. The kid's on vacation. Let him take in the sights. Am I right, feller?'

'Right as rain.'

The first fat drops were, in fact, at that very moment spattering the windowpane.

* * *

THE RAIN WAS BEGINNING TO LET UP. It was now early evening and Kraven had walked miles, a compulsive meandering trek through the maze of London. He was no longer aware of being abroad, had long since given over directional control to his feet. The city had sunk with the damp into his bones, claiming him once more. His New York self was otherwhere.

Kraven had pursued a path that twisted and looped around the city and often turned in upon itself. Now he had just emerged from New Bond Street and was making for Oxford Circus. Why, he could not have said. He was wretchedly tired and yet slogged on, walking on the cushions of raw, exquisitely painful blisters. But he would not think of quitting. Indeed, he was by now incapable of any coherent thought at all. His mind was a whirl of fragments, the multitudinous chaotic elements of his own life aloft in riotous dance with his impressions of the city, his red-rimmed eyes snapping scene after scene and tossing the shots into the mental mêlée. Wincing, and striving to smile as he winced, Kraven limped on.

Oxford Street itself had fallen on evil days, a seediness and a greyness that the lowering skies and the wind that whipped and skirled the paper rubbish about the pavements did nothing to mitigate. The grand old department stores, or some of them, fought a rearguard action against the loss of grace, but civility and elegance had fled else-where. Their strong fortress in Mayfair remained, to be sure, as did a few ill-defended redoubts in Regent Street, Jermyn Street and Piccadilly. But by and large they had pitched their standards to the south and west, in Kensington, in Knightsbridge, in Sloane Street, in the Brompton Road. Foreigners, of whom there was, it seemed to Kraven, an unconscionable number in London, jostling everywhere, babbling in their frenetic languages, peering at maps, puzzling at buildings and plaques and statues, foreigners actually photographed one another outside Harrods. Kraven had seen them do it.

But Oxford Street, though more crowded than ever during business hours, though swarming with tourists, had become honky-tonk. It was a blaring line of fast-food bars, liquor stores, jeans outlets, employment agencies, pawnbrokers, shoe shops. London had ceded Oxford Street to the Princips and Corombonas, native and foreign, the disorderly and unspeakable young, ceded it along with Piccadilly Circus, Leicester Square, Shaftesbury Avenue. Gone, all gone. . . Regent Street was going, and Lower Regent Street, and the Haymarket. Kraven turned south and then west, making for Hyde Park Corner.

But perhaps this was wisdom's way, a deliberate plan of containment: confine them here, here, and here. Meanwhile, the city was cleaner than Kraven remembered it, soot-free. And in this season the trees were in bud, blossom and leaf: London was green. And in the odd moments between rain showers when the clouds had parted, the city, washed and bleached, sparkled.

He turned off Piccadilly and on to Old Park Lane. It was now that his feet gave up. Quite simply, he could walk no more. Just ahead of him was the Inn on the Park. Perhaps a drink would lift his spirits. As he turned into the driveway, a taxi wheeled smartly in front of him, its wheels sending up a filthy spray. He leaped back heroically, wincing on aching feet, and spared himself a dousing. Meanwhile, a doorman in a truncated top hat stepped up smartly to the taxi and opened its door.

First to appear was a long, elegantly shaped leg, held in the air for a second, the toe pointing downward; then the head, beautiful and adorned with a blonde afro, smiling unseeingly left and right at an assumed audience; and then the rest of her, descending with a delicious wriggle and a sharp bump. To the doorman who had assisted her she blew a kiss. It was Dolly Divine. Kraven was on the point of calling to her when he saw a second figure scramble out of the taxi, a figure that shook him out of his weariness and brought a smile to his lips. For there, paying off the driver, was none other than Robert Poore-Moody. Kraven stepped behind a pillar and stared at him, hardly able to credit his eyes. But it was, without question, Stella's husband, a man who himself, evidently, was a victim of demons. Here, then, was Dolly's angel, the mysterious Bobby. Well, Kraven had promised Stella he would find Poore-Moody and, by God, he had found him.

Poore-Moody followed Dolly into the lobby; Kraven at a safe distance followed Poore-Moody. Once inside, Dolly took the old man possessively by the arm, and together they climbed the stairs to the mezzanine, she towering above him. Kraven watched as Dolly bent over Poore-Moody and kissed him on the top of his head. Poore-Moody seized her hand, held it to his heart for a moment, then kissed it passionately, and at last, reluctantly, let it go. He went to the lift. She stood where he had left her, waving to him until the lift doors closed.

'Dolly!' said Kraven then, stepping forward.

She turned, looked at him myopically for a moment, then grinned. 'Gee, look who's here. Hi, Marty.'

'So how's the Big Time?'

She frowned. 'Maybe not so hot.'

'Not lost your angel, I hope.'

'Nothing like that. You got a minute? I'm supposed to be meeting the girls inside. Come say hallo.'

Kraven looked at his watch. He was anxious to send off a telegram to Stella; on the other hand, he rather wanted to see Candy again. 'Well, just for a minute.'

He accompanied Dolly to the bar lounge. At the entrance she paused and surveyed the room, which at that hour was quite full. Sugar Plum, seated at one of the tables, waved to her. Dolly waved back and ground her way across. The muted hum in the room ceased; all eyes, it seemed, followed her progress. She smiled and nodded unseeingly at her audience.

'Candy not here yet?' said Dolly. 'Look who I found.'

'Well hi, Marty.' Sugar seemed no more surprised to see him than had Dolly. Perhaps such encounters were the norm in the show-business world.

'Hi yourself.'

Kraven and Dolly sat down and the room's hum resumed.

'How'd it go? How'd you and Bobby make out?' said Sugar.

'No need to break out the champagne,' said Dolly glumly. 'I told you not to get your hopes up.' She sighed.

'Oh no, Dolly,' said Sugar. 'What happened?'

'Bobby's got these theatrical contacts over here, big shots,' Dolly explained to Kraven. 'That's where we were today. Feeling them out, seeing if they'd bite.' She turned to Sugar. 'Not a chance,' she said. 'The Royal Shakespeare don't wanna touch it, not even if Bobby agrees to take the loss. Y'know, at first they thought we was just kidding. "Remarkable sense of humour, old boy!" They said maybe somewheres in the boonies, like maybe Harrogate, maybe. In the off-season. Only maybe. Well, I'll say this for Bobby: he's loyal. He told them where they could shove it.'

'Aw, gee, Dolly' said Sugar.

'I told Bobby maybe I should consider the boonies. I mean, what the heck. We have a hit up there, we can always open in London later. But you know Bobby. I open in the West End or I don't open.'

'So what now?' asked Kraven.

Dolly shrugged. 'We're looking for a new vehicle. Find a vehicle, says Bobby, and he'll take care of the rest. He says I'm a natural for musical comedy. Could be he's right. He didn't get to be a mult-eye millionaire just by whistling Dixie.'

Kraven fought to keep his eyes open.

'I know Bobby don't like me showing my whatsis around,' Dolly was saying. 'Men get kinda possessive, no offence, Marty. So maybe that's why he's talking musical comedy. I take his advice, that's a factor I gotta consider.'

'You ain't giving up on the *Follies*, are ya, Dolly?' wailed Sugar. 'What about me?' She turned to Kraven. 'There's this great number where all's I'm wearing's just these two itty-bitty snakes. Y'know, I'm this Egyptian queen?'

'*Antony and Cleopatra?*' said Kraven.

'Yeah, that's it, that's the one. Dolly promised.'

'Bobby's doing his best,' said Dolly. 'He's still got a couple a contacts.'

A gloom was beginning to settle, however. To Kraven, comfortably seated in the warmth of the Inn on the Park, the exhaustion of his hours-long London wanderings had returned. His eyelids were unbearably heavy. 'Cheer up, girls,' he said. '*Bardic Follies* is too big an idea to disappear. Someone will pick it up. Maybe Paris, West Berlin.' He struggled to his feet.

'You leaving?' said Dolly. 'Candy'll be here any minute. Let's have a drink.'

'Candy thought you were really cute,' said Sugar.

'C'mon now, Sugar!' admonished Dolly.

The news pleased Kraven, even excited him. But he had Underground miles to go before he slept. And there was still a telegram to be sent to Stella. 'You're staying here yet a while, aren't you? Good. Tell Candy how sorry I am I missed her. I'll be in touch. Please tell her that.'

'See ya,' said Dolly and Sugar.

* * *

DARLING STELLA, HAVE LOCATED ERRANT MONK IN COMPANY OF THREE, REPEAT THREE, UNFROCKED NUNS. FRA ROBERTO STAYING AT INN ON THE PARK, LONDON. SUSPECT HERESY. WIRE INSTRUCTIONS C/O AMEX, HAYMARKET. NICHOLAS.

* * *

KRAVEN FOUND IT DIFFICULT TO FALL ASLEEP. Aunt Cicely's efforts to dry out the room had produced an equatorial climate, the Matto Grosso in the rainy season. The air was hot, humid, unbreathable; the room stank of jungle rot. He lay naked on the bed, turning now to this side, now to that, his body wet, a helpless surface for condensation.

Through the steaming jungle he now flew, flitting, darting, away, away, through verdurous glooms and winding mossy ways. The slap-slap-slap of slippers going past his door returned him to his sole self. The door to Fishbane's room opened and closed. A bed creaked and creaked again. The unmistakable sound of soft flesh making violent contact with soft flesh announced itself.

The creaking, now rhythmical, began slowly but soon picked up speed. Grunts.

Kraven threw his pillow over his head.

A sharp cry.

'O Percy, o Percy, o Perce–erce–erce–eeeEEE!'

'Cock-a-doodle-doo! Cock-a-doodle-doo!'

Silence.

Kraven fell at last into a fitful sleep.

'He forced me,' Nimuë said bravely, 'to engage in prac-tices the vilest and the most perverse, acts that bring a blush in recollection to modesty's fair cheek. What cared he for maidenly innocence? What cared he for ought but satisfac-tion of his cruel and bestial lusts.'

In the panelled courtroom cries of horror, cries of shock. A sob, 'Alas, the poor, sweet child.'

His Lordship adjusted his wig and looked grave.

'The wretch,' said Princip, pointing an impassioned finger at Prisoner-at-the-Bar, 'lured the young virgin into his iniquitous den under a shameful subterfuge, which was no other than to help her polish her already brightly shining verse. I submit for m'lud's perusal and certain delight a not-untypical example of her exquisite poetry. M'lud will notice in particular the sentiment.'

His Lordship looked from the poem 'Cousinhoodship IV' to Prisoner-at-the-Bar. 'Tsk-tsk.'

'No sooner had she entered his rooms, this vestal of Apollo and the Muses, than he threw her upon his sybaritic couch and would have tried her *à l'outrance.*'

Cries of 'No, no. Oh, the fiend!'

'He would, I say, have tried her thus had I not rashly – and praised be rashness for it – burst in upon them. There is a divinity that shapes our ends, rough-hew them how we will.'

'That is most certain.' His Lordship frowned at Prisoner-at-the-Bar and turned again to the witness. 'What prompted you so to burst in, as you say, upon them?'

'Why, even in that was heaven ordinant. He had affronted me of late, had called me villain, plucked my beard and blown it in my face. . .'

'Is't possible?'

'I had his phonic number in my purse. Here's the transcription, read it at more leisure. I am not pigeon-livered.'

'Most commendable. Next witness.'

The next witness swayed in the box. 'The prisoner is a thief, a charlatan.'

'The name of the witness?'

'Alec Feibelman, traveler in ladies' personals, retired.'

His Lordship noted with compassion the venerable age and attendant frailty of the witness. 'Bailiff, provide a *sella*, or in the base vulgar a chair, a seat, a stool, for his honorificabilitudinity.'

'Thank you, m'lud. Know then that this vile rogue snatched from me my discovery of the Jewish Charlemagne and passed it current for his own.'

'O, the wretch! For shame!'

'Mine was not the good fortune of the fair and yet unspotted Nimuë.' La Corombona settled herself in the witness box amid gasps from the thronged courtroom. Her cheeks and lips were carmined, her full breasts pushed against the laces of her bodice. 'He took me in the blossom of my virginal innocence, an orphan whose only treasure was her untried virtue, rammed through the portcullis of an unmanned fort, and plucked the rose. What route through life was left me but the poxy way to Hell?'

Last came and last did go C.U.T. Quimby. 'M'lud, it grieves me to report that the prisoner is not at all who he purports to be. In brief, he is an impostor!'

A sensation in the court.

'Prisoner-at-the-Bar,' said His Lordship, placing over his wig a black square of silk, 'have you anything to say before I pass sentence?'

'M'lud, I have been most notoriously abused.'

His Lordship sniffed.

'M'lud, I am a human being.'

'So say they all. Be so good as to wait outside.'

Kraven was woken again during the night by another crowing of the cock.

TEN

KRAVEN ROSE EARLY THE NEXT MORNING, despite his restless night, and he was frustrated in his desire for a tranquil start to the day by Percy Fishbane, who padded into the kitchen even as he was sitting down to a cup of tea. Fishbane was clad in a woolly tartan dressing-gown that touched the floor and beneath which the tips of tiny tartan slippers peeped out.

'Morning,' said Fishbane cheerily. 'Ah, tea. Good-o.'

Kraven groaned.

'No, don't get up. Yours Truly will get his own cup.' He disappeared into the scullery for a moment, returned with a mug marked with a florid letter P, and hopped on to a chair at the table. 'Auntie likes to have a bit of an extra kip on the occasional morning, so me and you are going to have t'look after ourselves. How about some toast and jam, then?'

'Thanks, I'd like that.'

'Bread's in the box, butter's in the fridge, jam's in the cupboard.' Fishbane jerked his head in the several directions.

Mumbling to himself, Kraven set about preparing their breakfast.

'I heard you getting up, not that you made much noise, but Yours Truly's a light sleeper. Here's an opportunity, Perce, says I, for me and him to have a little chinwag.'

'I'm going to have to leave in a few moments. I've one or two things to take care of.'

'No doubt, no doubt,' said Fishbane imperturbably. 'However, you've still to have your tea and toast. Time in plenty for what Yours Truly has to say.' He took a mouthful of tea and swilled it around noisily before swallowing. 'What I'm going to tell you now your auntie knows nothing about, and until or unless I give the word I rely on you as a comrade in affairs of the heart to keep it that way.' He searched Kraven's face with his glittering eyes; Kraven nodded. 'As you have already guessed, this is a matter of no small delicacy.' He paused significantly; Kraven nodded again. 'Hence, I have to spend a moment putting you in the historical picture.' He spooned jam on to a corner of his toast and bit it off, chewed slowly, staring the while at the ceiling as if hoping there to find fit words. At last, he embarked upon his narrative.

To Fishbane's account of his early years in America, his loneliness, his enthusiasm for the Brooklyn Dodgers, his futile attempts to awaken political consciousness in the masses – 'it was like trying to incite the meek to inherit the earth' – his hackwork for left-wing journals, his growing conviction that he was being watched by the FBI – to all of this Kraven paid scant attention. His mind was occupied with Poore-Moody and Stella. But some of Fishbane's narrative penetrated his private thoughts.

'Her name,' said Fishbane with tremulous reverence, 'was Miriam Pechvogel.' His glittering eyes scanned the past. 'She had other names, of a professional sort, but Miriam Pechvogel was what she was born.'

Tuning in and out, Kraven gathered that Miriam Pechvogel, 'an *artiste*', 'a real swell dame', was the first true love of Fishbane's lonely life. Fishbane could not believe his good luck. What a woman of such opulent beauty could see in him he was unable to fathom. 'She used t'call me her bantam cock.' When he had met her, a little over a year before he was forced to flee the States, she already had two children

175

out of wedlock by different men. 'None of your booshwa petty morality about her. Philosophically, we were both advocates of free love.'

A shift in tone indicated that Fishbane's tale was approaching its climax. Kraven paid closer attention. Such was the lovers' passionate abandon that Miss Pechvogel in due course became *enceinte*. Percy Fishbane was to be a father. Meanwhile the FBI were snooping around, talking to the neighbours, even questioning Miss Pechvogel's children in the schoolyard. 'All I was was a harmless reporter, forty-five dollars a week, exposing the fascist government's union-busting tactics. You'd a thought I was an expert in nuclear physics!' A tip from a friend told of imminent arrests at the newspaper offices. Fishbane had put his passport in his jacket pocket and shipped out immediately, arriving in England with little more than the clothes on his back.

'Here's the point: I've a kid over there who must be in his twenties by now, who I've never met, and who I know nothing about. When I left New York, Miriam was in Chicago. She was in her fourth month, one of her last appearances before the public. In her line of work you can't go on performing right up to the last minute, now can you?' Fearful of wire taps and conscious of the need to move swiftly, he had been unable to get in touch with her. Later, the thought that he might jeopardize her career, that she might be blacklisted – 'they were opening people's fucking letters; they were coming down hard on people in show business' – prevented him from writing to her. By the time the Senator from Wisconsin was no longer a threat and the hysteria in the country had died down, Fishbane had lost his sense of urgency. He had already picked up his life again in England.

'Me and Miriam, that's water under the bridge,' he said. 'Besides, I'm happily situated now, and I hope Miriam is too. I love your auntie, and I've come to appreciate the benefits of intellectual companionship and the refinements that come of a booshwa upbringing. Not that I've turned me back on old truths. But I now know that good manners sometimes reveal a good heart.' He looked shrewdly at Kraven.

Kraven was not unmoved by Fishbane's story, but he had problems of his own. He looked pointedly at his watch.

'A little patience, that's all Yours Truly asks,' said Fishbane aggrievedly, 'hear me out. Why don't you have some more tea.' He poured some into Kraven's cup. 'I've put a bit by over the years, took a leaf from the capitalists' book. And why not? I've been a slave all me life. Whatever goes into my pocket don't go into the pockets of those fuckers. The poor sodding peons'll be trampled on regardless. So I've made the odd investment or two. Did quite well on Mexican silver, thanks to a tip from your auntie.

'Well, who'm I going t'leave it to? Here's where you come in. Undertake a few discreet inquiries for me in the Hew Hess of Hay. I can tell you where to start. Try and find Percy Fishbane's son. Who knows what he's up to? Given the sort of upbringing he's likely to 've had, chances are he's in bleeding prison. Miriam's circles, as you can well imagine, were not the most elevated, all things considered. But don't delay too long. Time and tide, you know.'

'I'll do what I can, of course. But my plans are rather unsettled at the moment. I don't know when I'm returning to the States.'

Fishbane made a dismissive gesture. 'It's no emergency. You can stay here as long as you like, three days, four, five. No need to go off to an hotel, even, on my account. As Yours Truly is pleased to tell you, this is Liberty Hall. But once you *do* get back there. . .' He looked up suddenly. 'Morning, Ciss. Have a nice kip, did you?'

Aunt Cicely in a fashionable silk robe stood at the kitchen door. 'There you are, you two. Who would like onions and eggs?'

177

'Suit me a treat,' said Fishbane. 'Me and your nephew 've had a very nice chat, Ciss, very nice indeed. We're better acquainted now, which was all that Percy Fishbane wanted.'

'None for me, thanks. I've some things to do in town,' Kraven told his aunt. 'I'll be back in mid-afternoon to get my bags.'

'Off you go then,' said Fishbane. 'Don't forget what I told you.'

'What was that, Percy?'

'Men-talk,' said Fishbane blithely.

* * *

What might await him back at Mosholu Kraven preferred not to think. At the very least he would be required to reimburse the college for his air ticket. This cost might be offset, however, if the IRS could be persuaded that the trip was a legitimate professional necessity. Hence, he was off to the British Library to acquire one or two date-stamped book-request slips. He turned into the grand forecourt of the Museum. A banner athwart the grim façade announced a current exhibition of Michelangelo drawings. He would pop into the Reading Room, acquire his evidence, and then spend a pleasant hour at the exhibition.

An unexpected figure was descending the steps before the main entrance and emerging into the bright sunshine. It was Candy Peaches. Say what you will about burlesque, it had taught her to perform so humdrum an activity with uncommonly sensuous grace. But there was nothing suggestive of burlesque about her appearance today. She wore a smart, almost severe navy-blue business suit, softened by a floppy lace bow at the neck of a white blouse. Her gorgeous hair was neatly arranged. She offered him a dazzling smile.

'Jesus, Marty, you look awful. What the hell've you been up to, or shouldn't I ask?'

London, for all its teeming millions, was a village. 'Sorry I missed you yesterday. I waited as long as I could.'

'Yeah, well, Sugar told me. How come you're limping?'

Kraven's feet, hastily bandaged that morning, were painfully blistered from his wanderings. 'Stubbed my toe getting out of bed.'

He gestured at the Museum behind her. 'Seeing the sights?'

'Y'might say that.' She blew him a bubble of gum, withdrew it, chewed, and grinned. 'Hey, buy a girl a cup of coffee?'

'A cup of coffee it is.' The Reading Room and Michelangelo could wait. She took his arm and together they wandered in search of a coffee shop.

Seated across from her at a small, wobbly table, their coffee before them, Kraven was enjoying this moment of intimacy with a beautiful young woman. From the depths of his tiredness he summoned his charm. 'I wonder whether you've made plans for this evening?'

She held up her hands in mock horror and flashed him her bewitching smile. 'Hey, am I safe out with you like this?'

Kraven, feeling encouraged and thinking he recognized the script, pressed on. 'So far you are, but I make no promises.'

'Marty, there's a couple of things I gotta make clear right off.' She counted them on her slender fingers. 'First, I'm not stupid; second, I'm not an easy lay.'

Kraven, thrown completely off his stride, said, 'Oh.'

She laughed at his consternation. 'Hey, c'mon now, we can still be friends.' She grinned impishly. 'Some of my best friends are guys.'

Kraven attempted a smile.

'Most guys, I tell them that, they think right away they're the exceptions. "Just lay back and relax, honey, you're gonna love this." ' She made a few swift passes with the flat of her hand held stiffly before her. 'I'm pretty good at karate. No, there's nothing wrong with my libido. It's just I like to think my body belongs to me, like I maybe have some say in its proper operation and use.'

'Most commendable,' said Kraven faintly. 'Still, that hardly seems consistent with your choice of profession. I mean, an ecdysiast is scarcely protecting her privacy. And the performance itself invites the kind of male response you're condemning.'

'Oh that,' she said. 'Well, there's privacy and privacy, but maybe you've got a point. It's worth considering anyway.' She took a piece of paper from her pocketbook and jotted down a note to herself. 'I'll take it up with my shrink. But stripping's not my profession. I sort of slipped into that through family connections.' She winked. 'Even Momma can still shimmy. She's got a little place out in Sausalito, Mimi-a-Go-Go. Every now and then she does one of her numbers for the old-timers. For me, though, burlesque's only moonlighting. The pay's good, you'd be surprised. I stripped my way through Ohio State, and now I'm stripping my way through graduate school.'

O brave new world that has such creatures in it! He was unable to mask his surprise.

'First impressions, Marty?' She laughed with delight.

'But what are you studying? Where are you doing your work?'

'Psychology, at Yale. Right now I'm working on my master's thesis: "Displaced Eroticism in the Fiction of Early Nineteenth-Century Women Writers." When I'm through with her, Jane Austen will never look the same.'

She glanced at her watch. 'Which reminds me, I've still a couple of hours ahead of me in the Reading Room. Let's get down to cases, okay? I've been straight with you, and I want you to be straight with me.' She placed her hand over his. 'I doubt your name's Martin Chuzzlewit, I know my Dickens. I also know Spinoza's Burly-Que, and I'm willing to bet you're not a customer. So I'm asking you right out, what d'you want with Dolly and Sugar? They're my sisters. They're not exactly mental powerhouses, and I don't want them hurt.'

Startled by this frontal assault, Kraven fell back on the truth. At any rate, he told her his name and his academic affiliation. As for his interest in the sisters, he had met three beautiful young women without male escorts. It was pleasant to talk to them. Surely that wasn't so odd? Certainly he meant none of them any harm. And look, it had paid off for him, hadn't it? Weren't he and Candy having a friendly chat right now?

'Did you follow me to the Museum today?'

'Certainly not!' Since this *was* in fact the truth, his voice carried conviction.

'You married, Marty?'

'Nicholas, remember? No, of course not.'

'Don't be so shocked. I was just wondering why you didn't give us your real name.'

Once again, Kraven was forced back on the truth. 'I've got into a rather bad habit of lying in recent years. Usually for no good reason.'

'I used to be like that,' she said. 'But then I grew up. Break the habit, Nicholas. Especially if we're going to be friends.'

'You're on,' he said. Ah, if only it were that simple.

They got up to leave.

'I'll walk you back to the Museum, if that's okay,' he said, 'but I think I'll put off my own visit for today.'

She took his arm. They walked in silence for a moment.

'Are Dolly and Sugar serious about *Bardic Follies*?' he said.

Candy grinned. 'Oh, they're serious all right. Once in a while Dolly gets a bug in her head. Nothing'll come of it. She's good at what she does. Really. She's one of the best in

181

the business. Sugar's pretty good too, but somehow she's never gotten top billing. Listen, I love them, they're my big sisters, so don't get me wrong. But legit? Not this time.'

'That scene from *Hamlet*, though, you'll admit it was extraordinary.'

'Sure, I'll admit *that*,' she said, 'but Dolly wants to open at the Old Vic, the Garrick at the very least.' She squeezed his arm.

'What about Bobby in all of this?'

Candy shrugged. 'Who knows? Dolly can take care of herself when it comes to romance. Maybe she's found herself an angel, maybe something more. She says he's cute. She should know.'

They had arrived back at the Museum.

'Good luck on Jane Austen,' he said. 'I enjoyed this afternoon.'

'Me too. By the way, in answer to your first question, I'm *not* free this evening. But there *are* other evenings. Keep in touch.'

She stood on her toes and kissed him gently on the cheek. He waited and watched until the Museum swallowed her up.

* * *

Aunt Cicely's particular friend was out when Kraven got back to Hendon to pick up his bags. He was at the lending library, in fact, where he did *so* like to pass an hour or two at least once a week. 'Mr Fishbane is a devoted reader of the Russian classics,' Aunt Cicely explained. 'He'll be back soon, but we have plenty of time before that for our little talk.'

They sat together in the front room, eating hot buttered scones and drinking tea.

'You've changed, Nicholas.'

'Not for the worse, I hope.'

'I don't feel I know you. It's as if you weren't *settled* in yourself, as if you were somehow uncomfortable in your own body. Adrift, somehow.'

'Things change, people change. Time passes. You've changed too, you know.'

'Mr Fishbane means well.'

'I'm sure he does.'

'You mustn't think ill of him because he's a bit. . .'

'Coarse?'

'Please don't say that. He's not had our advantages. But he's got strong family feelings, perhaps because he's all alone himself. He thought it wrong that we were so out of touch. He's a *good* man.'

Kraven relented. 'He must be, if he's your special friend.'

She smiled. 'But business first, Nicholas, dear. I want you to know the house in Hampstead is still yours, I never sold it. In fact, I've been letting it out on short leases – for the most part to American academics. There's a Professor Luft-mensch there right now. He holds a Chair somewhere in Inter-Personal Dynamics, whatever *that* is. But he's moving out tomorrow. You're free to do what you want with it once he's gone. And then there's *this* house, which will come to you eventually, together with whatever's left over of Grand-pa's and mine. There, so much for business.'

'Aunt Cicely – '

'No,' she interrupted him, 'not another word.' She paused. 'I didn't get on too well with your father, you know.'

'I know. I always supposed it had something to do with my bastardy.'

'You were *not* a bastard, Nicholas, not that it would make a ha'porth of difference if you were. Mummy and Daddy were married before you were born.'

'A shotgun wedding, though.'

'It almost broke Grandpa's heart. The *shame*, the *disgrace*! It's hard to believe nowadays the fuss that was made over something like that. But of course, Grandpa was frightfully moral. After all, he *was* a Victorian, the genuine article. He even named your mother after the old queen.

'Your father was charming, though, I'll say that; he had a way with him all right. Your mother adored him, absolutely adored him. But he was a dreadful womanizer. They *all* were, *all* the Kravens, even your Uncle Ferri, who was easily the most decent of the lot. Poor Victoria! She'd weep and weep at Felix's infidelities, and he'd jolly her out of it in minutes.

'But you know, Nicholas, I've lived long enough to envy my sister. I envy her the *completeness* of her love for your father. That was it, I think, although at the time I would have died rather than admit it: the sheer physicality of it. She *gloried* in it.

'When your father died, she felt that her own life was over. In some ways it was. You probably don't remember his funeral, you were just a boy at the time, poor little chap. Your mother went almost mad with grief. They wouldn't let her anywhere near the coffin. Good thing too. Barbaric business. The rabbi was a figure out of some Polish horror story.

'Well, now I've got Mr Fishbane and we rattle around in this house together and I *love* him. Oh, I know how he must look to the outside world, but *I* love him.' She turned suddenly. 'Oh Percy, you *did* give me a start!'

Fishbane stood at the door, a tam-o'-shanter on his head, a tartan scarf wrapped thrice around his neck, two books under his arm. 'There you are,' he said. 'A scene of family tranquillity such as would warm the heart of Tolstoy himself. And in the front room, too. It's my humble hope I'm not intruding.'

'Not in the least,' said Kraven affably. 'We were waiting for you to complete the picture.'

Aunt Cicely reached across the tea table and squeezed his hand.

ELEVEN

IT WAS TWO IN THE AFTERNOON of the following day. Kraven sat glumly in the Gaiety Bar of the Hotel Russell. Before him on a little table stood a half-finished glass of light ale and on a paper plate a ham sandwich curling at the edges. The room's purple-and-red decor was conducive to mordant thoughts. A man may rot even here, he reflected. A little while before, he had been to the British Library, not in pursuit of Candy alone, although he had certainly looked for her in the Reading Room, but because he had still to acquire his date-stamped book-request slips. There, sitting in a chair perhaps once occupied by Karl Marx, he had composed a poem inspired by Stella's telegram, found waiting for him at the American Express Office in the Haymarket:

> To Stella
> On His Absence from Her
>
> Since I accept (and must, perforce)
> This simulacrum of divorce
> And in my lonely cot must pine
> The absence of that flesh divine,
> Whose bounteous beauties would inspire
> An Orpheus to restring his lyre,
> What comforts now can cosset me,
> Who've lost mine own Eurydice?

My mind's the attic where I'll trace
The outline of that lovely face
And paint the tint of blushing rose
Upon sweet tissue adipose.
There, with ever-mounting zest
I'll show the curve of luscious breast,
Whereon, half-fainting, I shall stipple
My mistress' boldly-thrusting nipple.
Then the brush will try each part
That erst my prick, with livelier art,
No heady pleasure ever missed,
By far the better pointillist.
   No pagan in the days of yore
His idol ever might adore
As I this image in the mind,
This canvas whereupon I find
My Stella's mere reflection
Can cause me an erection.
   Alas! Fond Fancy's but a cheat:
Food for thought is airy meat.
The artist of the mind grows thinner
For want of a substantial dinner.
Out, out upon it! Woe! Alack!
I want my fleshly Stella back!

He felt his eyes closing, his head sinking on to his chest,
and jerked himself upright. This would never do. From
behind the square enclosure to Kraven's left the bartender
polished a glass and shook his head in sympathy. Kraven
plucked from his pocket Stella's telegram and turned his
back. He unfolded and reread it, although he already had its
message by heart.

DARLING NICHOLAS. ARRIVING LONDON FRIDAY 1500
HOURS. STAYING ESU, CHARLES STREET. BAD NEWS

How her arriving here might further complicate his life he
could not say. He did not know if he had missed her too: nor
did he know if he was glad she was coming. What had she
meant by the trashing of her apartment? Had she been
burglarized? Well, by tomorrow he would know. On the back
of the telegram, and in his self-elected role of lover, he
scribbled a tornada for this morning's poem:

> Venus heard me sigh this ditty,
> Took on me immediate pity,
> Promised a swift end to sorrow:
> Stella flies to me tomorrow!

Kraven lifted his eyes from the telegram and looked across
the room and into the dim alcove beyond. There, seated
alone at at a little table identical to his own, was a rotund
figure, a woman in a belted trenchcoat and slacks. She was
peering beneath the flat of her raised palm, seemingly
directly at him. It was disconcerting. The woman dropped
her hand and let out a shriek.

'Nobby!'

It was Diotima von Hoden, of course – here, as she had
told him only last weekend she would be, for a spot of
grinding at the British Library. Not a village, London was a
hamlet.

'Nobby!'

Kraven looked at his watch in the manner of a man
shocked at learning the lateness of the hour. From the alcove
came the sounds of a table overturning, glass shattering, and
liquid sloshing.

'Nobby!'

He dashed for the door, ran down the steps, and strode as

rapidly and purposefully as his still crippled feet would permit across the street and towards the Square.

'Nobby, wait! It is here Didi!'

He quickened his pace.

Behind him there was a wrenching squeal of brakes, an ugly thud, and then the melancholy demented wail of a stuck car horn. Kraven did not stop.

'Nobby! Only wait, my sweet little sausage . . . stop . . . halt . . . attention!'

People were looking at Kraven now, heads were turning. Panic gripped him. Sweat trickled into his eyes. His heart pounded. Someone, a passer-by, made as if to stop him. He dodged and broke into a run. A dog barked. The car horn wailed.

'Now then, now then, what's all this, then?'

Kraven, his eyes stinging, had run head-on into a policeman, a giant, who held him firmly and inescapably by the upper arm. Luxuriant ginger moustaches descended from his nostrils but soon curved cheerfully upwards to adorn his pink cheeks.

'There's someone after you, m'lad.'

'What?' Kraven turned around in rich astonishment. But he was unable to break thereby the strong grip of the law. Perhaps fifty feet behind them was Diotima, bent almost double, holding on to a lamppost and taking deep, deep breaths. 'Good lord, it's Mother!'

'Ah, it's your mum, is it?' The grip was minutely relaxed.

'Yes.'

'We'll have to see about that then, then. You come along with me, sir.'

With ponderous and stately tread the policeman escorted Kraven back to where Diotima, now upright, stood wheezing at the lamppost.

'What luck meeting up with you like this!' said Kraven, frankly delighted. 'We've the constable to thank, old girl.'

Kraven turned gratefully to the man, peering at his collar insignia. 'Thank you ever so much, PC 49!'

PC 49 released Kraven's arm. He touched his helmet with his forefinger and quoted the Bard. 'All's well that ends well.'

'Ta everso, peeler,' wheezed Diotima, her idiom keyed to the locality.

'Right, then. I'll be getting along.' The stuck car horn came within the purlieus of his attention. 'Tsk-tsk.' He moved off in sober pursuit of the sound.

'You didn't hear me calling? I cried out in full throat and yoo-hooed.'

'No, I'm afraid not. Look, I'm in an awful rush.'

'I've got the potion, Nobby. It's here with me in London.'

'Delighted to hear it. It's been marvellous seeing you again, but I've an appointment with my publishers and I'm already late.'

Diotima had got her breath back. Her eyes narrowed in concentration. 'But we must talk.'

'But not now, Diotima. I really must be off.'

'I stay at the Hotel Ispahan in Swiss Cottage, a hop, a leap and a chump from the station. But where do you stay?'

'The Inn on the Park.' Kraven spoke as one inspired. 'Come to me there tonight, about half-past eight. We'll have dinner in my suite, just the two of us. Champagne, music, and then. . .'

'Oh yes! Tonight, my treasure! Oh yes, oh yes!'

He waggled an admonitory finger at her and winked. 'Don't forget the potion, Didi.'

'Never doubt me, beloved.' She caught his hand and kissed his knuckles roughly. 'Tonight, Nobby Poore-Moody! Tonight, you beautiful little sausage you! Tonight!'

* * *

KRAVEN, WITH BLISTERED FEET, SAT NOW in the genteely worn lounge of the English-Speaking Union waiting for Stella. Two of her countrywomen occupied a far corner and discussed Spode, cashmere and the London theatre. They were much bothered, it seemed, by a draught, but the ancient waiter, perhaps deaf in fact, was certainly deaf to their complaints. Kraven smiled at them sympathetically. It was well known, his smile said, that in America there were no draughts.

He turned the pages of an old copy of the *Tatler*, glancing impatiently every few moments at his watch. He was on the brink of something. Love, it could not be other than love, flooded through him. And who could doubt that his love was returned? Ripe she was and bright she was, and she was his. She was also, some might say, Poore-Moody's, but that was a trifling technicality, a problem that the next day or two would solve. In fact, her loyalty to that elderly reprobate endeared her all the more to Kraven. That she should fly three thousand miles in compassionate pursuit of her mad monk was somehow touching. It was in Kraven's arms, however, that she would find her rest.

Stella's voice, emanating from the reception hall, broke in upon these happy thoughts. She had arrived! He rose to his feet even as she appeared in the doorway. They kissed long and passionately.

He held her by the shoulders at arm's length and gazed at her. 'You grow more and more beautiful,' he said. And so she did. She looked glorious. The dark rings of sleeplessness were on her a sensual fillip and conveyed a heavy warmth.

'Why didn't you phone? You're such a cheapskate! Christ, you could've called collect.' She kissed his earlobe, nipping it as she did so, gently, with her teeth. The tip of her tongue darted into his ear and out again. 'We've so much to talk about. All hell's broken loose in New York. I phoned the college, and then there's the apartment. And what about Robert?' She kissed him again, urgently.

The rattle of a teacup in its saucer reminded him that they were not alone. 'First things first,' he said. 'Let's get you settled in your room.' He jerked his head to indicate to her her compatriots, who were sitting rapt, no longer bothered by the draught.

Stella winked at them. 'Come on, first things first,' she said with Stellar lewdness. 'Get me settled in my room, why don't you?'

'My fiancée,' said Kraven.

'My British lover,' said Stella, and dragged him by the arm.

* * *

THEY MADE LOVE IMPORTUNATELY, wildly, selfishly. They lay in one another's arms, softly caressing skin now made tender, and they kissed and turned and rolled flesh to flesh. And soon they began anew, but gently; and, exhausted at last, lay side by side, her hand gently cupping him, his resting heavily on her cleft wetness.

'Hungry?' he said after a while. 'We'd better make a dinner reservation somewhere. The Red Lion all right?'

'It might seem a little indelicate,' she said, 'in view of our current condition, but I think it's time you told me about Robert.'

'Later. You're right, it's indelicate.'

'But Nicholas – '

'Later. Tell me first about New York. Did I understand you to say you'd phoned the college?'

'What the hell was I supposed to do? I desperately needed to get in touch. I thought they'd give me your London address.'

'I never told them I was coming, for pity's sake! God,

191

Stella, what have you done?' He leaped from the bed and began to pull on his trousers.

'How was *I* to know?' she said. 'Where are you going?'

Kraven had no idea. He sat down beside her on the bed. 'Tell me what happened.'

'What *you* would call "a regular cock-up", I guess. At first, they said you were in LA, insisted on it, but I told them I was holding your telegram from London in my hand. Then they said, yes, they'd already heard you hadn't shown up on the Coast and that there were some serious questions pending. Then I had to hold on for a bit. Then they said, who was this and would I have a word with your chairman? I thought I'd better hang up.'

'Ah well, not to worry,' said Kraven with a sigh. 'It would all have come out anyway.' He took her hand to his lips and kissed her on the knuckles.

'I admire your gallantry, darling, and I'm well aware that but for me you wouldn't be in this mess. No, don't deny it. I mean your dropping everything to find Robert for me.'

'Ah, that, yes. I had given you my word, after all. But Stella, I think I ought to tell you – '

She put her hand to his lips. Her eyes were moist. Well, Kraven had tried.

'What put you on his trail?' she wanted to know then.

'It's a long story. Besides, we're not to talk of Robert yet, remember?'

'You ought to phone the college, though.' She turned his wrist and looked at his watch. 'It's still early afternoon over there. Perhaps you can contain some of the fall-out.'

'Perhaps I shall in a bit. But there's more to tell, isn't there? What happened to your apartment, Stella? Was *that* why you had to get in touch?'

She looked at him in amazement, her eyes wide. 'Good God, Nicholas, not *my* apartment, *yours*!'

'What happened to it?'

'It was trashed, a fucking shambles, utterly destroyed.'

A neighbour on Kraven's floor, it appeared, had noticed Kraven's open front door, had knocked, peered in, and quickly withdrawn. He had told the super, who had told the police, who had questioned the other tenants. That was how Stella had found out. She had claimed friendship and taken responsibility for locating him. She had also seen the apartment.

Not a photograph or print or painting was left on the walls. The entire Kraven collection, family photographs, Opa's Sarah Bernhardt memorabilia, all ripped, all crushed, all tattered, all gathered in a heap in the centre of the living room on a bed of shattered glass, pottery shards and smaller wooden pieces: snapped picture frames and hacked-off table legs, inner white wood exposed like bone, a pyre never ignited. The barbarians had balked at actually striking a match. Instead, they had urinated on the heap.

An axe had been used on the furniture. The heavier wooden pieces bore ugly hackings and gashings. Here and there on the couch and the other upholstered furniture they had left their faeces, dessicating mounds mimicking the nobler heaps of Kraven possessions, in Stella's word, shit, the signature of the vandal. Only the great bed had been spared. On the walls, in several hands, appeared spray-can epigraffiti, offering ideological justification for the destruction: VIVA MAO, DEATH TO ALL CUNT PROFFS, UP PLO, SHAKSPIR SUCKS, PEOPLE POWER.

The news struck him with the sickening force of a blow to the guts. In the course of her telling, he blenched, all strength draining from him, fought to right himself, steadied, held on to her, listened, tried to make sense of her words.

So it was all over. The material representations of his past, his household gods, were shattered, and Sarah herself lay mingled with the shit and the dust. In one mighty bound the hobnail boots had leaped to the top of the stair. He was now, in a sense that Aunt Cicely could not have anticipated, adrift. The substantial sources of his being, his mythic roots, his sense of self – all these were gone: the highly polished, small table made by hand in Graz in 1847, for example, and figuring in the earliest family photographs, a table that had travelled unharmed from Vienna to Hampstead and, after Marko had claimed it, unharmed from Hampstead to New York. It was gone now, no different at last from the whole tribe of Kravens. Now even their shadows were gone, their images in sepia tones, in blacks and whites, instants of time once captured and secured, now gone forever, torn, crushed, pissed on and beshat.

Stella held him hard by the hand. 'I'm so sorry, darling.'

Kraven said nothing.

'But who could have done such a thing?' she said.

Kraven still said nothing. He knew well enough: it was Princip, of course, Princip and his gang of louts, his cohort of hooligans. The barbarians had swept on through. Such were the times. A bishop of Rome, he recalled, had once interposed himself between the Hun and his beloved city, had thrust his chest defiantly at the very spears of the invader: 'Over my dead body!' The Hun had been very happy to oblige.

'Nicholas,' said Stella with alarm, 'are you all right?'

'Thank you for taking care of things,' he said politely. Disengaging his hand from hers he got to his feet. 'Excuse me for a moment, please.' He walked to the bathroom with the painstaking deliberation of a drunk, knelt before the bowl, his head bowed piously above it, and then, very meekly, heaved the contents of his stomach into it.

* * *

CALMER NOW, KRAVEN PONDERED. Stella was soaking in the tub. Perhaps he should phone Mosholu, get that business over with before his present numbness passed. The

Union operator was pleased to make the connection for him. In the distant Bronx a telephone rang.

'English Department.'

'Mrs Trutitz? Nicholas Kraven here. If you'd just put me through to Professor Papadakis?'

'Ari's kinda busy right now, he's got Dean Pioggi in there with him. I don't know I should interrupt them.'

'Believe me, you should interrupt them.'

Kraven, cushioned by the sustaining numbness, held on. In the bathtub Stella splashed and ah-ed contentedly. There was a click in his ear.

'That you, Kraven? How was LA?' Acid dripped from Papa Doc's tongue.

'Ah, you see – '

'You weren't there, were you, feller?'

'The thing is – '

'Don't lie to *me*, guy. We've already heard from Dillinger. I mean, there he was before this learned body, people with *names*, Nicky-baby, you know, like this was the Big Time, history-wise, and the Dill's ready to introduce Mosholu's Number Two attraction, pun very much intended, you shit. Wait, it gets worse. Seems there's a guy from Harvard name of Hill, an international biggie, introduces one of *our* students, one of *your* students, guy called Feibelman, and this Feibelman announces to the assembled throng the Big Idea, which, according to the Dill, you had claimed as your own. We're lucky, I guess, we're not in the middle of a major plagiarism scandal. So you wanna tell me where the hell you are?'

'I'm in – '

'You're in London, right? No need to answer, bunky, we *know*. How's the season over there? Anything worthwhile at the Old Vic? What the fuck are you doing in London?'

'There's no need to be abusive.'

'Jesus Christ, are you kidding me? You figured, what the

195

hell, who'll know, right? You think that's the worst? I've hardly begun. You see, the Dean had this conversation with a former teacher of yours, guy by the name of Quimby, remember him? I told you about him, right, about his coming over here? The Dean happens to mention your name, Mosholu being so proud of you and all. Know what Quimby said? He said you're dead. Now ain't that a rib-tickler? Yup, he said you're dead. One of his most promising students, if a bit erratic, cut off in his prime. Said he attended your funeral. How about that?'

'I can explain.'

'Sure you can, feller. Thing is, I got this photocopy of a PhD sheepskin right here on the desk in front of me, London University. Just tell me this one thing: you the Marcus Nicholas Kraven whose name appears here in, let's see, in modified Gothic?'

'He was my – '

'Hold it right there. Is this your sheepskin? Yes or no?'

'Not *mine* exactly, it's – '

'Do you *have* one of your own?'

'No, I – '

'That's all she wrote. Misrepresentation in addition to simple, albeit grand, larceny. You're into Mosholu for maybe ten years' salary, medical benefits, pension, God knows what. Kinda makes your little jaunt to London look like peanuts. D'you have any idea how serious this is? Impersonating a doctor of philosophy! My God, you must be crazy! And how about Illegal Entry? Almost as bad, wouldn't y'say, Mal? Dean Pioggi is right here with me.

A mild but certain anger was beginning to dissipate the numbness. 'I entered the US, as it happens, with my own passport and visa. And there are simple explanations for what you slanderously call misrepresentation and larceny.'

'I'll bet. Only I don't happen to be simple. What's that,

196

Mal? The Dean says he's not simple either. You got a simple explanation for moral turpitude too?'

'I don't know what you mean.'

'No? I got a letter here from a certain female student, girl by the name of Giulietta Corombona. Let's see now. She makes certain allegations of sexual misconduct against a certain member of our department, said misconduct having taken place on college property; in fact, behind a closed college door. How about that? Something about a passing grade depending on her "putting out", by which she means performing certain unnatural, filthy, and shameful sex acts. Miss Corombona's preferences in English grammar and spelling are as perverse as her mentor's sexual proclivities, but she gets her point across, no problem there.'

'That's utterly ridiculous. Giulietta Corombona's – '

'Listen, we've been on the phone with our legal department, so we agree with you, it's not an easy charge to sustain, you're lucky. But another student claims – hold on, I've got her name here somewhere, yes Antonia Anstruther – she claims you deliberately position yourself in class so's you can look up her skirt. Now that kinda thing doesn't exactly help your case. Sure, Mal, sure. The Dean would like a word with you.'

'Hallo, Nicholas? Malcolm here. How *are* you, old thing? I'm willing to accept your resignation now, Nicholas, over the telephone. That would be best. But you'd have to send us official letters just the same, one for President Proudfoot, one for Ari here, and one for rotten old me.'

'I guess Dean Pioggi's said it all, feller,' said Papa Doc. 'The college won't prosecute so long as you don't grieve, okay? Both sides can do without the embarrassment, right? But you grieve and we got no choice.'

Kraven, who had been holding the phone at a distance from his ear for the last several minutes, decided to hang up. At that moment, Stella emerged naked from the bathroom. She glowed, all signs of tiredness gone. Kraven marvelled.

'Straighten things out at the college?'

Kraven smiled a smile he would himself have been hard put to explain. 'It seems,' he said, 'that I am absolutely free.'

TWELVE

AS THEY WALKED TOWARDS THE INN ON THE PARK, Stella spoke of what she hoped to accomplish. There was a little village in the Swiss Alps, Villars, not far from Vevey, where she and Robert had stayed years before, quiet, semi-rustic. She had phoned ahead. 'He needs rest and love. Above all, love.'

Kraven was bitterly disappointed that she had even conceived such a plan, but since he was quite sure she would be unable to pull it off, he simply asked, 'And how much time do you propose to devote to his convalescence?'

'Who can say?'

'He probably can use the rest, poor old sod, but love? What the hell d'you think he's been up to all this while?'

She tossed her head in anger. 'What do you know about love? You think it's just a function of your prick.'

She made a visible effort to control herself. 'Try to understand Robert. You don't know him. He's so sensitive, so easily hurt.' She took his hand. 'Finding out about us crushed him. Even so, he thought first about me and my happiness. *That's* why he wrote the letter, don't you see? He wanted to give me an easy out, he thought I wanted it that way.'

'And *don't* you?'

'That's beside the point. We're talking about *him* now and *his* needs.'

199

'My God, Stella! He's running around with a stripper. A burlesque queen. He's even got her sisters along. For someone who wants to fade out quietly, he's leaving with a most remarkable bang.'

She dropped his hand. 'Go ahead, make jokes. I tell you he's bruised.'

'His balls are perhaps.'

'Ssh, Nicholas!' Stella glanced from side to side. She placed a forefinger to her lips. It was an old fashioned, melodramatic, and utterly enchanting gesture.

It was true that he had been raising his voice. They had paused before the entrance to the hotel. There were people in evidence, people arriving, people waiting for taxis.

'Obviously you're going to have to see for yourself. You seem to think he's walking around in some kind of a trance. I tell you, he's *involved*, he's got *plans*, and they don't include being coddled in Switzerland. Look, he's going to put on some kind of a Shakespearean strip show for them. That's where the monastery endowment is going. Probably he hopes to make a bundle out of it; maybe he will.' Kraven felt that Stella was slipping from him. Couldn't she see what Poore-Moody was up to? Wasn't his hypocrisy plain? 'Did you ever stop to consider this: maybe he doesn't *want* to be saved? maybe he *likes* things the way they are?'

'That's enough, Nicholas, not another word. He's *sick*, he doesn't know what he wants. He needs his ego rebuilt. We destroyed that, you and I. How can I abandon him now? His letter was right about one thing: he's getting old. Who knows how much longer he's got? He's a human being. He needs love and understanding.'

'What about me? I'm a human being too. You think *I* don't need love?' He glanced despairingly about him. 'What about *us?*'

'*Us?*' she hissed. 'We're here today because of *us*. Now we must see what we can do about *him*.'

She swept past him and into the lobby. He could only follow.

* * *

THEY EMERGED FROM THE LIFT on the twelfth floor.

'What if he's not alone right now?' said Kraven. 'Don't you think the decent thing would've been to ring up from downstairs first?'

'Don't be ridiculous, Nicholas. You choose the oddest times to exercise your sense of decency. I'm his wife, remember?'

She knocked on the door. Silence. She knocked again. Aha, the sound of stirring. She knocked a third time. Someone was there, on the other side of the door.

'Yes, what can it be you want? Please to go away.' It was a woman's voice, hinting at hysteria.

Stella gasped. Kraven caught her arm. He raised his voice. 'Floor porter 'ere mod'm. Shampine and flars, complimongs of the management.'

'A moment, please.' A brief conference in indistinguishable vocables went on behind the door. 'Yes, yes, very nice.'

The door opened slightly. Stella gave it a violent push and marched in. Diotima von Hoden, knocked off balance, fell into a fortuitously placed chair. She sat rubbing her forehead where the door had struck it. She was wearing a man's striped silk robe tied loosely over her rotundity. Her grey hair frizzed wildly in all directions.

In the tousled bed, cross-legged, his back straight, sat Robert Poore-Moody. A lighted cigar drooped from his lips. His rounded torso was a forest of tangled black and white fur, through which two flabby hairless breasts, their nipples a delicate pink, protruded. Disordered sheets covered him to the waist. With his arms dropped, the palms of his hands outwards, he resembled an oriental idol.

'Robert,' said Stella, 'I don't know who or what this revolting creature is, but please ask her to leave.'

Her words had an immediate effect on Poore-Moody. With a groan he pulled the sheet from his waist and threw it over his head. Almost at once a small circle of discoloration appeared at head level. It grew brown, black, and then, out of a lazy spiral of smoke, the glowing tip of Poore-Moody's cigar broke its way. Stella rushed to the bedside and taking up a pitcher of water from the night table inverted it over her husband's head. He yelped but remained in place, bolt upright, the damp ghost of a Buddha.

Kraven watched from the open doorway, reluctant to enter.

'Just one moment, miss.' Diotima sprang nimbly from the chair and bounded between Stella and the shivering Poore-Moody. 'Just one bleeding minute, I say. By what right you are bursting in here? There are no laws in England? I think so, miss. By what right you are disturbing our peace? In London there are no bobbies? Beware, I say.'

'Robert!' Stella's tone was grim.

Diotima's face was now bright red. 'This is the bleeding limit! I ask you, where is your badge of authority? Who are you? Only answer me that!'

'His wife. I'm *Mrs* Poore-Moody.'

Diotima's elbows stopped in mid-motion. 'Robby,' she wailed, 'Robby, my dear tasty little sausage, is this true, this terrible thing she is saying?'

The head beneath the sheet nodded. The wilted cigar rose and fell.

'So.' Diotima dropped her arms to her sides, instantly calm. The mad look left her eyes, the heightened colour her cheeks. 'I go quietly, it's a fair cop.' She went briskly to the closet and gathered together her clothes. 'A moment to dress, please.' She made for the bathroom.

A groan issued from beneath the sheet.

'Robert, come out from under there. And you, Nicholas, for God's sake come in and close the door.'

They both did as they were told. This was a Stella new to Kraven, one perhaps known only too well to Poore-Moody. There was a brisk, no-nonsense determination to her, an attitude that would brook no disagreement, an assertiveness that turned grown men into small boys.

Meanwhile, Kraven was delighted to observe that Poore-Moody looked vile. Diotima must have been working him hard. A heavy stubble accentuated his pallor; his eyes were bloodshot. He glanced at Stella sideways and up. There was a boyish bashfulness to his voice. 'I don't know what to say.'

'Don't say anything for the moment. Just shake hands with Nicholas here. As soon as that witch of a woman has gone, the three of us are going to have a long talk. Above all, don't worry. There's nothing to be ashamed of; everything's going to be straightened out. But first, shake hands.'

Poore-Moody obediently held up a hand towards Kraven, who ignored it.

The door to the bathroom opened. Diotima emerged composed, every inch the sober academic.

'First,' she began, looking around calmly, 'I would like to say – ' But then for the first time she noticed Kraven. Her expression underwent an immediate transformation. 'Swine!' she shrieked, leaping nimbly across the room. Before he could prevent her, she struck the startled Kraven a stinging blow across the cheek. 'Swine! Whoever you are!' She assumed a boxing stance. Her eyes stormed. 'Swine!'

'She seems to know you,' said Stella.

'Never seen her before in my life.'

'A-*ha*! a-*ha*! Not know me? A-*ha*! Not know the Koh-i-Noor? Not know the Gaiety? What next? A-*ha*!' Diotima was prancing around making fisted feints at Kraven's jaw.

'She's mad then,' said Stella. 'Robert, can you do anything with her?'

'Now, now, Didi,' said Poore-Moody uselessly.

Kraven, at the centre of Diotima's circling, felt at once a trifle nervous and more than a trifle foolish.

But the fight went out of Diotima as swiftly as it had come. She shook her head as if clearing it and released a sigh. Her pose was now that of a gymnast come to rest after a complicated sequence of exercises, legs together, arms at her sides, head slightly bowed. Only her bosom betrayed her recent exertions. She had a word for each of them: 'Remember me, dear Robby.' 'Your claim on him is running out, madam.' 'Swine, one fine day we will be bleeding evens-stevens.' She left.

'Really, Robert, I understand in principle. I mean, I'm aware of your needs, your physiological and your psychological needs. But how could you? With such a creature?'

'Sit down, my dear,' said Poore-Moody courteously, patting the bed beside him. Stella acceded. There was something about them, it occurred to Kraven, of Victoria and her beloved Albert. No one need doubt who occupied the throne. The Prince Consort turned to the Queen's gillie: 'And you, sir – Mr Kraven, isn't it? There are chairs a-plenty.' He waved vaguely about him.

Kraven leaned back, half squatting, against a low sideboard. His studied nonchalance dislodged a thick pink satin scroll. It began slowly, slowly to unfurl. They all watched it, fascinated. It was an old fashioned whalebone corset, replete with laces, a *Panzer*, a tank, as Opa had once dubbed the variety. In her haste Diotima had forgotten a fundamental item of her costume.

'You ask me for an explanation, Stella. *You* ask *me*. You and your . . . your Nicholas here' – Poore-Moody gestured dismissively in Kraven's direction – 'the two of you follow me to England, no doubt making love all the way, and *you* ask *me* for an explanation. My sweet, you never fail to delight and surprise. Where, one wonders, did you learn so much about the art of defence?' He was absentmindedly playing with his stomach hair, curling it around his finger, releasing it, curling it once more, releasing it. 'I'm sorry,' he said. 'That was cruel of me and insulting to you. You deserve better.'

Kraven, transforming discomfort into a gesture of scorn, shifted from cheek to cheek. The lamp on the sideboard teetered.

'Nicholas, either sit in a chair or stand up. You'll have the lamp on the floor next.' Stella was peremptory.

Kraven stood up and folded his arms across his chest. Stella nodded her approval and returned her attention to her husband.

'How could I? you ask.' Poore-Moody considered the question. His expression suggested considerable puzzlement. 'I don't honestly know. She came to my room a couple of nights ago. There was some kind of a mix-up. She had the right name and room number but the wrong person. Anyway, we got to talking. She's something of a scientist, you know, an erotologist. That's what she called herself. Her name's Diotima von Hoden. She's had fascinating adventures all over the globe. You wouldn't believe half the things she's done. She claims to have discovered a powerful aphrodisiac, Didi's Potion. She had a vial of it with her, quite by chance, and she offered me some. You know how these things go. In a spirit of fun I agreed to have a sip. That's really all I remember. I guess I blacked out.'

Poore-Moody eyed them with a look of childish innocence. 'No, I'm not speaking figuratively at all. The fact is, I *did* black out. And each time I came to – three times, I think, in all – Diotima poured some more of the stuff down my throat. She was just about to give me another dose when you arrived.'

'Thank God we did.'

'Yes, yes, of course. But you know, Stella, it's marvellous stuff just the same. Diotima explained that after the body builds up a level of tolerance one can enjoy *all* the physical benefits *plus* the special fillip of full consciousness.'

'What's it supposed to do?'

'It's an aphrodisiac, Stella. What d'you suppose it's supposed to do?'

'But if you were unconscious, how can you possibly know it works?'

'Oh, I know it works.' Poore-Moody smiled mysteriously.

Kraven walked over to the windows and examined the view from the twelfth floor. Across the street a few of the magnificent houses built by the Regency nobility still remained. But down at the corner others had been razed to make way for yet another high-rise hotel, aesthetically meretricious, graceless, like the one from which he now contemplated the city of his birth. When he had left for New York there had been no Inn on the Park.

Behind his back Kraven felt Poore-Moody's nod in his direction, felt Stella's eyes on his back, felt the excluding privacy and complicity of husband and wife. He turned to face them.

'Aren't we forgetting something? Aren't we forgetting the saintly letter he sent you in New York? The ageing eyes piously fixed on the next world? The monastery endowment? Dolly, Sugar, and Candy? The Scheherezade number in Westchester? I could go on. Your husband is not exactly an innocent victim. Let's not shed too many tears.'

'Nicholas, how can you be so cruel, so crude?'

There was something these people knew that he would never understand, certain unwritten rules of behaviour inaccessible to him, refinements of social intercourse to which he was blind. Had he misrepresented Poore-Moody? He had not. Was not Stella this man's wife? Had he not known that Kraven and Stella had been lovers? He had. One did not hand out blame, of course. But one need not accept it either. Poore-Moody would have been screwing wherever opportunity presented itself whether Kraven and Stella had met or not. More power to him. Kraven hoped that at Poore-Moody's age he would have the necessary strength. But why did Stella feel that she and Kraven were somehow at fault? And why were they treating Poore-Moody as one convalescing from an embarrassing disease? Surely the old fellow's healthy relish for a little of what he fancied should ease her residual guilt feelings. One touch of nature made the whole world kin. Or so one would have thought but for the invisible lines that these wealthy alien presences drew.

'I'm at an enormous psychological disadvantage, my dear, naked in bed like this. How can I answer him?'

'But there's no need to answer him. Nicholas doesn't stand *between* us, Robert. He stands *with* us. Isn't that right, Nicholas?'

Silence.

'Nicholas!' she said sharply.

'Yes, yes.'

'Well then, why not get dressed if it bothers you so? You must be uncomfortable under that wet sheet anyway. We'll have our talk as soon as you're ready.'

'But I can't get out of bed.'

'Why not?'

'Kraven, d'you mind looking out of the window for a moment?'

Kraven turned his back. Beyond the rooftops he could see the great green expanses of Hyde Park and Kensington Gardens, divided from one another by the curved arm of the glinting, steely Serpentine.

'Just look at that, Stella,' whispered Poore-Moody hoarsely.

'Good God!'

'I told you Diotima was for real.'

'Jesus Christ!'

Suddenly the sun, escaping from white fluffed clouds, raced across the green and kissed the water. The serpent's skin had glittering golden scales.

'Er, Nicholas. . .'

Kraven turned even as Poore-Moody covered himself with the sheet again.

'Perhaps we should have our talk a little later. It's obvious Robert isn't ready yet. He's been through a lot. These things take time.'

'I'd like to have a talk with Stella right now, man and wife. Say an hour? Two at most? You understand, Kraven?' Poore-Moody grinned.

Kraven looked at Stella. She nodded. Well, they *were* still man and wife, after all. A last encounter? He would leave them to it.

Kraven walked across the room. Dignity, that was the ticket.

'So long, Kraven,' said Poore-Moody cheerfully. 'See you.'

* * *

KRAVEN SAT ONCE MORE IN THE LOUNGE of the English-Speaking Union. Two hours passed very slowly. Hungry, he went out for lunch. She was not yet there when he returned. He strolled around Berkeley Square, strode purposefully down Piccadilly to the Circus, returned to Charles Street. Still no Stella. He settled himself again in the lounge, listened to the variety of accents, mostly American, blindly turned the pages of *Punch*. At four o'clock he ordered watercress sandwiches and a pot of tea from the ancient retainer. He went out again, walked up to Oxford Street, over to Marble Arch, down Park Lane, and so back to the Union. No Stella. He sat once more, and attempted the puzzle in *The Times*. He checked repeatedly to see if she had returned. He set himself the task of producing a condensed version of *Paradise Lost* in twenty lines, or fewer, coming in at the wire:

> Paradise:
> Enter Vice,
> Satan
> Waitin'.
> Eve falls;
> Adam bawls,
> Falls too.
> What to do?
> Stole fruit;
> Ate loot.
> Man bad,
> God mad.
> No hope?
> How cope?
> Christ is come,
> Man's chum;
> Dies on Cross,
> Pleases Boss,
> Saves all:
> Lucky Fall!

He went to Shepherd Market and bought a sandwich and a bottle of beer, sauntered on, returned to the Union. Again, no Stella. At eleven o'clock he was told that the lounge was about to close. He caught a taxi on Curzon Street and asked to be taken to his hotel.

* * *

KRAVEN WOKE LATE IN SPITE OF HIMSELF. He washed and dressed hurriedly and dashed out of his hotel.

In Tottenham Court Road he hailed a cruising taxi and ordered the driver to Charles Street.

At the reception desk at the English-Speaking Union, he was told that Mrs Poore-Moody had had all her bags picked up early that morning. She was no longer in residence.

'Did she leave a forwarding address? Where were the bags taken?'

'Ah, that would be telling, wouldn't it?' The man viewed Kraven with deep suspicion. 'May I ask your name, sir?'

'Kraven.'

The man pulled a slip of paper from beneath the desk and perused it gravely. 'Would that be Dr *Nicholas* Kraven, sir?'

'It would.'

'Ah, that's all right then. I've a message for you, sir.' He read slowly from the slip of paper, ' "If Dr Nicholas Kraven should call, be so good as to inform him he can reach Mrs Poore-Moody at the Inn on the Park." I think I can safely tell you now, sir, that that's where the bags were sent.'

Depressing news indeed. Kraven turned to go.

'Excuse me, sir. Will you actually be *seeing* the lady in the near future?'

'I'm going round there now.'

'When madam's bags were packed for her this morning, a certain item was, most unfortunately, overlooked. The chambermaid found it not half an hour ago. Might I prevail upon you, sir, to convey it to the lady?'

'My pleasure.'

The man reached under the counter once more. With a fastidious finger and thumb and an expression of sober distaste he offered Kraven a small envelope in which had been sealed a disc-shaped object, in size a little larger than a cosmetics compact. 'Madam might have need of this.'

Kraven slipped the envelope into his pocket.

But if at the English-Speaking Union the news of Stella

boded ill, at the Inn on the Park it proved disastrous. Mr and Mrs Poore-Moody had paid their bill and – the clerk consulted his watch – had left the premises within the hour. Where they might have gone the clerk was unable to say, but Mrs Poore-Moody had left a note for a Dr Kraven, the gentleman now before him who had so identified himself. Kraven felt an unhappy tickling in the pit of his stomach. With a rudeness the clerk's face made manifest, he snatched the note from the polite hand, stuffed it in his pocket, and fled the hotel.

In Hyde Park, sitting woebegone on the first unoccupied bench he had found, he took out Stella's letter and read it. It was short.

Darling Nicholas,

You still haven't told me, dummy, where you're staying. Sorry about yesterday. Things came up. But as you know, my first concern in all of this – *our* first concern, yours as well as mine, I hope – is Robert and his rehabilitation.

My plans are changed. Instead of Switzerland, we're going to Germany, to Heidelberg. Surprise, surprise! Robert and I remember the town fondly from earlier visits. Do you know it at all? The hills of the Odenwald should be dotted with cherry blossoms by now. And of course it's a university town, peaceful in a delightful medieval way. Coincidentally, it's the home base of that ghastly woman Robert met at the hotel. He feels, dear sweet soul, that we treated her a bit shabbily. We should look her up, he says, and offer an apology.

'But what about us?' I hear you saying. Yes, indeed, what *about* us? Robert's wounds will take time to heal. Heidelberg offers hope of that, and in the long run my experience there might reap rich rewards for you and me. Be patient, darling.

Yours ever,
Stella

211

So that was it! Kraven felt something akin to disgust. His disappointment was swamped by anger. Decrepit Robert and his mincing-virtuous wife were in hot pursuit of dewlapped Didi and her magical potion. 'Perhaps we'll look her up.' He tore Stella's letter to shreds, crumpled the fragments, and threw them into a nearby rubbish bin.

What now was he to do? His career was at an end, an ignominious, farcical end. His past, his present, his future, all gone. He had no home, no profession, no reputation. And now Stella too had gone; indeed, had never really been there. He got up from the bench and distractedly wandered the park, his misery gathering strength, seeping through him.

THIRTEEN

A DAY OF BLEAK DESPAIR gave way at first to numbness, then to an itch to be doing something, anything, and finally to thoughts of Candy Peaches. He phoned the Inn on the Park and was obliged to hold on for a moment.

'Nicholas?' said Candy.

'Yes. How did you know it was me, for pity's sake?'

'I just knew.'

He suggested they meet at the first bench to the left through the entrance to Green Park, near the underground station, and she said, 'See ya.'

* * *

KRAVEN ARRIVED EARLY. He sat on the bench and, idly patting his pockets, discovered at his left hip an unexpected hardness. It was the envelope he had been given at the English-Speaking Union. Within was Stella's diaphragm case. It belonged to another life, not this. He opened it. The rubber dome, drily powdered, puffed clinically upward. He sat upon the park bench and contemplated its rotundity.

'Hey, what y'got there, Nicholas? You gonna get that bronzed?'

Candy Peaches stood before him grinning widely.

'Found it on the bench,' said Kraven, 'wondered what was

in it.' He snapped the diaphragm case shut and tossed it with the envelope into a waiting receptacle.

They went to a coffee shop in Shepherd Market. Candy brought Kraven up to date. Bobby's wife had arrived unexpectedly: 'A ball of yarn walking on toothpicks, an old broad with a yecchy Kraut accent, with this face, y'know, kinda looks like Bugs Bunny?' Candy, leaning towards him, exposed her upper teeth, drew back her jaw, and narrowed her eyes. Diotima, without question. She had left Dolly's suitcases outside the door. 'Poor old Bobby.'

Dolly had taken her ouster philosophically. You win a few, you lose a few. She had got in touch with her agent, who had found her an immediate booking in Paducah, Kentucky, where only two years before her Scheherezade number had won her a silver ribbon and a civic gold star from the Chamber of Commerce. Dolly and Sugar had left for the airport that morning.

'But you stayed on?'

'I like it here.' The British Library had proved more fruitful than she could have imagined, the British themselves were refreshingly polite, the atmosphere was 'conducive'. She hoped to finish out the academic year in London. Right now, she was looking for a flat or for rooms she could afford.

Kraven was reminded that he had a house in Hampstead, one which was soon to become vacant, but he said only that he might have a lead for her. Would he be able to get in touch?

Good old Bobby had paid for her room at the Inn on the Park through the end of next week.

'How about you, Marty?'

'Nicholas, remember?'

'Nickleby, I bet. When are you going back to the States?'

'It's a long story,' said Kraven ruefully. 'I'm not sure you have the time.'

'It's worth a try.'

In that instant Kraven realized that he wanted nothing more than to pour his many sorrows into the charming ears of this beautiful, willing and receptive young woman.

'You asked for it,' he said. 'But not here. Let's go outside.'

They wandered slowly hand in hand through London streets. The warm sun smiled on them. He told her how in a single week his life had fallen in ruins about him, how his expectations of the future had been reduced to smithereens. He told her everything, held nothing back. He was lucky, she said. His slate was clean. Now he could do whatever he wanted with his life, write, travel, anything at all. And Kraven, purged, began to feel growing in himself something of her optimism. Seize the day! Why not? He would move back to London. He had his savings, not inconsiderable, from a lifetime of work. Not only that, he was now, he had learned, the Blum heir.

And so he told her, hesitantly at first but soon enthusiastically, about *Tickety-Boo*. Valueless, he said, fledgling stuff, private spurts of mental masturbation, mere finger exercises. Yet he believed they revealed a talent, small perhaps, dormant still, but worth the rousing.

They were standing on the Victoria Embankment, across the sparkling Thames from the Jubilee Gardens. He caught her in his arms and kissed her exultantly. She did not object.

* * *

ONCE AUNT CICELY'S PROFESSOR OF INTERPER-SONAL DYNAMICS had moved out, Kraven invited Candy to look over the Hampstead house.

'It's a bit gloomy,' said Candy doubtfully.

'I'm going to throw all this stuff out,' he said. 'Paint the place inside and out, refurnish, remodel the kitchen, the lot. In fact, I thought you might be willing to help. Pick fabrics, that sort of thing. A woman's touch.'

'I'm not that sort of a woman. Haven't you noticed?'

'Even so. . .'

'What is it you *really* have in mind?'

'I have it in mind to woo you, win you, and wed you. But for the short term, I know you're looking for a place to stay. Why not move in here with me?'

She frowned as if in deep thought. 'No hanky-panky, huh? Landlord and tenant?' She bit her lip, then smiled. 'Okay, sure, we'll give it a try.'

For Kraven, her smile irradiated the gloomy room. He restrained an impulse to take her into his arms. They shook hands with mock solemnity.

* * *

ONE AFTERNOON FISHBANE PHONED.

'Perce here. Thought you might've forgotten me. Circumstances force me to wonder what's become of our little agreement.'

'Sorry?'

Fishbane dropped his voice to a horrible whisper; Aunt Cicely must have moved within earshot. 'The hunt for Miriam Pechvogel, a course; the hunt for Percy Fishbane's only son. How're you going to conduct an investigation from over here, tell me that? You was supposed t'be returning to the bleeding Hew Hess of bleeding Hay.'

'Ah, yes, *that*. Well, as you know, my life has somewhat changed direction since we spoke. I shall be living here for the foreseeable future. But I *shall* be going to New York in a couple of months, three at the outside. I've things to do there, an apartment to put on the market. I can begin making discreet inquiries then.'

'Time and tide,' whispered Fishbane. 'Time and tide. Don't delay more than you have to. As he told you himself, who knows how much longer Perce has got?'

'Rely on me,' said Kraven, meaning it.

* * *

ONCE THE LAST OF THE WORKMEN HAD LEFT and the minimal furniture and household needments were in place, life for the couple at 15 Beauchamp Close settled into a pleasing routine. Kraven had begun writing a novel and spent his weekdays at the desk in his study. Candy spent her days in the British Library or in *her* study, writing her thesis. On most evenings they sampled Hampstead's restaurants, returning home to read and listen to music.

A day came when Kraven, convinced that he had more than demonstrated his *bona fides*, let alone his heroic self-restraint, handed Candy a poem he had written for her, a poem with a *carpe diem* theme:

> Youth's here now and gone tomorrow –
> Cause a-plenty, love, for sorrow.
> *Now*, therefore, whilst time is fleeting,
> *Now*, whilst blood is strongly beating,
> Let us, on Love's altar lying,
> Like the Phoenix, ever dying,
> Burning in our sacred fire,
> Kiss and see the flames leap higher.
> Come, embrace me, four-and-twenty,
> Healthy bodies need Love's plenty.

He watched her eagerly as she read, her beautiful head bowed over the page; he watched her when she looked up at him, the strangest of smiles on her lips, and with slow deliberation tore the poem in half, and then in half again. There was to be no hanky-panky.

The weeks sped by. Summer was in the offing, and Kraven was talking of returning to New York 'to settle his

217

affairs'. They had eaten at Cerubino's, their favourite restaurant in Hampstead, and gone home in a mood of satisfied somnolence. The lights in the lounge were dim and warm and gentle. They listened to music on the radio. Kraven was stretched out in his leather chair nursing a scotch on the rocks; sunk into hers, her ankles tucked beneath her, her short skirt revealing a breathtaking expanse of white thigh, the light behind her glinting in her abundant and gorgeous hair, Candy nursed a stinger.

On the radio, the programme 'Windows on Spain' began to play a recording of Ravel's *Bolero*.

'*Bardic Follies*,' said Candy, smiling. 'Remember?'

'*Hamlet*, act three, scene four.'

Their eyes met and held as the sensuous music slowly, exquisitely slowly, increased in tempo and volume, its rhythmic repetitions taking hold of them, attuning their breathing, carrying them along, until, louder and louder, faster and faster, swollen beyond bearing it burst into its dissonant climax.

Candy suddenly leaped to her feet. 'Let's go!' she said, and held out her hand.

* * *

HE LAY ON THE BED AND WATCHED HER UNDRESS, a wondrously sensuous performance, erotic, self-mocking, exquisitely slow and teasing, limber and graceful. 'O my America, my new found land!' Majestic in her nakedness and beauty, her divine shapeliness, she came to him. 'Oh my,' she said, 'what's this?' and guided him into his place.

Later, he was struck by a sudden thought. 'Candy Peaches must be your name in Burlesque. What's your real name?'

'Candida,' she said. 'Candida Pechvogel.'

'And your mother's?' he asked eagerly.

'Miriam Pechvogel. Mimi. Why?'

Kraven took her once more into his arms. He kissed her cheeks, her nose, her lips. 'Cock-a-doodle-doo!' he crowed, 'Cock-a-doodle-doo!'

* * *

KRAVEN GOT UP BLITHELY THE NEXT MORN-ING, prepared coffee against Candy's wakening, and went out for a vigorous walk on the Heath. He returned almost two hours later, a bag of fresh poppy-seed bagels in his hand, to an empty house and a note taped to the hall mirror:

Dear Nicholas,

I'm going back to the States. No, it's not some crazy impulse – I've been booked for a month.

It wouldn't have worked out anyway. Not with us. Look, I like you a lot. Honest. It's been great. Last night was great. But you were getting too serious. (Or playing at it – with you it's sometimes hard to tell.) The point is, all I ever wanted was friendship. Nothing too heavy, no unnecessary complications. (Does 'Nicholas' *mean* 'complications'? The same root, maybe – in the original Sanskrit, or something?)

I've got plans I'm not about to change: student teaching next term, getting a start on my PhD, a career that's just beginning. I need space. Let's leave it at that.

Candy

From his slack hand the bag of bagels, bought for Candy, dropped down and shed the seeds across the floor. He stood for a moment, pale and speechless, then ran from room to room calling her name, half-trusting to find her. He rooted in vain within their common laundry bag, hoping to find in soiled T-shirts, panties, bras, an assurance of her continued presence. Alas, alas. In desperation, he phoned Heathrow and had her paged; miraculously, they found her and she came to the phone.

'Nicholas?'

'Don't go,' he said.

'My flight's boarding. I've *got* to go.'

'I'll come to New Haven. We'll talk.'

'Give a girl a break.'

'Give *me* a break. I *need* you, Candy. Besides, I've found your fa – '

'Nicholas,' she said firmly but kindly, 'grow up.'

A *click*, and the line was dead.

FOURTEEN

BETWEEN THE SIDE OF THE HOUSE AND THE
STONE WALL that had separated the Kravens from their
Harrogate neighbours grew a magnificent old oak. It stood
there still, although it would probably not survive the
transformations the building speculators had in mind. The
tree was already in leaf, already concealing what had been
Nicko's most secret place. Kraven made his way through the
wet high grass and stood with his hand on the great wrinkled
trunk, looking up. No, not even from here: the secret place
was invisible beneath the huge green umbrella, hidden by the
very arms that formed it.

About fifteen feet up, the central trunk diverged into three
heavy upsweeping gnarled branches, which then became the
source of all subsequent ramifications. At their common base
these three formed a hollow, like the inside of a small barrel
or the crow's-nest of the HMS *Victory*, and quite roomy
enough for a small boy. Nicko had even been able to sit
down in it, for a natural ledge, a kind of arboreal goitre,
bulged halfway down one inner wall. Here had been his
mizzen mast, his mountain peak, his fortress turret, his
Spitfire cockpit.

Two feet or so beneath the secret place, a single sturdy
branch, a sport, a bastard growth, sprang from the central
trunk. It hung downwards, heavy with offspring of its own,
to form a leafy bridge from the parent tree to the stone wall.

221

Here it rested before turning skywards itself. This branch, this drawbridge, gangplank, mountain trail, had been Nicko's route to his secret place. Once on the wall, it was as easy as toffee.

Nobody had known about the secret place, certainly not Marko. Kraven patted the friendly trunk. Perhaps still up there, up aloft in the castle keep, was the treasure box. He strove to remember its contents. A catapult made by Wipers Willie (much-decorated hero of Flanders in the First World War, the Kraven's gardener and Home Guard defender in the Second) and capable, Willie had said, of smiting battalions of Nasties hip and thigh; some pre-war marbles in a fine net bag, cat's-eyes, blood-eyes, aggies of all sorts; a *Wisden's Cricketer's Almanack* for 1938, a wad of cigarette cards secured by an elastic band, a genuine police whistle.

He walked back to the paved path through the tall wet grass, over the track he had recently beaten down. Turning he looked back at the oak, at its overarching green immensity. Perhaps also up there still were Nicko's bow and arrows. They had been up there that morning and all through that day in the spring of 1941, when the trees had burst into their first leaf and the flowers exploded in vivid colour, and hidden in his secret place Nicko had taken careful aim at the Beast, and the Beast had suddenly clutched his heart while reaching for a rose, had clutched his heart, crumpled up and died.

* * *

KRAVEN HAD GONE UP TO LEEDS BY TRAIN and rented a car at the station. He could have changed trains, but arrival by car had seemed somehow grander. He had left Harrogate a little boy; he was returning a man (in a Ford Cortina). Why he had travelled north he could not have precisely said. The fact of Candy's abrupt departure offered no obvious explanation. He had phoned Percy Fishbane to tell him of his discovery.

'A *girl*, you say?' The old man was indignant.

'Yes. Candida. She calls herself Candy Peaches.'

'Naow, you must've got it wrong. A girl! What about her mum, then?'

'There's no mistake. Miriam Pechvogel is alive and well, and owns a strip joint in Sausalito.'

'Strewth!'

'Your daughter's a graduate student at Yale. A letter should reach her there without trouble. D'you want to take down the address?'

'No hurry. Bit of a shock, this. Not a *son*, then? Needs chewing over.'

'But you said – '

'Never mind what I effing said. What I'm saying now is, no effing hurry.' And Fishbane had abruptly cut the connection.

It had been drizzling in London. The drizzle had grown into rain and the rain into downpour as the train hurtled northwards. Leeds was awash. He stood at the bar of the Queens Hotel looking glumly past the barman's shoulder and out of the window at the traffic island, fighting the paralysis of the will soaking into his marrow and gluing him to the spot.

Traffic around the island had been heavy. Several major arteries converged there. (Had Nicko actually released the arrow?) On the island itself Edward the Black Prince, Hero of Crecy and Poitiers, Flower of England's Chivalry, Upholder of the Rights of the People in the Good Parliament, grandly equestrian, was growing wetter and wetter. (Probably Nicko hadn't released the arrow at all, and even if he had, the distance from the boy's perch to the spot in the garden where his father had died was far too great for an arrow from a toy bow to have travelled. Besides, Nicko's arrows had been tipped with suction cups, for pity's sake!) Growing no less wet than princely Edward were four Leeds Worthies, native sons, representatives of all the centuries from the sixteenth to the nineteenth, each in an admirably sober attitude, together forming a restraining rearguard for the flamboyant Plantagenet. ('Good,' Nicko had thought as the Beast fell. Kraven distinctly remembered Nicko thinking that.) In the van, as it were, and neatly counterbalancing the Four Worthies, near-naked nymphs danced in wanton gaiety, each holding aloft her lamp, together determined to lead the Hero, Flower and Upholder down the primrose way to the everlasting bonfire. They too were wet, but in their case a certain shiny lubricity seemed quite suitable. (Yes, when the Beast fell, Nicko had most certainly thought, 'Good! Serves him right!') Kraven ordered another whisky.

From the Queens Hotel Kraven drove to the cemetery, but the gates were locked, no one responded to his summons, and he returned to the car wet and yet relieved. He sat for a moment considering what to do. Harrogate, then. But the road to Harrogate took him back through the city. In a mutable world the ugliness of Leeds was a rare earnest of permanence. The rain, far from washing clean, had only slimed over the city's characteristic grimy red brick. On Swinegate stood an idiot holding up for the passing motorist's distraction a sign whose clumsy lettering dripped in the downpour: 'THE LORDIS OOMPA88IONS FAIL NOT; THEY ARE NEW EVERY MOANING. Lamentations 3:22.' Kraven drove on. His route brought him at last to the A61, the Harrogate road.

As Leeds thinned out and began to merge with the countryside, the sky lifted and brightened. Scraps of blue appeared. The sun shone, at first hesitantly from behind torn shreds of white, soon boldly from a deep blue sky. Kraven opened the Cortina's window and began a favourite hum.

The road dipped and lifted its way through the margins of the glorious Yorkshire Dales.

Entering Harrogate, the A61 led past the West Park and the War Memorial – alas, poor Willie, a fellow of infinite jest, of most excellent fancy, dead now surely, long since gone – down Parliament Street and up Ripon Road. Kraven had half intended to put up at the Majestic, a massive red-brick pile with many gables and green turrets that stood on a vast park-estate, four stars, very grand indeed. But he drove past the Majestic and turned left instead just short of Duchy Road into the spacious forecourt of the Barrow. The Barrow would serve well enough, two stars, solidly provincial. It was built on a generous Victorian scale of the sooty grey stone that distinguished Harrogate architecture.

He was given a large airy room on the Barrow's north side. From his window it was possible to see, across the tennis courts and beyond the far bordering trees, Duchy Road. In fact, he found he was looking directly at what had been the Kraven house. The suddenness of its appearance before his eyes, the sheer unexpectedness of it, gave him what Aunt Cicely would call 'the willies'. It had been his plan to lead up to a first sighting only after a preparatory wandering about the town. Assuring himself that all he had seen, after all, were the roof and the upper storey, he left the hotel and began his tour.

Harrogate had not changed much physically in thirty years. Well, the railway station was new, or somewhat new, its sterile modern exterior no more than a superficial skin over its gamier predecessor; the Central Cinema had become a bingo hall; the St James's had disappeared altogether. Farrah's (Estd. 1840) Harrogate Toffee was sold all over town, everywhere but in the original Georgian shop, which was now maintained as a sort of tourist attraction, 'a glimpse of Harrogate's colourful past'.

Nobody came here for the waters any more, the myth of their sulphuric medicinal efficacy having apparently been exploded. Why, even the Pump Room itself had been turned into a museum! The poorly among Yorkshire's 'quality' and 'brass' no longer convalesced here. But others came with jingling coin, the conventioneers, TUC, IBM, ITV, CPC, and a healthy number of See-Britain-Firsters. Nor was it surprising. What had never entered Kraven's mind until today was the fact of Harrogate's beauty.

His route took him past the Kursaal, whose very name evoked its origins in the spacious days of Victoria and her beloved German princeling and from whose stone and iron façade flowers in ornamental baskets now depended, past the Royal Baths, and up Parliament Hill to the Memorial and Prospect Square. There were flowers everywhere, and well-trimmed public greens, benches where the weary might recreate themselves, neatness, cleanliness. The New Yorker he had become was awed.

He walked down Montpellier Parade glancing in at the windows of the elegant emporicula. Hadn't there once been a toyshop along the Parade? Yes, next door but one or two to the Imperial. His father had taken him there, and Opa, and Onkel Ferri. The toyshop was gone. But the Imperial still sold cakes and pastries and served teas, albeit now under the management of Betty's, once a rather less exalted establishment across the Square: the hobnail boots had climbed another stair.

He crossed the Floral Roundabout to Cold Bath Road. Up the hill was his school and the classroom that Miss Hudson had ruled as her demesne – 'Miz'oodzn,' as her terrified pupils had called her, Nicko among them, she of the parrot nose, the acerbic tongue, and the threatening battledore. The school was still there, a grim dark Gradgrind of a monster, its dead eyes catching the blessed sun and throwing back to heaven a blind and bilious yellow glare.

226

Not a sight or a sound of a child today. He shuddered and hurried on.

Not far beyond the school began Valley Drive, and the Drive, as it curved and plunged towards the Pump Room, was magnificent yet: house after house in unbroken contiguity, grey-stone Victorian façades, a paean to that earlier and stouter, somehow more solid and certainly nobler age. Most now were broken into flats, or called themselves hotels, or took in boarders. But the houses still stood, outwardly unchanged, and that was something. A pair of elderly ladies, genteely poor, mere wraiths in antique black, fluttered past him hand in hand, talking in German. Refugees, he supposed, who had beached like driftwood here, perhaps during his own years, and who had held out here, weathering on an alien shore.

Crossing the road at the foot of the Drive, he turned into the Valley Gardens. Here old people sat warming sluggish blood in the April sunshine, here mothers and nursemaids pushed their prams, here idlers idled and layabouts lay about. In the Gardens springtime had blossomed extravagantly but, however vivid and abundant the flowers, with decorous and ordered restraint, a casebook demonstration of nature methodized. Kraven strolled, enchanted. He passed a local shepherdess and her swain, arm in arm, hip sliding agreeably against hip, and heard something of their bucolic raptures:

'It was a Thursday, remember? And we did it in the park?'

'Yes.'

'Remember?'

'Yes.'

Their eyebeams, twisted, had thread their eyes upon one double string. Kraven found himself aching, not for Candy, but for what of love she had represented.

He left the Gardens and made for the Old Swan Hotel, where a double whisky encouraged him to persevere. But in

what? And whither? Except for the Crag and one or two odd
corners, he had already done Harrogate. Swan Road would
only take him back to Ripon, Ripon to the Barrow, and the
Barrow at last to Duchy Road and the house. Yes, yes, the
town was beautiful, but so what?

Thirty years before, he had sat with the other children in
the cinema on a Saturday morning, had followed the bouncing ball, had screamed lustily with the rest: 'A lit-tle bit of
heav-en fell out the sky woon day, and set-tled down in
York-shire and said, "I'm go-ing t'stay," and when the
an-gels saw it, it luked so neat and "raight," they joost
sprin-kled it with star-doost and named it HAR-RO-
GATE.' But for him there had been no more significance in
the action of the angels than in Mummy's sprinkling of salt
into the pot of farfel.

Where *was* that cinema? The Odeon, wasn't it? Ah yes, it
lay beyond the station. One had to cross Station Bridge.
Nicko had never spent much time in the area, a relatively
new part of town, sensible houses built in the late '20s and
early '30s for the upwardly immobile lower middle classes, a
place in those years unaccountably hostile to Jewish refugees.
But the station itself, now modernized, held memories. It
was to the station that he had fled, empty suitcase in hand,
when determined to run away from home. London had been
his goal, London and his father. He had been found on the
platform by Onkel Koko, arriving himself for a weekend in
the country, who had approved of his plan but suggested
that he return home first for dinner, such undertakings as
Nicko's being laudable in themselves but unwisely begun on
an empty stomach. Koko had also pointed out that a
threepenny-bit would not take Nicko far, perhaps no more
than a half a mile. As they had made their way across
Harrogate towards Duchy Road, devoting an appropriate
allocation of their consideration to the relative merits of
Lancasters and Flying Fortresses, Koko had suggested that

it was perhaps a trifle ignoble – not at all the Kraven thing – to abandon a lady, namely Mummy, in her time of need, a time when her first line of defence, namely Daddy, was necessarily detained in the nation's capital. Koko had admitted that he was himself unsure what it was best to do, but he had no doubt that Opa would be able to advise Nicko on the best possible course.

* * *

ONE DAY NOT LONG AFTER THEIR REMOVAL to Harrogate Nicko rushed from the garden he was still exploring, the garden in which he was still seeking out his Secret Place, to the back door of the house, the so-called Tradesmen's Entrance, where his mother was talking to Wipers Willie, the gardener. He and Willie got on extremely well together, but he had no time for his friend now. He had just remembered it was Friday.

'Is Daddy coming up today?'

'Yes, dear.'

'May I – '

'Nicko, darling, don't be so rude. You're interrupting.' She turned back to Willie, leaving the boy to stamp his foot impatiently. 'Now, where were we? Eighteen-and-ninepence, is it then?'

'Ay, moom, and then there's the booket of horse doong for them roses, that's eightpence, and woon-and-tuppence-ha'p'ny for the new nozzles on the hose. That cooms ter, let me see. . .'

'One pound, seven-pence ha'penny,' said Nicko.

'Smart lad, that,' said Willie.

'Here you are, then, Willie. And you'll be back tomorrow?'

'After m'noovers and a little soomthing t'wet m'whistle. Drilling's hot work.'

229

'Mummy, may I go?'

'Go where?'

'To the *station*, of course. To meet *Daddy*.'

'Whatever next! That's *much* too far. All those streets to cross, and the traffic near the station! Perhaps when you're a little older.'

'But I know the way, and I'd cross at the belishas, and I'd promise to be careful!'

'I'll teck th'lad toot station,' said Willie, 'in me bike.' The bicycle had a small front wheel surmounted by a large basket, the near upper bar of which served as handlebars.

'We wouldn't dream of troubling you, Willie.'

'No trouble a tall, moom. Th'lad can sit int basket, coomfy as can be.'

'Oh please, *please* let me go!'

'All right,' said Mrs Kraven doubtfully. 'But you must sit quite still and not be a bother. Thank you so much, Willie. If you could just let him off at the main entrance. He knows the platform.'

'Coom on then, lad. Don't stand about gormless, 'op in.'

And off they went, wobbly at first, along Duchy Road, and then smoothly as they turned into Ripon. What a grand way to travel! Nicko, in the gun turret of a Lancaster, scanned the skies for the Luftwaffe. Once past the Barrow Hotel the road dipped sharply. Harrogate spread out beneath them. Down they zoomed, the air whistling past their ears, down towards the Kursaal and the Royal Baths.

But from here it was all uphill to the centre of town, hard going. Willie got off the bicycle and pushed it up Parliament Street. 'Yer a heavy little booger,' he said. He was sweating and before long he had to pause for breath. With trembling fingers the old man took a Woodbine from behind his ear and lighted it. 'Half a tick, then,' he said.

'Will you show me your wound again, the one from Wipers?'

Willie rolled up his sleeve and showed Nicko his scar. It was at least four inches long, a deep rift on the white pitted surface of his forearm. No hair grew there.

'May I feel it, Willie?'

'There it is, then.'

Nicko ran his finger along its length. It was unexpectedly cold and damp, and something ticked away beneath it. It made Nicko's tummy squiggle delightfully.

'Does it still hurt dreadfully?'

'Only when I laff,' said Willie grinning. He carefully stubbed out his Woodbine on the heel of his boot and settled the remnant behind his ear. 'Off we go, then.'

Willie pushed the bicycle to the top of Parliament Street, turned left before the War Memorial, and once past Betty's Tea Shop remounted. For a second or two they wobbled wonderfully. At last they were at the station. At the main entrance Willie lifted Nicko out of the basket.

'Shall I wait with'ee, lad, joost till th'dad cooms?'

'I'll be right as rain. Thanks awfully for the lift, Willie.'

Nicko ran into the station. The train from Leeds was already in. He saw his father coming through the wicket. He had someone with him, a WREN officer. Why, she looked just like Deanna Durbin! She was holding on to Daddy's arm, and they were laughing and talking together. Perhaps she was to spend the weekend with them. Nicko certainly hoped so.

The boy hid behind a kiosk. His idea was to trail them out of the station and then, when the time was ripe, to pounce and surprise them both. He hugged himself to restrain his excitement. What fun!

But his father was helping the lady into a taxi at the stand. She let down the window and put her face out, smiling. His father kissed her warmly. Well, apparently she was not to stay with them. If Nicko was to pounce, he had better pounce now.

'Daddy! Daddy!'

'Nicko!' Felix Kraven looked surprised indeed. 'Is Mummy with you?'

'She's at home. I came all by myself, with Willie. He brought me on his bicycle, Daddy. He let me feel his wound, the one from Wipers. We're best friends.'

Felix Kraven looked far from pleased. The lady, too, had lost her smile.

'Is that *your* little boy?' She looked from father to son with a *very* odd expression. Perhaps, thought Nicko, she doesn't like surprises.

'Yes, Angelica.' Felix Kraven sighed. 'That's Nicholas.'

'How d'you do, Nicholas.'

'How d'you do.'

Why was she blushing so? She must be very shy.

'Well, that's that, I suppose,' she said.

'I'm sorry, Miss Crawford, truly sorry. I would have told you. There wasn't time.'

'There's not much point in it now, is there? Goodbye, Mr Kraven.' She turned away, then turned back. 'And goodbye to you too, young man. Take Daddy home to Mummy, there's a good fellow.' The taxi window snapped up abruptly. Felix Kraven shrugged.

Had Nicko understood at the time the significance of this incident at the station? Whatever he had understood, he knew better than to say anything about it to his father. And even though the lady was the spitting image of Deanna Durbin, one of Victoria's favourite actresses, he said nothing about it to his mother either.

Felix had been grumpy all the way home, responding only with grunts to his son's chatter. Supper that night was a gloomy affair, with Felix complaining about the blackout and the shortages and the bombings and how exhausting it was to travel up to Yorkshire and back down to London every few days. Victoria tried in vain to cheer him up. Opa told for the umpteenth time the story of his first sight of Sarah Bernhardt, but to no avail. Nicko kept quiet. He was sent to bed early.

Saturday wasn't much better. Daddy wouldn't play with Nicko in the garden, he wouldn't take him for a walk, he didn't care about Willie and Wipers. He just sat sulking in his chair in the morning room reading his rotten old papers, grumbling to Opa about this and that, muttering that the war was going badly, that Hitler was virtually on their doorstep, that maybe he and Koko should have sent the children to America. 'Sarah Bernhardt had a great success in America,' said Opa. Saturday was completely ruined. It was best to stay out of Daddy's way.

Happily, by Sunday morning Felix was more his old self. Nicko knew that everything would be all right when Daddy tried to tap open his soft-boiled egg and discovered it to be an empty inverted shell. He showed great surprise and complimented Nicko on his clever trick. This was an old trick of Nicko's, but it caught Daddy every time. Opa pinched Nicko's cheek.

After breakfast Daddy took Nicko out for a long walk, all the way to the Crag, and this time they took the mountaineers' way down, not the sissies' path to the side. Daddy knew all about mountains. He had scaled the Alps and the Andes. And one day he and Nicko would climb to the peak of Everest, the highest mountain of all. That would take some doing, and today they were putting in a little practice. Since they would be the first to the top, King George himself would pin medals on them and grant them knighthoods. 'What do you think of that, Sir Nicholas?' said Daddy in his careful English. But they would have to wait for war's end, of course, and for Nicko to grow up a bit.

They got back in time for Sunday dinner, a magnificent meal, in spite of wartime rationing, one of Nicko's favourites: mashed potatoes and bangers and fried cabbage-

and-onions, absolutely scrumptious, and for afters Mummy's world-famous utility cake. What could be better? Mummy cleared the table and carried the dishes into the kitchen while Daddy and Nicko talked of cricket and Opa nodded in his seat. Sunday was Gladys's day off and she had gone to the Pine Woods with her soldier sweetheart. She said she loved the smell of pine.

After a bit Daddy and Nicko followed Mummy into the kitchen. Daddy gave a gentle slap to Mummy's bottom and kissed her on the back of the neck. He had an announcement to make, he said.

'Nicko and I are very, very sleepy after our exertions of the morning. No lady can possibly understand the effort expended in climbing not only down but also up the mountaineers' path at the Crag. It is a task for heroes. And so, we are tired, it goes without saying. But we understand that you are tired too. Accordingly, today we will *all* enjoy a nap, not just Opa.'

Mummy blushed and giggled. Nicko groaned. He had been looking forward to playing the hunter's game this afternoon, with Daddy in his usual role as the Frightful Beast.

'But after we're rested and have again a full measure of vim, there will be just time enough before my train for us to go to the pictures.'

'Hooray! And Opa too?'

'If he wants. But Betty Grable is not Sarah Bernhardt.'

* * *

KRAVEN ROUSED HIMSELF from his contemplation of the tree and walked towards the house. A board hammered into the ground announced that a magnificent block of modern luxury flats would soon arise on this desirable site. The announcement was signed Dobbs and Glissando, Architects, Wigan, Beirut, and Los Angeles. His Italian shoes, elegant, lightweight, informal, a splurge on Madison Avenue to celebrate the end of the previous academic year but hitherto deemed too expensive to wear, were soaking wet and undoubtedly ruined. The walk to the oak had done that. Bits of undergrowth and soil clung to them, and they were dusted with yellow-white pollen. He could feel the wet creeping round his toes. And his trousers too were wet, up to his knees. He felt suddenly cold and plunged his fists deep into his trouser pockets. What was he doing here? He began to shiver.

The front door was boarded shut. The house seemed to be in the last stages of decay. Most of the windowpanes were gone; shards and slivers of broken grass littered the ground at his feet. The weather of many seasons had scavenged the house's innards. It must have been unoccupied for a decade and more, preparing for the wrecker's ball.

He peered through the window of what in Kraven days had been the study, then a noble room, wood-panelled, furnished in comfortable dark-wine leather, books of the previous owner lining the walls, a fine blue and white Chinese rug on the polished floor; peered gingerly because of the jagged edges of glass in the window frame and accumulations of bird and fieldmouse droppings; peered, and recoiled in shock. Two gigantic wolves, their fangs bared, their red eyes glittering, were leaping at him across the room. No, not wolves, two watchdogs, German shepherds. He prepared to run on legs spongy with terror, his mouth dry, but his legs refused the brain's command. The dogs had made no sound. He forced himself with pounding heart to look into the room again. The dogs were still in mid-leap, frozen en route to the jugular. There was only one dog. Its reflection leaped at a slightly odd angle in an oval mirror that leaned against a shattered packing case. Dust and debris were everywhere. The words *Up Leeds U* were crudely painted on a rotting panel wall. A cobweb furry with dust ran from the tip of the dog's nose to the floor. The dog was stuffed, preserved in vicious attack, silently snarling, ready for the kill. It leaped from a low metal stand disguised as a log athwart bracken. Since only its hind legs made contact with the stand, it achieved balance with the aid of a steel rod that ran from a point in the log's centre straight up into its rectum. No wonder the poor creature was out of sorts. Kraven's heart resumed its normal rhythm.

So the study had come to this. It was here that they had sat *shiva* for his father, sat on the floor for seven days of misery, while the new spring sun shone outside and the sounds of reawakened life darted in through the open window. It was here that they had sat *shiva* for Tante Carlotta and Tante Erica and Onkel Gusti, blown to smithereens with the air-raid shelter in far-off Hampstead at the end of the same evil year, victims of a freak bombing, inexplicable, one of the many ironies of the war, and there had been little enough of them left to bury. Onkel Ferri had spent three months in a straitjacket after that, screaming until his voice gave out, and then screaming with no sound at all. When at length they had let him out, he was at thirty-seven an old man, but calm, philosophical, and already the Compleat Mourner. By then Opa had already begun his withdrawal from the world. It proved a slow process, but with the Divine Sarah's help he had made it in eight years.

The sun had gone. It would probably rain again. The leaden weight of the heavens had begun to press down. Was there any point in spending the night in Harrogate, here among his ghosts? He had seen all there was to see. If he wished he could drive back to London and not bother at all with the train. It wasn't much more than two hundred miles. He looked at his watch: it was only five o'clock. A cold wind soughed through the trees; the house creaked and keened, calling him. He felt an impulse to climb in through the study window, to curl up on the littered floor, to sleep. In panic, he turned his back on the house, strode rapidly along the path and out into the road. He could be in London tonight: he *would* be in London tonight.

The rain began, slowly at first. Kraven started to run, but within seconds it was pelting. The light went out of the sky. He was soaked to the skin. There was not much to be gained by running any more. Panting, he slowed down to a walk. The Barrow was just around the corner.

'Don't have t'ask if it's raining, do we then?' said the hall porter amiably. He had the round pink face and short-clipped hair of the English sergeant-major, but he stood like a question mark, slovenly, unpleasing to the eye.

Kraven had squished his way to the porter's desk and now stood in a pool of his own creation. The water streamed from him, from his hair, down his neck, his eyes, his cheeks; it dripped from his nose, his chin, his fingers. His clothes clung to him, cold and wet. Damp wool had rubbed his crotch sore. He was not amused.

'I'd like my key, please. And be so good as to have the Cashier prepare my bill. First a hot bath and a change of clothes, and then I'm leaving. Let's say an hour.'

'It were joost a joke, sir,' said the porter in alarm.

Was *that* supposed to be a joke too? Kraven couldn't tell. 'A sudden change in plans.'

'They'll charge you fort full twenty-fow'r hours.'

'So be it.'

'And you forfeit your breakfast, sir, that's worked in toot nightly rate.'

'Let's leave it to the Cashier, shall we?'

'Oh aye, but I thought th'd like t'know.'

Kraven squished his way to the lift and rang the bell. The gate opened and Kraven stepped into the lift. 'Don't 'ave t'ask if it's raining, then,' said the liftboy cheerily. It must be a local joke.

237

In the bathroom a grand Victorian bath stood on massive clawed feet. It served all the guests at Kraven's end of the corridor. A sign near the lightswitch urged the bather to be kind enough to rinse the tub after use. Happily for Kraven, whoever had preceded him there had been obedient to the prompting. Kraven drew the water and soon immersed himself, rediscovering the simple sensuous delight of a hot bath, a pleasure that a decade of showering in New York had rinsed from his memory. The steam rose visibly; the condensation formed in large droplets on the ceiling and on the walls and ran in tearful columns to the floor. Weeping walls, that was the local phrase for them, that's what Gladys had called the scullery walls. 'Them's weeping walls,' she had told him when he'd asked where the water came from. Nicko had found that funny, but not Gladys. 'I'm the won as 'as t'wipe'm, moogins.'

Alas, poor Gladys, buxom, limber Gladys, a young woman as ugly as an old potato. She had had an endearing way of snitching up her nose if she was either pleased or displeased. She had exuded sex, even a child was aware of it. Kraven had a momentary recollection, a mere feathery teasing at a corner of his brain, impossible to say whether of something that had actually taken place. He had joined Gladys in her bed in the attic. It must have been a Sunday morning or she'd have been up and about her duties; on the other six days she got up when it was still dark. She lay on her back and held him between her legs, where it was moist and warm and tickly. He liked it there. Her flannel nightie was rucked up under her breast. She held his child's body under the arms and moved him up and down, up and down, between her legs. She moaned a happy moan. She smelled a good smell too, a smell he had never come upon on any woman since. He thought of hay and new sweat and warm milk. 'Th'moozn't tell thy moom, moogins, or she'll 'ave me out ont dole.' He had known not to tell without her prompting, but had he known why? And in any case, had it even happened?

Gladys would be sixty today, an old woman, if she was still alive. Good God, bouncy Gladys sixty! He shed a tear for her, stretching himself out at full length in the tub, a girl of whom the very memory and after all these years still had the power to move him: a masthead pointed skyward from the water. It was a sincere tribute and bespoke a Kravenesque taste for the bitter-sweet. Meanwhile, the hot water was a soporific. Lazily he soaped himself.

On the next weekend that Felix Kraven had been able to come up to Harrogate, there had been no WREN officer with him. Father and son played in the garden all Saturday afternoon. Felix had been the lion, a 'ravaging, ravenous, rampageous Beast', and Nicko had been the White Hunter, bravely stalking his dangerous quarry through veldt, scrub and jungle. Sometimes the Beast had become aware of pursuit and turned on the Hunter ('Roar-r-r!'), sending him scrambling, shrieking and laughing, for cover. The game had gone on for hours. Every now and then Opa had joined in, leaning out of the kitchen window and holding his stick like a rifle: 'Look out, Hunter, look out!'

The Hunter's gunpowder caps, hard to come by in war-time, had fallen into the damp grass ('O bother!') and wouldn't fire. Never mind, there was still the bow and arrows. Unobserved by the Beast, who fortunately had taken a moment to put away the deckchairs in the potting shed, Nicko had climbed up to his secret place. He had picked up his bow from his hidden armaments and selected an arrow.

Kraven, one towel around his waist and another around his shoulders, stood at his Barrow window, his body still radiating hot-bath warmth. The rain had scarcely let up, but the sky had lightened somewhat, which perhaps augured well for the weather. But it was impossible to see the house. It had disappeared, lost behind the trees that swayed in the wind, lost in the rain itself and in the still poor quality of the light, a pervasive green-wet dimness. He turned from the window and began to dress.

'Time to come in, you two,' called Mummy from the kitchen window.

The Beast emerged from the potting shed.

'Where's Nicko, Felix?'

The Beast looked all about him. 'Come along, Nicko, it's teatime.'

Rats! Just when the game was getting going. The White Hunter remained silent in his secret place. It wasn't time to finish yet. It wasn't fair.

'Nicko, the game is over,' called the Beast a trifle sharply.

He was looking in the wrong direction, ha-ha!

'Baked beans on toast,' called Mummy, 'and for whoever is good, a poached egg.'

Silence.

'Nicholas, it is no longer a choke.' Daddy's mood could change in a trice. 'When you are called, you answer.'

But to answer would be to give away the secret place. Nicko made not a sound.

'I say, Victoria,' said the Beast, momentarily distracted and resuming his careful English, 'look here, a perfect rose. But surely it is weeks before its proper time.' He struck a pose, his right hand over his heart, his left raised towards Mummy in the window, and began to sing, 'The first rose of summer. . .' Mummy blew him a kiss. And he reached to pluck the rose even as Nicko took careful aim with his bow and arrow. Daddy looked suddenly startled, clutched at his heart, gasped, and collapsed, his face in the rose bed. Mummy screamed.

'Good,' thought Nicko. 'Serves him right.'

But he had come down from his secret place after that.

Kraven buttoned his shirt and contemplated the present. His slate, he assured himself, was indeed wiped clean. Had

240

he not reason enough, then, to rejoice, reason in overplus? Had he not stumbled quite through the wreckage of his past? He had, he had. Alone once more, he would begin again. *Quand même!*

Sitting on the low stool in his Barrow room and pulling on a sock, Kraven discovered he was weeping. He was weeping uncontrollably, his shoulders heaving, tears streaming down his cheeks. He sobbed for a long time. He sat on the low stool and grieved – not so much perhaps for what he had lost as for what he had found.

Joseph Heller

CATCH-22

Hilarious and tragic, at the heart of *Catch-22* is a savage indictment of twentieth-century madness, and a desire of the ordinary man to survive it.

'Blessedly, monstrously, bloatedly, cynically funny, and fantastically unique. No one has ever written a book like this'
Financial Times

'Not only the best novel to come out of the war but the best novel to come out of anywhere in years'
Nelson Algren, *The Nation*

'Wildly original, brutally gruesome, a dazzling performance that will outrage as many readers as it delights. Vulgarly, bitterly, savagely funny, it will not be forgotten by those who can take it'
New York Times

'An apocalyptic masterpiece'
Chicago Times

VINTAGE

Philip Roth

SABBATH'S THEATER

'Sabbath explodes like some mad genie out of his bottle...[*Sabbath's Theater*] has more firestorming prose than any other novel I have read this year'
Anthony Quinn, *Observer*

'A work of near-heroic vitality and cunning'
Justin Cartwright, *Sunday Telegraph*

'Soaring above all other novels I read this year...A postwar American masterpiece'
James Walton, Books of the Year,
Daily Telegraph

'I finished *Sabbath's Theater* with my heart and blood pumping and thumping, the pulse racing to the last savage lines, the pay-off'
Linda Grant, *Literary Review*

'In time this will be seen as Roth's best novel so far'
James Wood, *Guardian*

VINTAGE

Arno Strine, a modest temporary typist, has perfected the
knack of stopping time in its tracks and taking women's
clothes off. He is hard at work on his autobiography, *The
Fermata*, which proves in the telling to be a provocative,
very funny and altogether morally confused piece of work.

'The book is bursting with sex and beauty, wound together
profoundly and pornographically. It is bountifully
Rabelaisian and intensely refined...I have never read anything quite like it...*The Fermata* should be celebrated'
Mary Gaitskill

'Lots of nakedness, quite a few surprises...His novels have
the brazen, daring timidity of love letters you know you'll
never post'
Sunday Times

'Witty, dry and thought-provoking, a great addition to
Baker's unique observatory of contemporary life'
Vogue

'The funniest book about sex ever written'
Kate Saunders, *Literary Review*

VINTAGE

Kurt Vonnegut

SLAUGHTERHOUSE 5

Prisoner of war, optometrist, time-traveller – these are the life roles of Billy Pilgrim, hero of this latter-day *Pilgrim's Progress*, a miraculously moving, bitter and funny story of innocence faced with apocalypse, in the most original anti-war novel since *Catch-22*.

'An extraordinay success. It is a book we need to read and re-read...Funny, compassionate and wise'
New York Times Book Review

'A marvellous excursion...the writing is pungent, the antics uproarious, the wit sharp as hyperdermic'
Daily Telegraph

'One of the best living American writers'
Graham Greene

'One of the master alchemists of modern American fiction'
Sunday Times

'A work of keen literary artistry'
Joseph Heller

VINTAGE

Also available in Vintage

Thomas Pynchon

THE CRYING
OF LOT 49

Suffused with rich satire, chaotic brilliance, verbal turbu-
lence and wild humour, *The Crying of Lot 49* opens as
Oedipa Maas discovers that she has been made executrix of
a former lover's estate. The performance of her duties sets
her on a strange trail of detection, in which bizarre charac-
ters crowd in to help or confuse her. But gradually, death,
drugs, madness and marriage combine to leave Oedipa in
isolation on the threshold of revelation, awaiting *The
Crying of Lot 49.*

'An exuberant, off-beat talent...This strange writer indulges
us to the extent of being wildly funny, but the comedy is as
black and turbulent as storm clouds'
Norman Shrapnel, *Guardian*

'For the reader who has yet to make acquaintance with this
important comic talent...an appropriate introduction...
defiantly, purposefully outrageous'
Spectator

'The best American novel I have read since the war'
Frank Kermode

VINTAGE